MARSHAL OF SUNDOWN

Jackson Gregory was born in Salinas, California. He graduated from the University of California at Berkeley in 1906. His early career was in journalism in the East, primarily for the New York City News Association. By 1913 he was writing Western and adventure fiction for the magazine market. *The Outlaw* (1916) was his first Western novel, published by Dodd, Mead. "Silver Slippers", an early story appearing in Adventure Magazine, was filmed as *The Man From Painted Post* (Artcraft, 1917), starring Douglas Fairbanks, a story later expanded to form *The Man From Painted Rock* (1943). *Six Feet Four* (Pathé, 1919) was the first of Gregory's novels to be brought to the screen, directed by Henry King. *Judith Of Blue Lake Ranch* (1919) was the first of his Western romances published by Charles Scribner's Sons where Gregory's editor was Maxwell Perkins. The style and types of stories he told appeared to be a combination of Zane Grey and F. Scott Fitzgerald, the latter another noted author edited by Perkins. *The Bells Of San Juan* (1919) was serialized in four parts in Adventure Magazine in 1918 and, following book publication, was filmed in 1922 by Fox, starring Buck Jones, a popular movie cowboy of the time. Buck Jones particularly liked Gregory's stories and often used them for his film vehicles, including *Hearts And Spurs* (Fox, 1925) based on *The Outlaw*, *Timber Wolf* (Fox, 1925), *Desert Valley* (Fox, 1926), and *Sudden Bill Dorn* (Universal, 1937). Tom Mix starred in the screen adaptation of *The Everlasting Whisper* (Fox, 1925). Beginning with *Redwood and Gold* (1928), Gregory returned to Dodd, Mead as his book publisher, and for the next decade and a half would publish one and sometimes two Western novels a year. His best novels would certainly include *The Shadow On The Mesa* (1933), *Into The Sunset* (1936), and *Secret Valley* (1939). Perhaps the New York Times said it best about a Western story by Jackson Gregory: "It is the sort of book that, once started, one gallops eagerly and absorbedly through, hating to put it down until the final page."

MARSHAL OF SUNDOWN

Jackson Gregory

GUNSMOKE

First published in the UK by Hodder and Stoughton

This hardback edition 2009
by BBC Audiobooks Ltd
by arrangement with
Golden West Literary Agency

ISBN 978 1 405 68284 8

British Library Cataloguing in Publication Data available.

Printed and bound in Great Britain by
CPI Antony Rowe, Chippenham and Eastbourne

CHAPTER I

WHEN Jim Torrance, riding up from the south, crested the live oak-studded knoll from which he saw the rip-roaring little town of Sundown for the first time, the place looked as clean and pretty as a fresh picture, and as peaceful as the little dove cooing on a dead limb over his head. But that was because Sundown was still a good three miles away, and besides it was only mid-afternoon and not yet first-drink time.

"I'm turning off here to go into town, Skeeter," he told the boy helping him with his handful of stock. "You go straight on with the horses. You'll know the place when you get there; just watch for an old wheeltrack turning off where there's a dead pine leaning over a big white rock. Likely I'll overtake you anyhow. It's only about seven miles."

"Gee, Jim," said Skeeter, "me, I'd like to see Sundown, too. I've heard a lot about it."

"Not today, kid. In two-three days I'll pay you off and you can ride where you please. Better hobble Barney and old Molly when you get there. I'll see if maybe I can get you a pie in town."

The boy, convoying the dozen head of likely looking saddle horses and the two heavily laden pack mules, rode on through the oaks, down the farther side of the knoll, into the straggling pines on the slopes beyond, and vanished in the creases of the hills which grew more rugged and more thickly timbered as they rolled away toward the far blue mountains in the north. Jim Torrance sat where he was a moment, rolling a thoughtful cigarette and looking toward Sundown with lazy-lidded eyes.

In the late October sunshine, as yellow as butter, under a sun-drenched sky as deep a violet hue as the towering

5

mountains in the far background, at the end of a dusty road, wavering chalk-white across the valley lined with quivering aspens in their brilliant autumn dress, was a clutter of houses—and that was Sundown, where colors clashed and laughed, the warm red of bricks, the white of adobe walls, the weathered brown of shake roofs—and down in the valley there was a girl with a bright red neckerchief, riding a dappled gray horse. She was at considerable distance, on another road approaching Sundown from the north.

Jim Torrance and the girl rode into town at the same time; they were for an instant abreast as they came in front of the Stag Horn Saloon. He was seeing many things today for the first time, since, on the single other occasion of coming into this neighborhood, he had kept straight on from the farther side of the knoll where he had left Skeeter, and had not come any nearer Sundown. So also for the first time he saw Sally Dawn Cannon. She did not appear to notice him at all, though at the sound of his horse's hoofs she glanced his way. It was the most fleeting of glances, indifferent, flashing elsewhere.

He had the trick of taking in everything with those keen dark eyes of his, of registering swift impressions, of filing them away for possible future reference. He thought, "She's a little beauty if there ever was one." Not quite like other girls either, a sullen, smoldering beauty, with brooding, smoky eyes.

He passed her and dismounted under the big poplar with butter-yellow leaves that cast its black blot of shade in front of the saloon, and she rode straight on. As he jingled down to the edge of the wooden sidewalk, he turned his observant eyes upon the two men who were standing there; they were watching the girl go by and spoke of her.

"Prettiest girl inside a hundred miles, Bordereau," said one of them—a short, stocky, immensely broad man, dressed in store clothes like a town dweller, yet with the hard hands and weathered face of a rancher.

"Yes," nodded Bordereau, and rolled his cigar and squinted after her. A tall, darkly handsome man in frock coat and high hat, quiet-voiced, even unctuous, it was a simple thing to mistake Steve Bordereau for a prosperous undertaker. "Yes," he said again, "she's been getting better looking all the time. Classier now than Florinda, even."

"If she was dressed right, she'd be." Then the heavy-set man laughed. He said, "Now if you just had a girl like her in your place, you'd double your intake!"

Steve Bordereau pursed a full lower lip.

"It's an idea, Murdo. I'll get her."

"Like hell you will!"

"What's this, Thursday? I'll have her upstairs at midnight just exactly one week from tonight. Midnight. Dressed right, too."

"Bet?" challenged Murdo. There was only one way to settle things with men like these two, one of whom owned and the other helped operate the Stag Horn.

"Two to one," said Bordereau coolly. "Five hundred of yours calls a thousand from me."

Murdo stared at him, seemed about to agree, then shook his head.

"You've got something up your sleeve, Steve. I know you. No bets."

Jim Torrance tied his horse at the hitching rail under the poplar, hung his spurs over the saddle horn and went into the saloon. There were not half a dozen men in the place, cattle hands from the look of them, and only one bartender behind the longest and most famous bar in this part of the country. Torrance photographed them all with that low-lidded glance characteristic of him; his survey began with the bartender and came back to him, taking stock of his pale-blue eyes, his pale, sleek hair that looked like the pictures in the barber shops, his mustaches like a buffalo's horns. Jim Torrance spun a silver dollar on the bar, ordered his drink and asked:

"Know anyone up around here named Jim Torrance?"

"Howdy, Stranger," said the bartender. He set forth bottle and glass and leaned forward conversationally on his elbows. "Jim Torrance?" he repeated. "Can't say as I do. What's he look like?"

"About my size and build," Torrance told him.

"Who's he askin' for, Jurgens?" rapped out a voice from one of the men lounging over a round table farther down the room. "What's he want?"

"You'd be sure to ask, now, Sam, wouldn't you?" grunted Jurgens. "Well, he's asking for a man name of Torrance, Jim Torrance."

"What you want him for, Stranger?" demanded Sam, and got to his feet, a little dried-up man of fifty or thereabouts, seeming to rattle around in his blue overalls and faded blue denim shirt like a dried pea in a weathered pod. He had just about the shrewdest, brightest little eyes that ever twinkled and gleamed and widened and narrowed in a man's face, eyes that just now, and at most times, were as eager as a six-year-old's at Christmas time. He came hurrying forward.

"It's old Sam Pepper," Jurgens advised Jim Torrance. "The damn' grasshopper's got his nose in everybody's business and knows most everything."

Old Sam Pepper, a wisp of a graying man standing something like five feet and a half in his high-heeled half-boots, peered straight up into Jim Torrance's face. All the men in the room had looked the stranger over pretty thoroughly, as was but natural and customary; strangers weren't everyday occurrences in and about Sundown; but no man of them all regarded him with such frank and thoroughgoing interest as did Sam Pepper.

He took stock of everything—Torrance's checkered shirt and neck scarf, his worn chaps, black and shaggy and dusty, the two crossed belts dragged low by their twin burdens of guns and cartridges, the worn, dutsy boots beginning to grow lopsided on their high, rocking heels. But his greatest and gravest concern was the stranger's face. He made Jim Torrance out to be tall and lean and gaunt, but as hardy and sinewy as a man whose muscles and tendons were all fine drawn steel wire; he stared up into a pair of keen, hard, dark eyes with their trick of being low-lidded as though always he was squinting at the sun, or probing under the surface of other men, and a mouth that was set and stern and somehow grim, a mouth that did not seem ever to have learned how to smile, a mouth, one would hazard, that knew less how to soften than to grow savage and cruel.

Sam Pepper was intrigued, but then, as Jurgens had suggested, he was forever growing curious about affairs not his own and men with whom he had no dealings. He said a second time, and more briskly, "What you want him for, Stranger?"

The stranger ignored him as a wolf hound ignores a poodle.

"Seems to me I've seen you somewheres," Sam Pepper hurried on, just to make way for his second question. "What's your name, Stranger?"

Then another man spoke up in a deep, throaty voice that sounded downright jovial in contrast to Sam Pepper's reedy, rasping utterance, and Jim Torrance looked down the shadowy room to the speaker, a big, sturdy, bald-headed fellow a dozen years younger than Sam Pepper and some two or three times as big.

"Askin' for Jim Torrance, be you?" he demanded. "Well, me, I know him. Seen him lately, too. I and him was pardners for a short time, over to Miller's Camp. A man about your size; yep, about your build, too."

Sam Pepper snorted for any to hear. Then in a lowered voice, hardly above a discreet whisper meant for the stranger alone, he said: "That's only Lying Bill talking, Stranger. Lying Bill Yarbo. The truth ain't in him and never was. Anything he says goes just the other way round; if he'd of said he hadn't never saw or heard of Jim Torrance, well you'd know they'd been together not ten minutes ago."

Lying Bill Yarbo shoved back the little poker table and came stalking forward.

"If you're of a mind to advertise your business all over town, Stranger," he said, for men to hear out on the street a block away—and they were long blocks in Sundown— "why you just let that feller that's talking to you—Sam'l Pepper, his name is, whereas it ought to be Peeper—know about it and you won't have to pay to get it published." Then a heavy frown dragged at his shaggy, black eyebrows. "What's he been saying to you about me? What's he been whispering?" He balled up an oversized fist and took another forward stride, whereupon Sam Pepper whipped back and darted toward the door; and men laughed, and the bartender, bored as most of his fraternity grow to be habitually, almost smiled. Jim Torrance's expression, or lack of the same, was undisturbed.

"You say you know Jim Torrance?" he said mildly. "Might I ask if he's around town, or has been lately?"

Lying Bill Yarbo took a deep, preparatory breath, then began his rumbling recital.

"Like I say, him and me was pardners over to Miller's. But that was quite a while ago, 'bout fifteen-sixteen year. Sixteen year, that's what; I'm remembering now. It was when there was that big explosion the Billings boys was to blame for, a dozen men blowed higher'n kites. I rec'lec' how a leg with the boot still on it was blowed in through the cabin door where me and Jim was having us our dinner. That was Cy Patten's leg, and Cy got well and made him another one out of one that got blew off a piano over to Molly Blaine's place. And now, the other day, not more'n say two weeks ago, you could of blowed me over with a puff of smoke when a feller sings out, 'Hi, Bill!' and I look around and see Jim Torrance. Seems as though—"

Jim Torrance downed his drink and went out; the last words he heard were Jurgens', saying, "I never heard tell of that there explosion over to Miller's, Bill," and Lying Bill Yarbo answering crustily, "Shucks, there's lots of things you never heard about." He saw Steve Bordereau and Murdo standing in the shade where he had left them; the girl had passed out of sight. He continued along the wooden sidewalk, avoiding the trap of a broken board for bootheels, and presently heard hurrying steps behind him. Then Sam Pepper, breathless with haste, his short legs making two of one of Torrance's strides, came up with him.

"Seeing how you're a stranger in town," said Sam Pepper, "and are looking for information, I got to warn you that Lying Bill Yarbo—"

"I've been warned," said Torrance.

"I'll ask folks that I see, folks that might know," Pepper ran on. "Who'll I say is wanting to know? What name, Stranger?"

For a split second Jim Torrance appeared to be considering. Then he said, in that same somehow incongruously mild tone of his, "I'm Torrance. Jim Torrance."

Sam Pepper's eyes flew wide open, his jaw dropped and he came to a dead halt. Of a sudden there were a dozen questions he was on edge to ask. But Torrance stopped a moment and looked at him in a way that dried up all questions. Then Torrance went on, and Sam Pepper, fairly itching with a brand-new curiosity, stood where he was and watched.

He saw Jim Torrance go into the one other saloon Sundown boasted—a squalid, dingy barroom and dance place frequented by the more patently riffraffian of the community's population, swarthy breeds for the most part, with a sprinkling of low-life whites—and still waited. Torrance came out and Pepper darted in. In short order he ascertained that the stranger had asked whether a man named Jim Torrance had showed up there of late. Out Sam Pepper hurried again and saw Torrance go into the Stage Stop Hotel and reappear within two or three minutes. Again Pepper made inquiries; yes, a stranger asking for a man named Torrance was just in here. And out Sam popped again, this time to see his latest and greatest interest in life, his new mystery man, step into the bake shop. He came out with something in his hand that looked like a pie. No doubt it was a pie. Just the same, Sam Pepper made sure.

"Yep, it was a pie!" he said under his breath, out on the street again. And when the newcomer mounted his horse and rode away, carrying an apple pie, Sam Pepper goggled after him. It didn't seem to make sense somehow.

CHAPTER II

LYING Bill Yarbo, the next day, told one of the most intriguing lies of his Munchausenesque career, in that it was one which later seemed to be borne out in fact. All this was much to Lying Bill Yarbo's surprise.

Sam Pepper, that queer combination of curiosity and cowardice, speaking about the matter in a way he had, since nothing that happened was out of the circle of his interest and commentary, made an observation which fitted the case as a cowboy's new boots fit his Chinese feet. Sam Pepper said:

"Shucks, it's again natur' that any man, lyin' steady with every breath he draws for twenty year, won't make a miscue and blunder into the outside edges of the truth once in a while. It's like as if you took a gun and blazed away a thousand times, and even if you tried not to hit it you'd spot the bull's-eye sooner-later. Accidents do happen."

Lying Bill Yarbo rode into Sundown about noon and was seen—by Sam Pepper, of course—to rock somewhat unsteadily on his heels, then make a bee line to Doc Jones' Drug Store. Sam Pepper sniffed the air like a hunting dog on a hot scent, and made his own bee line. It wasn't like Lying Bill Yarbo to be drunk this time of day, and what did he want at the drug store anyhow?

Inside, Lying Bill was getting patched up, painted with iodine until he looked like an Apache on the war trail, hung together with strips of bandage and doused with Wizard Oil, so that face and hands were all crisscrossed, doused with forty-rod whisky that soothed what ailed him and lubricated the floodgates of his speech.

"I was riding up in the hills a piece," said Lying Bill Yarbo. "I cut acrost Nigger Crick and went up over the

12

saddle and down into Desolation Valley, and I seen three fellers down in there that I knowed. One of 'em was that very same Jim Torrance the feller in town was asking about yestiddy, and another was a half-breed I used to see around Tucumcari, and one was another feller; and so I rode down to pass the time o' day, and I seen three more fellers that was sorta hiding in the brush. Quick as a flash I made out what they was up to, 'cause they was getting set to murder another feller. Then them fellers made out that I'd seen what was going on, and they piled onto me. The whole six of 'em, being it was six that I counted, and there mought of been more. And we fit."

Sam Pepper giggled.

"Most likely they kilt pore old Bill Yarbo, bein' so many ag'in him," he offered humorously.

Lying Bill Yarbo glared him down.

"We fit, like I said," he said ponderously "Me, I grabbed one man and slung him ag'in the crowd, knockin' 'em all galley-west. And they begun shootin' and so did I, and I reckon I kilt some of 'em and the rest got enough and run for it. I was that mad by then I'd of kilt 'em all, only I was sort of shaky and unsteady from fighting so many, all the same time, and so the living ones escaped."

"Most likely," Sam Pepper observed out of the corner of his mouth to the druggist's boy, "he fell off'n his horse and rolled down a ten-foot drop of cliff somewheres, and most likely he wasn't inside ten mile of Desolation Valley, and most likely—"

That was as far as Sam Pepper got with his surmisings, for Lying Bill Yarbo had ears like a lynx and heard every word and doubled his fists and sort of leaned forward. Sam Pepper skipped to the door and stuck there, too interested to permit of full flight, too much afraid of Lying Bill Yarbo to draw closer.

But the tale was told, and, though Lying Bill Yarbo elaborated it and put in some fancy stitches, nothing of any great import was added. It was, of course, a lie made out of whole cloth. The truth of the matter had been expressed unknowingly by Sam Pepper. Lying Bill Yarbo hadn't been within miles of Desolation Valley that day, and he had gotten a bad spill when the young, half-broke horse he was riding shied at a rock rolling down into a bit of mountain trail. The rider, his wandering thoughts far afield, had come mighty close to going over a hundred-foot fall of granite rock instead of a mere ten, and was lucky to be alive, with no bones broken.

But the oddest part of the whole thing was to follow. Sam Pepper was right and knew it in his bones; just the same he couldn't sit still until he visited Desolation Valley. It was only a dozen miles or so to the northwest of Sundown, and within an hour of hearing the story he rode out of town, heading eastward to fool 'em, then circling and turning toward Desolation. And he came dangerously close to being the second man to fall off his horse that day, when he found what he hadn't the least expectation of finding.

Already, high in the blue air, the turkey buzzards were spiraling. Sam Pepper won the race from them. He found a man lying dead, arms outflung, wild black hair hanging straight against bloodless temples, a neat blue hole in his forehead.

"Why, cripes! I know this feller!" gasped Sam. "I seen him raising merry hell around Sundown only a couple days ago. He was looking for Steve Bordereau, and Steve was out of town right then, and he shot his mouth off to say some day him or Steve was going to kill each other. And I'll bet a man—"

Lying Bill Yarbo, when the news was brought to him, turned as red as a beet; even that bald and shiny pate of his, usually a pale pink, became a rich crimson. He swallowed a time or two; his Adam's apple went pumping up and down and he seemed to find difficulty in breathing. But he was not Lying Bill Yarbo for nothing. He began to laugh.

"That's only one of 'em I kilt," he proclaimed. "I dug a hole and buried the rest of 'em. Must of overlooked that feller."

With much laughter, with men slapping their own legs or the other fellows' backs and vowing that Bill Yarbo was the very king of all good liars, Lying Bill Yarbo himself rode out of town hurriedly and was not seen for a week.

"Ashamed, that's what he is," proclaimed Sam Pepper gleefully. "He's gone to hide his old bald head. Most likely he's that shamed that he'll never come back, which would be a good thing for one and all!"

And then—as though Sam Pepper didn't already have enough on his mind to put a man into what was locally known as a state or a dither—all he had to do was climb the high pine hill pretty nearly centering his ranch, and from it look over to the old Hammond place, all of a sudden and without his knowledge taken over by a stranger who said that he wanted to see Jim Torrance—and who, if you asked him, said that he was Jim Torrance!

"It's beyant me," muttered Sam Pepper when he had climbed the hill and had settled himself on a flat rock whence he could see far and wide. He saw the stranger going about the small house and barn and bunk house, pottering like a man at home; he saw the boy Skeeter and the dozen head of horses, likely looking stock, and the pack mules. "Must of bought the place," he speculated. "Wonder how much he paid? Wonder what he's up to? Wonder who the kid is? Wouldn't be his boy; might be a kid brother. Wonder what makes his face look like it does, like he was thinking black and mysterious thoughts! I got a notion to go over—" His spare shoulders twitched and he made a wry face, squinching up his sharp-pointed nose. "If he is hiding some evil doings, and I found out—and he kotched me—he'd commit murder as quick as I'd spit terbaccy juice down a knot hole."

Meantime the stranger, all unaware of the fact that he was being spied on whenever Sam Pepper had the leisure—and Sam always had plenty of leisure when there was something to be nosed out, and nearly always there was something afoot that invited his investigation—went about his work on the old Hammond ranch toward making it again what it had been a long time before, a tidy place to live on. First of all he and the boy mended fences; then they restored the old corral down by the barn, and after that they gave their attention to the barn itself. Those chores done, they did things to the old house. It was an ancient adobe with a plank shed addition like some noxious excretion that needed amputation. They tore the shed down and piled the lumber behind the house against some future use, as firewood perhaps. Then they carted out a lot of refuse and burned it; they cleaned out the well and installed a pair of new buckets on a new rope. Hour by hour the place brightened.

Jim Torrance's premises were at last invaded by Sam Pepper, who could no longer resist making an exploratory expedition. He came over ostensibly to be neighborly but with eyes and ears taking in everything. It happened that at the moment a red hawk lighted on a pine top within what Sam Pepper would have described as rifle distance. Jim Torrance snapped a gun from his dragging belt and set a bullet free—just like brushing a gnat away—no more premeditation, no more precision, you would have said; just an involuntary gesture. Yet it remained that the red hawk came straight down, a dead fluff of feathers.

"Don't like 'em," said Jim Torrance gently, and holstered his gun. He turned and looked Sam Pepper in the eye exactly as he had done that day in Sundown. "I've got doves around here that I do sort of like. The hawks bother 'em. Me, I've got no use for any sort of birds that go sticking their beaks into quiet folks' affairs."

And he kept on looking at Sam Pepper exactly as he had done in Sundown.

Sam Pepper went home.

As for Jim Torrance, he smiled, if you could call it a smile, and went into the house. He shed his work clothes and dug some town clothes out of a canvas roll. He shook them out, brushed them, used a hot stove lid as an iron and pressed them. He called Skeeter in and said: "Kid, at last I'll let you go on your way. Here's what's coming to you, with enough on top of it to buy you board and lodging for a few days. Adios and luck."

It was just one week from the day he had arrived in Sundown, just a week plus a few hours from the time he had overheard Steve Bordereau saying to Murdo, "I'll have her upstairs at midnight a week from now."

Jim Torrance rode into Sundown that night about ten o'clock. It was a Saturday night. That meant that the small town would be swollen like a tumor with that virulence which a horde of drinking, gambling, here-we-go, devil-may-care hell-rousers had the knack of injecting into an evening when they were at large. With them, cowboys, and ranchers and dry-gulchers and mule skinners and desert rats, up from the Big Sandy, and the rest of the denizens of the ridges between lowlands and highlands; the thing to do of a Saturday night was come to town.

They came to town.

When at ten o'clock Jim Torrance looked in at the Stag Horn Saloon it was upon no such quiet picture as he had mentally photographed that still afternoon of his first arrival. Now the place was jammed; the air was blue with cigarette and cigar smoke; a big, new magical-looking wheel turned out noisy music if you dropped a quarter into it, and quarters dropped like rain while voices shouted other voices down; and along the bar, upon which three busy barkeeps slammed down the drinks and raked in the silver, there was no space for a new invader unless he scrimmaged for it.

Jim Torrance, shaven and with his hair freshly combed, wearing a brand-new bandana about his throat, walked through the long room, looking things over. He kept thinking: "He'll have her here at midnight. That's two hours yet. Upstairs."

So he had his conventional drink and loafed through the place looking for its upstairs. He found a staircase, masked, until one looked sharply for it or knew where it was, by a pair of doors with veilings over them. As you came in from the street, all you had to do was turn right, instead of left where the barroom was, buck the doors, go upstairs and find the room where the wheel spun, where the faro layout invited, where chuck-a-luck and the rest of the popular games spun along wide open.

"I'll poke along upstairs at twelve o'clock," said Jim Torrance to himself.

A quirk of bitter humor moulded his lips into a half smile that was the next thing to a sneer, for he thought: "I am like Sam Pepper, getting the disease known as elongated proboscis. What business is it of mine?" Just the same he was quietly determined to stick his long nose into the Bordereau-Sally Dawn affair.

Shortly before midnight he found his way upstairs. On the upper landing, standing before closed doors, was a thick-bodied, beefy looking man who challenged him with a long probing look.

"Looking for somebody?" he asked.

"I want a run for my money," said Torrance. "I can get it up here, can't I?"

The doorkeeper didn't ask any more questions. The stranger didn't look like a tin-horn. Anyhow, ten minutes would show whether he was a cheap skate or the real goods. He said: "Go ahead, Stranger. Right through them doors. You'll find your game."

Torrance entered a big room, bigger than the barroom downstairs, that would have surprised him had it not been that the place was so widely known that he and thousands of others had heard of it from far off. It was the particular room to give Bordereau and the Stag Horn their dubious reputations. Elegance, nothing less, was the keynote here. On top of elegance you had abundance. Whiskies and brandies were of the best that the Southwest knew, and the Southwest knew its liquor. There was champagne that didn't sicken you; and the whiskies and brandies and wines flowed as from a spigot that aped the purse of Fortunatus. What was more to the point, you didn't have to pay for what your throat yearned for. There was a sort of politeness in the room; your host was M. Bordereau, and his one desire appeared to be to go to any extreme to make you feel at home, to make you feel cordially received, to get you cordially warmed—and put you in the mood to shoot your wad at one of his gaming tables.

Therefore the beefy man at the doors. It was his job to gauge all comers by the dollars-and-cents measure. You'd get anything liquid in the house that you wanted, free, not a cent for it; but you'd leave, at quitting time, nothing less than a hundred dollars. Maybe a thousand or ten times that. Steve Bordereau was wearing diamonds.

There were already some forty of fifty people in the room, men for the most part, though there were a few women, the dazzling, hit-you-in-the-eye, effulgent type, those adventuresses that the West drew at that time from all the world.

And there was Florinda.

Steve Bordereau himself, in his long-tailed coat and trousers with stripes down them and patent leather shoes, was very much in evidence. He knew everyone by his first name and was a genial host and friend. He was as smooth as an eel in oil, yet remained as hard as lava rock. Before them all he was a courtly gentleman with Florinda on his arm; not ten minutes before he had grabbed her by the hair and slapped her face and told her, as though she needed telling, what she was. But before his public he bragged about her.

This part of the establishment had been a gradual, natural growth. At first there had been just a poker room set aside for those who, when they wanted poker, wanted high stakes. There were several of them—old Tom Clark, the mine owner; Gaston Dubordieu, the gambler; three younger men, Juan Garcia, Walter Voorhees and Dick Hathaway, sons of three of the biggest cattle kings within a score of miles in any direction—and twenty miles was quite a step when you did it on horseback. These and their ilk at times brought others, and Steve Bordereau saw wisdom in accommodating them. So he had built on the second story, bricks laid on top of honest adobe, with not only a front but also a back stairway. He added a roulette wheel and a faro layout and dice and card games, and he made his regulations to shut out the nickel-shooters and admit only the dead-game sports.

Further, of late he had added two other luxuries—a deep Turkey-red carpet and a young lady in evening dress.

"She and the carpet add a nice homey touch," he said sentimentally.

The young lady—Florinda—greeted the boys smilingly and chatted with them; she encouraged them in extravagant notions and sat briefly with them at their tables, dropping in and fluttering away like a butterfly. She lifted her long-lashed eyes and widened them in horror at pikers' bets; she clapped her hands when some young fool took the bit in his teeth and began to plunge.

"And she's a real lady," Steve Bordereau boasted of her. "One of the fine old Spanish family of Valdez y Verdugo. The Señorita Florinda de Valdez y Verdugo, that's who she is! The real goods, no gutter-snipe. Not from Mexico— from Spain. You see, she just happened to be visiting in Mexico City when all her folks got slaughtered in that Jerez revolution. The family fortune was swept away, nothing left but the Verdugo jewels that she's wearing tonight." Without stint, he had spent sixty dollars for the double handful of glass diamonds and rubies and emeralds.

To Florinda, not ten minutes ago, he had said in one of the private rooms: "You damn little fool, watch out for the booze tonight. Get tight just once more and I'll kick you clean from here to the border dive where I picked you up, and where that *novio* of yours will pop a knife into you like sticking a pig."

As Jim Torrance wandered through the long room, looking at the games that were already running, glancing at faces to see whether any were familiar, and then stood up at the bar, he saw Florinda for the first time. She was not six feet away and chanced to turn at that moment and their eyes met.

"You!" she exclaimed.

He stared coldly at her. And Steve Bordereau noted her exclamation and Torrance's impassive, masklike face.

Bordereau came forward and explained to Torrance that up here a man did not have to pay for his drinks. It was all on the house.

"Drink hearty," he said. "Have a good time, Stranger."

Jim Torrance set a ten dollar gold coin spinning.

"I pay for my drinks, unless I'm drinking with a friend, or go thirsty," he replied.

Bordereau shrugged. To the man behind the bar he said: "This gentleman is new here, Charlie. Let him have things his way."

"Sure," said Charlie, and to Torrance, "What's your relish, Stranger?"

Torrance had his drink, but out of the corner of his eye he saw Bordereau signal the girl aside. He couldn't overhear their words but thought that he could come pretty close to guessing their burden. Bordereau would be saying: "Say, you know that man! Who is he?" She would have to confess that she didn't know.

But Florinda was saying more than that. A shiver twitched at her bare shoulders as though she were cold. She said rapidly:

"I don't know who he is, but I am afraid of him! There is something terrible about him. Did you see how he looked at me?"

"You do know him," snapped Bordereau.

"I saw him once, only once; that's all. Down in Nacional where I was dancing at the place of One Eye Perez where you found me. The way he looked at me just now, he looked at a man like that that night—and before the sun came up that man was dead. That is all I know. I swear it!"

"I wonder!" He looked at her suspiciously.

Jim Torrance amused himself for a while at one of the tables; faro was his game when it wasn't poker, but to-night his eye was less for the card the dealer slid from its rack than for the several doors opening into the long room. It was full midnight now, and the sullen little beauty with the smoky eyes, Sally Dawn, was nowhere in evidence. He was glad, because he wanted to have Steve Bordereau fail to make good his boast, yet it remained that he was disappointed, too.

Then he saw Bordereau look at his heavy gold watch and hurry out through a door at the far end of the room; that way was the head of the back staircase, and also, as Torrance later discovered, a series of small private rooms— a dressing room, an office, small rooms for poker. He thought—because Bordereau had looked at his watch: "He's going to get her now. He looks smug and somehow like he'd raked in a jack pot."

He was right. Almost immediately Steve Bordereau returned, and Sally Dawn came with him. The gambler threw the door wide with a gesture; he extended a dramatic arm in another wide gesture, ushering her in. Then a hush fell upon the room as she stood framed in the doorway.

CHAPTER III

STEVE BORDEREAU was a show-
man of sorts; else he'd never have made the Stag Horn
so widely publicized across hundreds of Southwestern
miles. He knew values and how to emphasize them.

A murmur went up when all eyes were drawn to Sally
Dawn. She was pale, with no rouge on her cheeks, and her
lips were scarlet. She wore long ruby-red earrings—ruby-
red but not rubies. No others of Bordereau's glass gems
adorned her. Her gown was exquisite, costly and in marked
contrast to La Florinda's flashy one, a beautifully simple
thing of white satin. She carried a large black ostrich-
feather fan in her left hand. Her eyes looked enormous.

"My friends!" sang out a triumphant Bordereau, "I have
a new surprise for you, and here she is! It is Miss Sally
Dawn Cannon, and I guess some of you already know her,
the daughter of the late cattle king, Big Bill Cannon. She
has consented to come here to be still another hostess, like
the Señorita Florinda de Valdez y Verdugo, and to be
friendly with all my friends. And to start with, she asks
everyone here to drink her a little toast! Nothing in the
house is too good for tonight, and it comes to you with
Steve Bordereau's compliments."

Sally Dawn smiled upon them. It was a lovely smile,
thought Jim Torrance, and he thought also, "Well, money
can buy most things." Bordereau's announcement was
greeted with cheers and hand clappings. Torrance went on
with his faro, playing as though he did not care whether
he won or lost, and so he started winning. He saw Sally
Dawn go straight to the Mexican girl; Florinda showed
her beautiful white teeth in what went for a glad smile of
greeting. The two girls spoke together a moment, Sally
Dawn eagerly, Florinda appearing more reserved; perhaps

she was striving for a hauteur to match the proud names Verdugo and Valdez.

Then men began surging forward, flocking for the most part about the new girl; in champagne of Bordereau's providing or their own choice of liquor they drank her health and happiness. And to Jim Torrance, still at his faro table, it seemed that she was the gayest of the gay ones; he thought that he had never seen eyes sparkle and glimmer as hers did.

Then she was swept away by a small party who wanted her at their table, and La Florinda went her own way with her own friends, hovering with them over a roulette wheel, and Torrance finished his game, pocketed his winnings and moved farther down the long room. He stood there at the end of the bar, his glass twirling slowly between lean brown fingers, his eyes, always low-lidded, looking lazy, yet secretly watchful.

He marked the face of every man and woman in the place; he took stock of winners and losers, of hard drinkers and hard players. When any newcomer arrived—and men were coming in all the time, the room filling and overflowing—he saw them. When some went out from time to time, he took note.

A very few departed early through the front doors, going down the front stairs and about their business, homeward bound perhaps. Several went out through one of the three doors set in the wall toward the rear end of the room. He gathered, without asking, that these were off to play poker in private rooms. He spotted the men, two of them, who would play for the house. Perhaps later Steve Bordereau would play for himself.

Again the new girl caught his attention, and his eyes still further narrowed until they were mere light-flickering slits. She seemed gayer than ever, eager, electric; he thought he had never heard such bright laughter. The warmth of color now staining her cheeks might have resulted, along with the exhilaration gripping her, from the wine that had flowed so generously.

And then he saw her eyes, and knew instantly that he had her all wrong. They chanced to meet his across the room—frightened, panicky, desperate eyes. Whatever reason the girl might have to bring her here, she was scared half to death.

She had just risen swiftly from a table where she was being made much of by four men. Steve Bordereau, who had never lost sight of her, hastened to her side; his hand, firm and agile and powerful, came to rest on her arm. As the men at the table rose, too, one of them drunk and leering, Bordereau said cheerfully:

"Go on ahead boys; we'll be back with you in two shakes."

The four went out at one of the rear doors. Bordereau, with his hand still on the girl's arm, stooped closer, his face close to hers. His words, so softly spoken were they, did not carry any farther than he meant them to carry. Then, though the girl for a moment stood very stiff, she turned to go with him, out of the room at the rear. The two passed quite near where Jim Torrance stood at the end of the bar.

The girl said, "That man is a beast, the one who wants to pay me to be his mascot—"

Bordereau said: "Shut up, you little fool! You'll do what I tell you!"

She answered, in a queer, strained voice, "You can't make me do a thing like that."

She had pulled back, but they were passing on again.

Bordereau said angrily, "You know I can make you do anything!"

She said, scarcely above a whisper: "I won't. I'd kill you!"

They went on then. A door opened and closed after them.

"Know a man around here named Jim Torrance?" Jim Torrance asked the nearest bartender.

"No. Never heard of him."

Jim Torrance paid for his drink with a silver dollar. As things happened, he did not wait for his change. Above the noise in the room, he heard the shot, not loud but clear and eloquent enough. Nor did he wait to note whether any others heard and marked it too. Two or three swift, long strides brought him to the door through which the gambler and the girl had just passed. There was a hallway with another set of doors on the farther side; a couple of shaded lamps gave their dim, colorful light. He saw Bordereau and Sally Dawn.

Bordereau had not yet fallen, but had his back against the wall and appeared to be sliding slowly sideways. The girl had dropped her big black fan; the only thing she held was a small pistol. There was a look of horror on Bordereau's face, a look of horror, almost twin with it, on hers. Her fingers opened slowly and the pistol clattered to the floor.

"I have killed him! I am glad! He—"

From her, Jim Torrance looked swiftly at Bordereau again. The man was down now; he had flung up an arm as he lurched; a hand brushed his face; Torrance saw the bloodstain there. He started to shrug; what affair was it of his?

Then he heard a clamor as a door was thrown open against a wall and men called out and came running. At the same moment he saw the head of the back staircase.

"Get out of here, quick; on the run!" he commanded. "They're all Bordereau's friends, not yours."

She didn't move; she didn't appear to have heard. He stopped to pick up the fallen pistol and her black fan; he caught her by the arm and ran with her to the stairs. They plunged downward together, the girl half falling, half carried by the strong hand that bore her along. Together they darted out at the rear of the house.

His one thought was to get her clear until she could have her own friends at her back, until the Bordereau pack had cooled a bit. He ran with her to the front of the building where horses were. He meant to throw her onto a horse, to pile onto another and be off with her that way. Then he saw the one wheeled rig, a buckboard as lean and light as a greyhound, with a pole team.

"Yours?" he demanded, seeing that there was but the one team here, knowing that most men came on horseback, and arguing that she, if she had dressed at home, would have mussed her dress on a saddle and hence had come in the buckboard.

She gasped out something, he couldn't make it out. Well, it didn't matter. He swung her up bodily over a wheel to the seat; he ran and untied the horses; he slipped the reins into her hand.

"Get going, on the run," he commanded. "I'll grab my horse and follow."

His horse was tied only a few feet away. He jerked the tie rope free, swung up into the saddle—and saw that she had not stirred; there she sat, a slim, white, rigid figure on the seat. He rapped out again, "Get going!" and lashed the horses over their rumps with the end of his tie rope. The horses were off at a run, frightened; the girl began to sway, then to lean sideways, reminding him of Bordereau settling to the floor.

With the horses running, he spilled out of his saddle to the tail end of the buckboard, keeping the tie rope still in one hand, leading his own horse. As he came to the back of her seat he saw that the girl's hand lay loosely at her sides; she had dropped the reins and they were about to vanish over the dashboard. He made a wild grab for them, caught them just in time—and just in time caught her, too. She had fainted dead away.

"Here's hell to pay," he growled. Never had he had his hands so filled—with the reins of the runaway team, his own horse's lead rope, and now an unconscious Sally Dawn.

He managed to ease her down on the seat, her head and shoulders on his knee; he gave the lead rope a couple of turns about the guard rail at the back of the seat, thrust the free end under him, anchoring it against any but a severe tug by sitting on it while he used both hands for a fighting second or two, getting the runaway team under control. Then he looked back through the starlit dark of the night to see whether they were followed and made out that they were not as yet. He looked ahead and briefly wondered where he and the girl were headed. There had been no time, no chance to choose a direction.

They were speeding north, and his ranch lay to the

north of Sundown, so, at the first side road, a wavering, little-used lane through the pines, he swung homeward. If the confounded girl hadn't slumped into a faint on him she could tell him where she lived, where she wanted to go now; he himself hadn't the least idea. Now the only thing he saw to do was carry her to his place; they might not look for her there—and even a Sam Pepper couldn't see in the dark.

He kept the horses on the run on the down grades, saving them on the pulls, letting them blow a time or two. When he pulled up at the side of the gray and ghostly road where the old dead pine leaned over the big white rock, the girl stirred and moaned sobbingly and sat up. He got down, tied the horses in the dark under the pines, put up his hands to her, and said curtly, "Better hop down."

"Where are you taking me?" she asked then.

"My place. It's only a step beyond the gate there. Then I'll come back and get rid of this team somehow; they won't be able to follow the tracks tonight, but tomorrow they will. By that time I can get you home."

She did not stir to get down.

"Why not now?" she asked.

"Suit yourself. But if Bordereau's dead— Well, where will they look first of all for you?"

She put her face down into the shelter of her hands; he stood close enough to see how she shuddered.

Once again he tried to shrug away all responsibility, yet somehow he couldn't quite make a go of it. He didn't like Steve Bordereau and he didn't care much for the gambler's crowd of friends; further, he remembered two things— how the gambler had gripped her by the arm, and how a strange terror had dilated her eyes. He stood a moment looking up at her uncertainly; then he simply reached up and lifted her down in his arms.

"Come along with me; I won't hurt you any. Whatever you do now, you had better take time to think."

She slipped out of his arms and answered quickly, "Yes."

He led the way, opened the gate and showed her the house; it was dark but the dull gray adobe walls were re-

vealed by the glimmer of the stars. He waited for her at the
open door; he heard her teeth begin to chatter.

"Step in and I'll light a lamp; we'll have no light until
the door is shut."

With the door shut and a smoky-chimneyed coal oil
lamp burning wanly on a box that served as table, she did
not look about her to see what this bare room was like
but lifted her eyes straightaway to his; they were no longer
sullen but were bright with burning anguish.

"I killed him," she said. "I wanted to kill him—and I
did."

"Maybe not," he told her. "A man doesn't die every
time a bullet from a small caliber gun hits him."

"If I did kill him, I can only hope that I won't live long.
If I didn't— Well, I might as well be dead." And then she
demanded: "Why did you step in? Why are you trying to
help me? You don't even know me."

"I meant to take you straight to your folks, but you toppled over and we had to start on the jump, and I don't
know where you live. That's why I brought you here—"

"I can't get his face out of my mind—how he looked
when he slumped down. He— Oh, God!"

"Look out!" said Jim Torrance sharply. "Don't you start
going to pieces!"

There was not a chair in the room, so she dropped down
in a corner, her face hidden in her hands as it had been in
the buckboard, as though she were fighting desperately
thus to shut out something she could not bear to look at.

"How far from here," he asked her, "to your home?"

"It's not far, just across the hills, but there's no road."

"What do you mean?"

"I'd have to go back the way we came, almost to Sundown; the road turns off there. And I'd be sure to meet
them—"

"Just across the hills? We could make it on horseback."

"Yes." She stood up. "I'll go now, right away. My
mother is desperately ill."

"And you left her to go to the Stag Horn!" His tone
was as good as a slap in her face. He softened it somewhat,
however, when he saw the anguish seeming to burn higher

and higher in her eyes, and said: "Well, your folks will be taking care of her. But about going right now—"

"I haven't any other folks. There is just Mother, and I think she is dying. I left her alone with an ignorant, shiftless and pretty nearly heartless Indian woman. That's why I must hurry."

He realized that there was a lot he did not know about this girl. He asked: "What about your team? It is yours, isn't it?"

"Yes." She looked down at her gleaming white gown, soiled and rumpled now, and set her hands to it as though she wanted to rip it off her body. "I drove over, so as not to muss this thing! The team? What do I care—"

"I'm going to ride along with you," said Torrance, "anyhow until you sight your house. Now you just wait here while I go saddle a horse for you; it's in the pasture, so it'll be a few minutes."

"Hurry!" she begged him.

He went first of all to where he had left the buckboard. He swung the team back into the road, still leading his own horse, and drove on at a run for a good mile. Where there was a possible though roadless way down into the dark, timbered canyon, he drove down into it, a winding way among the trees. There he left the buckboard; the horses, hastily unhitched and unharnessed, he turned loose, trusting that they'd return home in the course of time but not in any great haste. After that he hunted in the buckboard against the mere chance that the girl's fan or the gun he had dropped there had stayed with them on their rapid flight from Sundown; he found neither.

He met Sally Dawn, a slim white satin shape, at the gate.

"Where have you been? I thought you had gone away!"

He told her briefly, then at last went for a horse for her, cinched on his spare saddle, wondering how the devil she was going to manage with that dress on, and returned to her.

She managed all right. As a matter of fact she had thought of the problem before he did and had solved it after a fashion. While he was away with the team she had found a sharp knife and some string in his kitchen.

With a sort of savage delight she ripped that satin gown fore and aft so that it hung in two panels like a divided skirt. With the string she bound the two separate divisions about her legs from ankle to thigh. When he saw her mount it was like seeing a young page from some old court.

The way they rode, the girl leading along dim, dark trails, it was but four or five miles to the old King Cannon Ranch. The first winking light which she was first to glimpse was, she told him, home. He spurred to her side and put his hand on her horse's reins.

"Listen! You said you left your mother alone with the Indian woman. Well, listen!"

The night was still, and sounds carried far and clearly. There were men's voices; there were drumming hoofbeats, still in the distance. That meant that already there were several men here, others soon to arrive.

"I don't care! I've got to go to her. They won't dare—"

"Wouldn't Steve Bordereau have dared a pretty good deal?"

"He can't now!" Her voice was brittle. "I'm glad! Now, let me go."

"No. Keep your hair on. Wait here for me. I'll ride down, find out how things stand, and be back before you know it. You wait here!"

He dipped forward in the saddle and shot away, and what he had commanded her to do she did. There was a quality in his voice which as much as said, "When I say you've got to do a thing, you've got to do it."

A thin little night breeze blew around her and she shivered, not so much with cold as with nervous dread. She listened to the hammering of his horse's hoofs, and they sounded like far, sinister drumbeats. She lost sight of him down in a hollow brimming with black night, and for a little while she stared into the utter dark down there and felt its symbolism sweep over her like a palpable, drowning tide. When she raised her eyes and looked straight up at the millions of twinkling lights bespangling the wide sweep of cloudless sky, they seemed infinitely farther away than ever before, and as chill as a wintry morning glinting on frost.

She began to listen for his return long before she heard it. The thing that put a new dread into her was the slowness with which he was riding. She told herself: "He's just saving his horse. He has ridden it hard tonight. And it's uphill."

But when he returned to her and didn't speak out immediately, she understood that something terrible had happened. He came very close; this time, instead of putting his hand on her reins, he put it on her hand.

We've got to take things the way they come, youngster. In this life, we don't deal ourselves all the cards we've got to play."

"It's my mother!" she gasped.

His hand closed, hard and firm on hers.

"Yes."

"She is dead!"

"Yes."

"And I wasn't there! Let me go now; let me go! Quick!"

"Hold it. Hold it, youngster." It was he who held her. "You can't go now, not right now. There's a bunch of roughnecks down there that— Well, I'd rather deal with coyotes. They're a lot of low-lifes of the Bordereau crowd. They're half drunk and mean, and they say— Well, they're talking wild. They won't stay all night. Let them go first."

"I don't care, I don't care!" She wrenched furiously to break his grip. "I'm going—"

"Steve Bordereau's dead," he said bluntly. "They were talking about it down at the house."

"I tell you I don't care about anything now! She wouldn't be dead if it weren't for Steve Bordereau—he ought to have been killed long ago. Let me go. You can't stop me—"

"Can't I?"

He removed his hand only to scoop her out of her saddle and onto his own. Then he swung his horse about and turned back along the way they had come.

CHAPTER IV

THE following day had Sam Pepper running around in circles. Pop Smith, down at the General Store, said, "Sam reminds me of a dog chasin' his own tail." Hank Webber, the stage driver, said, "He'll have a fit afore the day's over." Lying Bill Yarbo remarked, "He's goin' to blow up an' bust; an' me, I don't want to be anywheres near when *that* happens." He put thumb and finger to his nose.

But under the circumstances there was no one—excepting Lying Bill Yarbo of course—who really censured the inquisitive little man for his state of excitement. Things had happened, the sort of things which were bound to interfere with Sam Pepper's proper attention to his own victuals and drink and everyday affairs.

Sam Pepper fairly danced up and down.

"It all begun with Sally Dawn Cannon being at Bordereau's gambling room! Her! What do you s'pose made her go to a place like that? All dressed up, they say, like a queen, in white silk with diamonds and ever'thing. Why wasn't I there? And then look what happens. She kills Steve Bordereau! Kills him! Her! What about that? Why? What made her? And then where'd she go? Talk about mysteries! Just vanished—poof! Like that. And that ain't half of it!"

No, that wasn't half of it. Sam Pepper was all over town, out of town, back to town, everywhere; he must have asked ten thousand questions that day. He said over and over:

"Sally Dawn's mother died last night, while all the rest of hell was popping, and I want to know why. And most of all, tell me this: Can a dead woman walk? The old woman's dead body's vanished, too, ain't it? How in hell? Where? Why? A woman dies and her body vanishes, and all you lunkheads do is squat and let things happen and don't even try to find out about 'em!"

So tremendously did all these occurrences obsess him that for the moment he lost all interest in Jim Torrance, and so failed of coming in contact with the one person who, if by any chance he had cared to do so, could have set Sam Pepper right all along the line. For Jim Torrance was at home all day, pottering around his ranch and letting his thoughts travel almost as far afield as curious Sam's.

Last night he had prevailed, at first by physical strength and then by the suasion of cool logic, upon a girl in the grip of such frenzy as came close to making her into a mad thing. She screamed at him until he shut off her screams with a hard hand; she fought, scratching and pummeling and biting. Until she wore herself out, she evinced a strength surprising in such slender feminine shapeliness. But in the end she melted, exhausted, in his arms, and he talked with her, and after a while she listened.

"It's tough, but you've got to take it. Don't you suppose other folks have had to take it, no matter how tough? Your mother, in her time, your own kids in their time, if you ever have any."

"I won't! I never will! Life is so ugly, like a big fiendish brute, like a gorilla. I hate it!"

"Life's all right," said Jim Torrance, sounding vastly indifferent. "It's sort of like taking a trip through the woods; you've got your ups and you've got your downs, all kinds of steep places and level places, too; and deserts after you pop out of the shade, and sun and rain and nice little sections of both heaven and hell."

"It's cruel and merciless, and it's vile."

"You knew your mother was a mighty sick woman; you knew she had to die before long—"

"I might have saved her! That was why I let Steve Bordereau make me do things I hated. He—"

"Never mind Steve Bordereau now. I'm talking about your mother. She is dead, and you can't help that. You can go down to the house where she is if you want to; I won't hold you back any more after you've had time to think. Only I'll tell you what'll happen if you go now. There's a tough bunch hanging around, and they're all Bordereau bums; and they're half drunk, some of 'em, and the rest are more so. They'll grab you; they'll yank you off to Sundown or somewhere. God knows what they'll do with you, but you could be sure of one thing. By the time you got back home, if you ever did, your ma'd be buried somewhere. Likely enough you'd never even know where."

He had set her down at the base of a big pine. Slowly she slid down close to the ground; she lay there, flattened against the earth; he couldn't hear a sob from her then and it was too dark for him to see how she writhed.

He waited a while, then spoke emotionlessly.

"I'll go down to the house again pretty soon. They won't pay much attention to me, as why should they? They won't stick around all night. There will be only the Indian woman left. I'll scare her off. Then you can come."

Late that night it was Jim Torrance who dug the grave on the knoll back of the house near that other grave, already six years occupied by the former cattle king, Bill Cannon. He found mattock and shovel in the tool shed, and some planks. And it was Jim Torrance who, just before daylight, bore in his arms a thin, wasted figure, blanket-enwrapped. All had gone; none had any thought of the dead woman except the Indian woman, and she had been glad to flee the place when Torrance gave her her chance. The girl had had her vigil on her knees by her mother's bedside while Torrance was digging. She did her weeping alone; when he came for her she stood up and helped him. She said, when they came to the knoll:

"I don't want anyone to know even where she is. They were so cruel to her. I mean Bordereau and Murdo and those men you say were here tonight."

So they replaced the dry sod over the unmounded grave; they scattered pine needles over it. Torrance even dug up a couple of small bushes and planted them on an already pretty nearly obliterated rectangle.

"And now?" said Jim Torrance. "What about you?"

"I don't know. I don't care. Oh, I'll go away."

"Where? Friends?"

"Anywhere. Friends? No. I haven't anyone. I don't want anyone."

"I see." He rolled a cigarette; rolled and rolled it until it was as smooth and hard as a lead pencil.

"I haven't thanked you—"

"Don't." He kept on rolling that cigarette of his. Then he cocked an eye at the eastern horizon. "It'll be sun-up real soon."

"Yes. I must hurry. While it's still dark. I've got to slip away as though—as though I were a murderer!" She broke into a shrill, sobbing laughter.

"Slam the brakes on," he said. He lighted his cigarette, then held it before his moody eyes, studying the red glow of its burning end.

"You have been mighty good to me," she said. "You don't know me; I don't even know who you are. Why?"

"Why what?"

"Why have you gone out of your way, gone to so much trouble to treat me like—like a friend?"

"I don't like Steve Bordereau," he said, clipping his words short. "I don't like Murdo, his side-kick."

"I see." And she added, her own words clipped as short as his and shorter and with their bitterness, "It was Clark Murdo first, Steve Bordereau next and working with him, who ruined us."

"You haven't answered me," said Jim Torrance, and didn't seem interested in her relations with Bordereau and Murdo and her sequential opinions of them. "Now what?"

"I've told you—"

"Only it won't work." He flipped his cigarette away, then strode to where it had fallen, to grind it out under the toe of his boot. "I listened to the men talking at the house before they drifted. Me, being a Johnny-come-lately, I don't get it all. But I do get this: Maybe they won't string you up the way they'd handle a man—but maybe, too, there are things a girl like you would hate just about as bad. They're plugging all the roads. You try to skip and they'll get you."

"It's Clark Murdo," she said angrily. "That's who it is. If Steve Bordereau were alive, it would be Bordereau. But with him dead"—she said it as steadily as though she were not remembering—"it's Clark Murdo."

He lifted his shoulders as much as to say, "What's that got to do with me?" He reached for his Durham bag, then changed his mind and pulled his hat off to run his brown fingers through his thick black mane of hair.

"You'll come along with me," he said. "Back to my place. I'll get you away, clear, from there. Let's get going."

"I can't understand—"

"You don't have to understand. Anyhow, there's nothing that wants any understanding. You're free, white and—you're grown up." She must be eighteen or nineteen or a barely possible twenty; at that ripe age a girl was a woman. "I'm asking you to come along. If you don't want to, remember the road's open both ends."

She came along. She was half dead with stress, grief and weariness. At the house she had kicked off that hated white satin gown and donned riding breeches and boots. She forked her horse the way he did, and they rode.

They rode through the dark under the pines, as silent and dark within themselves as the black pines were. They came up to the top of a thinly timbered ridge and into the wan glow of a new day, two self-contained black silhouettes against a pale-blue wall glinting with fading stars. And when the first roseate flush crept into the lower sky they returned to Jim Torrance's new ranch.

He made coffee, fried bacon, stirred up flapjacks and presented them as brown as October acorns. She wouldn't eat, she couldn't—but she did. He said:

"I've just moved in here. It's still mostly like a pigpen. But I've got some clean blankets. You lie down; maybe after awhile you'll get some sleep."

He slammed the door after him and concerned himself with various ranch chores which kept him near the house. Most of the time, under his low-drawn hat brim, his eyes were watchful. He saw her when, about four hours later, she came to the door. Before she could get well into the open he bore down upon her.

"Get back inside. I'll tell you a thing or two."

First to tell her was something which she already knew

but needed to ponder. Sam Pepper's ranch was adjoining, and Sam had developed the habit of going atop a hill to spy on the newcomer.

"I had a skinny kid named Skeeter helping me," he said. "He's gone now, but most likely nobody noticed. You'll find some of my old clothes in that back room; there's a pack needle and thread. You can make 'em into the sort of misfits Skeeter wore. From a distance you'd look enough like him. There's an old hat of mine in there too. All you got to do is just be a spindling, gawky boy; that ought to be easy."

She didn't say anything.

Later Jim Torrance saw several men riding along the road in front of his place. They passed on and out of sight. Presently they came riding back. He said to himself, "They found the buckboard."

This time they turned in at his gate, and he met them on the wheel track that served as a rutted road.

"Howdy," said Jim Torrance.

"Where's the Cannon girl?" said one of them, a skinny man like a hungry coyote. "Seen anything of her?"

"Who?" asked Torrance.

"The Cannon girl. King Cannon's kid. She killed Steve Bordereau last night, grabbed all the loose money she could get hold of and made a get-away."

"You don't say," murmured Jim Torrance.

They looked at him shrewdly. One of them, a gimlet-eyed, lanky young hellion, said sharply:

"You was in town yourse'f. You know all about it. She headed out this way. We found her buckboard. Where's she at now?"

Torrance's shrug at its best, as now, was eloquent.

"Me, I'm a stranger in these parts. I'm up here alone, save for the kid over yonder," and his gesture indicated a slim, slight figure on a hill nearly a mile away working at a fence. "If you think we've got the girl hid up our sleeves, look for her." His gaze, as stern as an eagle's, came back to their faces. "A flock of grown men trying to run down one lone girl? You make a man laugh."

"Got any meanin' back o' that, Stranger?" demanded the sharp-eyed, lanky man.

For a moment Torrance appeared to consider the matter. Then he gave them a second shrug and strode away, going off to the corral, which he, like the slim, slight, distant figure at the fence, was making a pretense of mending. He knew that in the house they'd find no trace of her; he himself had seen to that.

He saw them when they came out. They stood a while talking among themselves; then they went out to the barn, passing quite near where he was. He gave no evidence of paying them the slightest attention, but none the less he noticed when they came to a halt and looked across the fields to the hilltop where the solitary, unhidden figure was. He knew, too, how her heart was pumping then under that old ragged shirt of his which he had made her put on for the masquerade. In that, in old hacked-off trousers of his and his worst hat, she looked as little like the Sally Dawn Cannon he had seen in a white satin dress at Bordereau's as a scarecrow looks like a crescent moon. They might decide to take time off for a word with the "kid." Well, she knew her part. If she saw them start her way, she was to climb into the saddle of the horse tied to a fence post, to ride leisurely over the brow of the hill—and then to dig her spurs in for all she was worth.

They went on into the empty barn. Torrance heard them talking in lowered voices before they came out. Again they looked over to the hilltop where the figure of what was supposed to be Skeeter, the kid Torrance had brought along to help with the horses, was busier than ever at the fence.

"Maybe the kid's seen her?" said one of the men, looking at Torrance.

He got a third shrug.

"Maybe," said Jim Torrance.

The men then went away. But they stopped before they got to the gate to call back:

"Sorry we bothered you, Stranger. Guess she didn't come this way after all."

Any man with half his wits about him could have seen through that studied remark as through a clean windowpane, and Jim Torrance wasn't missing anything obvious today. He told himself thoughtfully: "They'll be back about dark, or maybe one of them will stick around, hid in the pines. They know damn well she did come this way."

He kept busy another hour at the corral, then went into the house for ten minutes, smoking and letting time pass. After that he saddled a horse, got a crowbar, shovel and hammer, and rode lazily across the fields to lend a hand at fence mending. The girl, watching him coming, turned frightened eyes upon him.

"They've gone?"

"Gone, sure. Not far, though. And they'll be coming back."

"You mean—"

"Yes. They found the buckboard where I ditched it, and back-trailed this far. They're not fools—or if they are, they're not plumb fools. I've a notion anyhow one of them is watching us now."

She shivered. She said faintly:

"I'm afraid. What will they do to me? What am I going to do?"

"Keep right on mending fence for a spell. You know these folks better than I do. Does it mean much to you, one way or another, if they get their hands on you?"

Her shiver now was a shudder. He was glad of that, glad that she realized what she might expect. She said all in one breath, "I'd rather be dead!"

He helped her set a post straight and began tamping the earth about it.

"I'll get you out of this—if you want to go with me."

"Yes! Yes, I do! Oh, you are so— But why? Why do you do all these things for me?"

The shrug she got from him was worth all the three he had bestowed on the men seeking her. He said:

"Pretty soon I'll go back to the house. You'll keep on here, working as hard as you can. But keep an eye open for me. When you see me mosey out to the barn, you take your time, pile on your horse and ride slow and lazy-like along the top of the hill, heading south. That will bring you in ten minutes down into a hollow where you'll cut into a trail. Turn north there and keep straight on for about three-four miles, where the trail forks and there's a spring. Wait there. You won't have to wait long. I'll be with you."

Her eyes had been lowered while he spoke; now there was a flutter of her lids, and then her eyes, opened wide, looked up at him wonderingly.

"You haven't even told me your name," she said, as though that mattered.

"Torrance. Jim Torrance."

"I'll do just what you say."

So in a little while, with few more words spoken, he left her. She, though her overtaxed body trembled, kept on at her intrinsically useless toil. He, pottering about house and barn and corral, kept an open eye. He saw Sam Pepper come out at his favorite vantage point, and was relieved rather than discomfited, for seeing what he knew must be there was easier on the nerves than just fancying it. Also, just once, he caught a glimpse of a figure skulking among the pines and knew it for that of the gimlet-eyed young hellion.

"Now we know," muttered Jim Torrance. "And knowing is better than guessing, any day."

He bided his time until the sun was red and flattening down by the western hilltops. Then he gave the signal which he knew King Cannon's daughter had so long and anxiously awaited. He did not turn his head after that to see what response she made. He rode down the wheel track, out through the gate and toward Sundown. He rode slowly until he had passed the first timber-masked turn in the road; then he swerved off into the wood and began circling through it. In twenty minutes or so he would strike back into the trail the girl was to have taken. Down in the hollow it would be dusky then; no one should see him come up with her.

CHAPTER V

"**W**HERE are you taking me?" was the first thing she said. Then, ashamed that she should always be thinking of herself, she added hurriedly: "But you! What about your ranch? Your horses? Who will take care of them? Or are you coming right back in an hour or so?"

"We're going up into the mountains," he told her. "No chance down the other way where they'll be on the lookout for you. They'd think nobody would tackle the mountains now."

She knew what he meant. It was late October; the days had been full and ripe with sunshine, but there was in the air the bitter sting of winter. And when winter came, spring could be very far behind. A sudden storm would choke the mountain passes with snow.

Apprehensively, as though the heavens could assure her, she looked up at the sky. Just now it had been a clear, shiny blue, but in the last few minutes a film had crept over it.

"Yes, it's apt to snow before morning," he said indifferently. "We'd better be on our way, hadn't we?"

"It's going to storm. If not tonight, then surely tomorrow or next day. And can we ever hope to get through to the other side? The passes are up ten thousand feet!"

"Sure," he said. "Sure. Let's ride."

And so they rode.

Together, they were aloof—she because of her fear, fear of what might be following and fear of him, the unknown; he because of a strange, baffling indifference. Why, she kept asking herself, why did he succor or seem to succor her? She could not at any step make him out. Maybe he, like the others, was out to drag her down. She did not know. She only knew she did not want to think of it. Without his aid she was utterly lost. She merely took the one chance, the one open trail. It might come to a dead end,

41

to a frightful dead end, but it offered her the one chance, and King Cannon's daughter took it.

Dusk thickened so fast that darkness, like a black blanket, dropped down over their heads within the first half hour. Still, looking up, one could see the frail light clinging like a gossamery mantle to the mountain tops—and she chose to look up. She saw the first star and it heartened her.

"Know your way through the mountains?" he asked her, abrupt, out of a long silence.

"Not very well. It's been such a long time—not since I was a little girl— No, I don't!"

"Neither do I!"

Then he chuckled. That, like the star, somehow put hope into her. When a man chuckled— It was like a boy whistling. It was too dark to see his face, so she could forget the sinister look of it. She gripped the horn of her saddle with both hands, clung on tight—and inwardly prayed to a merciful God.

Neither spoke again until they came high up on one of the ridges that flowed down from the loftier mountains, and they stopped to blow the horses. Then the girl, feeling strangely light-headed and fearless and utterly indifferent of fate, said unemotionally:

"The storm is sure to catch us. I suppose we'll starve and freeze to death."

"We won't starve," he said, matter-of-fact about it. "I've got a food pack along, you know. And maybe you noticed the extra blanket thickness under your saddle? Extra, doubled blankets there, and under mine, too; so we won't freeze."

"You'd thought of all these things!"

"Sometimes it pays to think a couple of jumps ahead," said Jim Torrance.

"I've tried to! I couldn't. I—I can't now!"

"Sometimes," said Jim Torrance, "it pays to do just what you've got to do—sail ahead and take on your thinking when you can. Let's ride some more."

He led the way and she followed, because it seemed to her that everything had gone out of her, leaving in her breast no will of her own. At every forward step into the ever darkening wilderness her fears mounted, yet like a chip borne along on a black unseen tide she went the way the tide commanded.

Within a couple of hours they came as straight as a string to a little long-deserted cabin neither of them had ever heard about. Whether they were led by chance, by the instinct which guides the wanderer through the proper mountain passes, or by a power she had prayed to, they did not ponder. After all, their horses were largely responsible; in the dark they had followed a trail along the bottom of a vast canyon and had struck into the continuation of that trail across a timbered upland flat. Torrance's horse came to a dead stop in front of the cabin before either of them saw it.

They went in and he made a fire in a wreck of a rock fireplace.

"It's early yet, but we can't see what we're doing," he said. "So we stay here over night and step along at daybreak."

He went out to care for the horses and presently came back with his blankets and food pack. She was crouching by the fire, head down, her face in her hands, her hair down about her shoulders.

"Hungry?" he asked.

"No. I couldn't eat."

It was a small one-room place. He arranged her blankets on a strip of canvas in a corner near the fireplace and put his own down in an opposite corner.

"Scared?"

"Yes," she told him, and looked up then, her eyes full on his. There was a shadow of fright in her eyes, yet somehow they seemed to remain fearless.

He slipped a gun out of its holster and held it out to her.

"Sleep with that in your hand. You'll get a better rest."

She shook her head. "No. I have shot one man, God forgive me. I'll never do it again."

He slid the gun back into its place, saying lightly:

"Bordereau had it coming to him. Don't let a little thing like that ride you. Good night."

"Good night," she said faintly, and went to her corner to lie down and tuck herself into her blankets.

It was bitter cold that night, with the wind howling from midnight on, and putting its fingers like icicles through a hundred cracks in the cabin walls. Jim Torrance kept the fire going, bringing in dead wood for which he had groped in the dark under the pines. When dawn came it was a pale, chill dawn; the ground was white with snow but no snow was falling.

Their breakfast, though the fire served them, was sketchy. The best part of it was the steaming black coffee made in an old tin can. When he brought the horses up she said, "If they come this far they can follow our tracks."

He didn't say anything but led the way, steering for a high notched pass in the mountains some miles ahead. On the more gentle slopes they rode swiftly; for the most part the climbing was slow and laborious. The sun rolled up, red and genial, and dissipated some of the morning chill. But soon thereafter a sharp wind began blowing and a thin gray film spread widely across the sky and they saw the gossamery snow wraiths swirling about the higher peaks.

"Our tracks won't last long," he said to her over his shoulder. "It's coming on to snow again."

She was glad; even now, as through her troubled sleep last night, there was always the haunting dread of a pack of men, like wolves, hunting her down. She had never gotten far enough to think what they would do with her, whether they'd hang her high to some pine tree, as they'd certainly do with a man, or— But just the thought of their hands on her had grown into a nightmare. And now, if God sent His white snow to cover the earth, she was free!

But when the snow did come and their faint tracks were lost for all time, her moment of exultation was short. For the cold penetrated, biting to the bone, and the mountains grew at every step more rugged and cold and inhospitable. The mountains grew inimical; rather they had always been that way, but she had never thought about it until now. They crushed and killed when they could, which was often enough. Men had their way down in the valleys and foot-hills, making things over—but let them try their puny hands up here! The stern old mountain straight ahead of them was now as it had been a hundred, a thousand, ten thousand years ago; august, it was an enemy entrenched behind its towers. Nor was it merely passively inimical; at times it poured down torrents of stone and gravel in what folk called landslides, which buried deep the intrepid invader of its kingly solitude. Itself, never stirring, was like a general directing devastating forces. On a day like this it was a simple matter to feel that old mountain's stubborn hostility.

"It's going to kill us," she said. "It's going to mash us like a worm someone steps on."

"You're all on edge," said Jim Torrance, and they rode on.

The skies thickened; the snow came down at first in chilled pellets, then in fluffy feathers that clung to their shoulders and knees and whitened the ground. Good-by to tracks now!

So for a little while both were content; nothing could be more welcome than a flurry of snow to shut the gate in the face of any possible pursuit. But within another hour, as they climbed together, it became obvious that they had to do with something altogether different from any mere light sifting-down of playful snowflakes. The wind burst storming through a high pass and flung hard frozen pellets in their faces. They spurred on; they came swiftly into a more sheltered region, but here the snow was falling so heavily that the air was gray and thick with it. This, then, was not just the advance notice that winter was on its way; it was winter itself, lionesque and raging.

"You see, I was right," she said, when they stopped a moment in the lee of a sheltering cliff. "The mountains and the storm are allied against us. It will grow dark, we'll be lost—there'll just be smooth white mounds in a day or two for markers, and we'll be under them."

"You don't sound like you cared much."

"You don't care either. I could tell when I first saw you."

But he shook his head, flicking snow right and left from his hat brim.

"You're dead wrong. I've got me a few jobs to do first.

And one of them is to get you out of this. Let's poke along."

"You are Jim Torrance?"

"That's what they told me when I was a little shaver. Why?"

"There's been a lot of talk about you; I suppose you know that. I heard men talking at Steve Bordereau's place. They said that you came looking for a man named Jim Torrance, and that that's what you call yourself."

"Men say lots of things, don't they?" he said lightly.

"Let's poke along," rejoined Sally Dawn.

Hours later—hours of floundering through already accumulated snowdrifts in the higher passes with scarcely a word spoken, head-down hours buffeting the storm—the two came to a spot where it seemed they could go no farther. Iron-flanked mountains, lifting their naked fronts high above timber line, seemed to constitute an impassable barrier; and so heavy were the low skies, so thick the air with storm, that dark was already on its way long before its appointed time. The two wayfarers came to a halt; their knees brushed as their horses pressed close together for warmth and the feel of companionship.

"All I know of this man's country," said Torrance, "is from a few words of hearsay that I didn't pay much attention to at the time. We can't be very far from Pocket Valley, and we're headed right as far as general direction goes."

"Pocket Valley is the first place they'd look for me," said the girl, "if they ever guessed we'd headed this way at all."

"Sure. But we needn't go right into the Valley at first. The man who told me about it said something about the old Red Shirt mining camp on the ridge above Pocket."

"The bottom fell out of it years ago. My father was interested up there when— There's not a soul there, now, especially at this time of year."

"That's what I meant. Some of the old shacks are still standing, I reckon. We could hole up there a day or two. I could make my way in and out of Pocket for supplies."

"If we can ever find our way!"

"Sure we can." She couldn't be altogether certain, but thought that he was smiling ever so slightly, and that the smile was quite unforced, as he added, "You see, we've got to!"

So they rode on, riding this way and that on the steepening slopes, finding a way where none seemed to be, climbing higher and higher in order to attain those vantage points which afforded best views across the broken country and down into any such regions as might prove to be Pocket Valley. They hurried all they could, running a race with the swiftly advancing night. Sudden dark overtook them on one of the high, lonely, storm-battered ridges, in as unlikely a place for a camp on a night like this as could be imagined; and when on the whistling wind there was borne the dismal howl of a hungry timber wolf, the girl's shoulders twitched with something more than cold, and the man admitted to himself that things could be far better and cheerier. But he said steadily enough: "We'll make out. We'll find shelter under a cliff. We'll get through the night, and in the morning we'll find Pocket Valley in two shakes. It ought to be just over yonder to the northeast and only a few miles off. If it hadn't got dark so early—"

"Look!" she exclaimed, and grasped his arm in her eagerness. "A light!"

His hand gave hers a good hearty squeeze; at the moment both were unconscious of their involuntary gestures. He, too, glimpsed the light, weak and wan and seeming far away, somewhere in the black void beyond and far below them.

"It's the settlement down in Pocket Valley," he said with assurance. "What we see is the lights shining out of windows. So we must be on the ridge we were heading for, and the old camp must be so close that we could throw a rock and hit it."

"If we could only see it! But it's so dark!"

"We'll take it slow now; we've got some sort of trail under foot; our horses will take us right. And if we don't have any luck, well we can get down to Pocket in no time at all."

He led the way and she pressed along close behind him,

not to lose him in the thick night. Twice his voice was hurled back to her by the wind, but she could not make out his words. Then she almost bumped into him; he had stopped and was dismounting.

"We're there!" he called triumphantly. "Look sharp and you'll see a cabin of sorts; it's so close you could almost reach out and pat it with your hand. We've just passed another. Light down and we'll take stock of our night's quarters."

Stiff with cold and weariness she slid down from her saddle; his hand was out to steady her. Then he shoved a sagging door open and she stumbled into the cabin's pitch-black interior.

"Wait a shake," he said. "Here are some matches. See what it's like inside. I'll tie the horses and you look around. If it's all right, we'll stay here. Or I can poke into one of the other shacks. I'll be back with you in a jiffy."

Their cold fingers fumbled together as he handed her a half dozen sulphur block-matches. He moved a few steps away in quest of a tree to tie the horses to, lest, seeking shelter from the storm, they wander off. Almost immediately he returned to meet her at the door, and to hear her excited whisper:

"We're not alone up here! There's a light in one of the other cabins; I saw it through a back window, and saw a man moving about. Do you think it is some of the men from Sundown, looking for me? They might have ridden ahead and waited here."

"Did you strike a match?"

"No. I was just trying to—my hands were so cold—and I saw the other light."

He went with her to the little window. Fifty or perhaps a hundred yards away was the other cabin; it, too, had a small square window, and through this shone glimmeringly the pale light cast by a candle or a glow from a fireplace. Presently he, too, saw a figure moving across the window; he couldn't see at all clearly, but it seemed to him that the fellow was gesturing as a man might if talking with someone else.

"Of course it might be anybody," said Torrance, "but

the chances are it's some lone crazy prospector and nobody from Sundown at all. Just the same I'd better step over and take a look-see from close up. And no matter who it is, I think we'd better stick here for the night. We'd have a devil's own time getting down to Pocket, and when we got there we'd be pretty sure to run into someone that knows about Bordereau. I won't be long."

"I'm coming with you!"

"Fair enough. Let's step."

So again they went out into the storm to grope their way toward a light which for her might have the least or the greatest significance. They went boldly, since the shrieking wind blotted out any sound they made and since they need have no fear of being seen. They drew close to the lighted window. At one end of the room a candle-end on a box, stuck in its own grease, was guttering out; it left the farther end of the room in wavering gloom. They saw clearly the man who had been moving about so restlessly and who now stood still; they made out indistinctly the form of another man lying on a corner bunk. The two were talking, but not a word was to be overheard. It seemed that the man standing was taking orders; that he didn't like them; that none the less he was accepting them.

Sally Dawn gasped out, her lips close to Jim Torrance's ear:

"They're after me! It's Clark Murdo, Steve Bordereau's pardner! I can't see who the other man is but it's bound to be another of Bordereau's men. What are we going to do?"

"Let's get back to our cabin," said Torrance. They turned away but he stopped and swung about and seemed tempted to linger. "No use," he muttered. "That candle will be out in a minute. I'd give my hat though to see that other man's face. I've got me a notion, Sally Dawn! I sure have!"

"What? What is it?"

He hesitated, then said roughly:

"No; I'm crazy, I guess. Come on, let's get under shelter."

"But can't you see—"

"No. Neither can you. It's too dark to see anything. Maybe daylight will tell us something."

They made their retreat as hurriedly as they had advanced. Once she spoke, saying in a mystified voice:

"I wonder who that other man was? I can't understand Clark Murdo being bossed like that. And he was being ordered about, wasn't he?"

"He sure was; he didn't like it but was taking it. And that's what gave me my notion."

But beyond that cryptic statement he would not go.

CHAPTER VI

TORRANCE brought in a saddle blanket which he fastened snugly over their window and then with splinters of wood from floor and walls he made a tiny fire on the rock hearth, purely for the sake of a little light in which to explore the premises. The place reeked of long desertion and was as bare as Mother Hubbard's cupboard, yet walls and roof were tight and sturdy. There was a rear door that led into a dugout some ten feet square.

"I'm going to bring our horses in," he said. "The dugout will house them where nobody's going to find them unless we get found first. And long before morning their tracks will be wiped out."

The horses entered the cabin willingly enough, and, though they sniffed and snorted when once inside, were at last coaxed and threatened into the dugout.

"Now," said Torrance, "we'll eat the rest of our larder, make up our beds the way we did last night and call it a day."

"A day! It's been a year, hasn't it?"

But she smiled as she said it, a faint and quivering and altogether uncertain smile, yet one not without its courage. And she added, "We've at least a few bites of food, but our poor horses—"

"Each one gets a double handful of grain," he assured her, and again she thought, "He thinks of everything!"

He lifted a corner of the blanket over the window to peer out, and reported:

"Our neighbors' house is dark. Mr. Murdo and his friend have gone to sleep by now, and you and I are going to build up our fire and keep it going until nearly morning; there's not one chance in a million of a ray of light or a spark giving us away. What's more, they haven't the vaguest notion anyone's about, or they'd have covered their own light. I stumbled over a dead pine when I was leading the horses; I'll have plenty of wood before you're ten minutes older."

"I'm going to help you," said Sally Dawn.

"Look here, you're tired and—"

"Have it your way," she said, and he went out and closed the door—and she opened it and followed close at his heels. She heard him chuckle.

They built up their small fire and crouched before it and got warm and began to yawn. She lay down in her corner and stared up at the dimly lit rafters and then looked out of the corners of her eyes at him, still squatting before the fire, and wondered. It was hard to read anything in that dark face of his, especially by so treacherous a light; the faint flicker of the flames at times seemed to reveal only a grim sternness that was twin with brutality, at other times to soften the features so that they appeared touched by a smile that had actually in it a hint of tenderness. She fell asleep, with Jim Torrance still motionless at the hearth.

She awoke with a start and sat up rubbing her eyes and staring about her. The room was ablaze with light and her first thought was that the cabin was on fire. Then she saw him standing there, looking down at her in that quizzical way of his, half smiling and half frowning, and saw that he had an enormous fire blazing in the fireplace; the room was cozy with heat and as bright as day. She sprang up confused.

"They're gone," said Torrance. "I saw them ride away half an hour ago. It's daylight now. They were in their saddles while it was still dark."

"You stayed awake all night, watching!"

"I kept an eye open part of the time," he admitted. "And I noticed that though you were asleep you didn't seem exactly comfortable. A good thawing out over a hot fire won't hurt either of us."

"Jim Torrance, what on earth are you made of? Steel?"

Already she had grown to love to hear that chuckle of his.

"Once upon a time, when I was very young," he told her, "they taught me a poem. It was all about what little boys and girls are made of. I forget about the boys but it said about the girls:

> 'Sugar and spice
> And everything nice,
> That's what little girls are made of.'"

Suddenly her face clouded; he remembered his first impression of her, a sullen, smoldering little beauty with brooding, smoky eyes. Her mouth, which had been softened by sleep, hardened.

"I haven't been nice to you," she said. "I'm afraid I haven't been very nice to anybody. The world wasn't nice to me—it made me hate it and it made me bitter inside."

"Shucks," he said lightly. "That's nothing. You're just a kid, that's all, and kids have got a right to cry and then sulk when they get their fingers burnt."

"I'm not a kid! I'm twenty—almost twenty-one."

"As bad as all that? Quite an old lady, huh?"

"A thousand years old this morning; I can almost hear my bones creak when I move. And what now, Mr. Jim Torrance?"

"The wind blew itself out about midnight," he told her, "but it's been snowing harder than ever. We've got to have something to eat. If we go into Pocket Valley you might as well give yourself up. In this storm no one else is apt to come along this way, so I leave you here alone for a little while; I poke along into Pocket; I bring back some provisions. Inside three hours I ought to be back. And, if I hurry along," he added, "I can still make out by their tracks the

way Murdo and his friend went. They headed down toward
Pocket; I can find out if they turned off anywhere."

She went to the door and looked out over a white world.
Snow was drifting down in large feathery flakes; trees were
dressed as in ermine; the sky was thick and gray. She
thought that she had never looked out over an expanse so
still and so lonesome. Her mood was not one to appreciate
its beauty, inescapable though it was.

"Of course you're right, and of course I can't go into
Pocket or back to Sundown, and of course I'm afraid to
stay here alone—"

"I'm going to leave a gun with you."

"I told you I'd never touch a gun again!"

"Oh, but you will, some time." He slid one of his guns
up out of its leather and dropped it to her blankets. "I'm
starting right away. My horse is already saddled; the quicker I get going the quicker my tracks will be covered and
the quicker you'll be having breakfast. You can count on
me being back in about four hours at most; if I'm not back
then— Well, you'd better saddle and go on down into
Pocket."

She looked startled.

"Why shouldn't you come back?"

He shrugged.

"I sure expect to. But a man never can tell, can he?"

A sudden suspicion suggested itself to her.

"You think you know who the man is with Clark
Murdo? Someone you know?"

"I can't be sure yet," he returned, and once more
sounded curt and hard.

"I know! You think it's that other 'Jim Torrance'!"

"You're doing enough guessing now for both of us," he
grunted, and went into the dugout for his horse.

She watched him ride away through gauzy veils of falling
snow which grew heavier until they almost blotted him out
before he vanished in a scattered growth of mountain ce-
dars. She closed the door reluctantly and went back to the
fire for comfort and companionship.

As for Torrance, he made what speed he could as soon as
he turned into the white furrow, already smoothing over,

that Clark Murdo and the other man had made; for he realized how heavily a few hours in this solitude could bear down on one—especially on a girl who had endured as had Sally Dawn Cannon. He had told her he might be gone four hours; he hoped to return within half that time.

The track left by the men whom he followed ran straight along the flank of the ridge, curved about a blunt shoulder of the mountain and then wavered downward among stunted pines, its course at all times indicating Pocket Valley as its objective. Now and then Torrance caught glimpses of the tiny village looking like a child's toy town roofed and based in fluffy cotton. As he rode lower down the slope a pine forest, all black and silver, shut off his view; still the single track left by Murdo and his mate led on. But when he had penetrated the forest some five hundred yards, that track split into two fading trails. While one kept straight on down into the valley, the other turned off almost at a right angle into a dark and thickly timbered ravine.

"And now I make a bet," said Torrance as, without stopping, he kept on down toward Pocket Valley. "It will be Clark Murdo who has kept straight on, the other man who has turned off into the canyon."

His next glimpse of the settlement, afforded when he was almost at his destination, showed him several pale smudges of smoke barely visible against the gray curtain of the sky. He estimated that he had been nearly an hour making his tortuous way down the mountain; by now it was long after the time of an invisible dawn and folk would be astir.

Until now he had followed along the track which he was wagering had been made by Murdo. At last, however, just before he rode out of the rim of the wood into the open, he altered his course, keeping to the timber for half a mile, not quitting it until he could approach Pocket Valley town from a more southerly direction.

"No use telling friend Murdo that he and I rode the same way," he judged. "And, in case he is curious, by the time he gets around to looking for my trail it won't be there."

Among the score of houses constituting the town of Pocket Valley he had no difficulty in picking out the one he wanted, nor was the sign over its front porch necessary as a guide. It was a long, low building of rough logs on a foundation of granite blocks; at the rear was an open shed to which he rode to stable his horse. He saw what he both hoped and expected to see: another horse, still saddled, was tied here worrying wisps of straw in a pole manger. He swung down, tied his own horse, and noiselessly went up the steps to the back door. Before he knocked he heard voices.

Then one of those voices called out to him, "Well, why don't you come in?" and he opened the door and entered directly upon a big barnlike room in which a round-bellied stove was blazing red-hot and in which three men stood about, all three with glasses in their hands.

One of the men was Clark Murdo.

"And so I win the first bet," said Jim Torrance to himself with considerable satisfaction.

The other men he had never seen. One he correctly took for the proprietor of the place. He disposed of the other man with a flick of his eyes; his real attention, though discreet, was bestowed upon Murdo. That individual's eyes were for an instant round with astonishment, then narrowed and cold and noncommittal.

"Howdy, Stranger," said the owner of the place. "Ride in on a snowflake?"

"Sort of getting ready to get hungry," said Torrance, and came on to the stove, spreading his hands out toward it. "If there's a store here I've come to the right place, haven't I?"

"Right as rain. Store, saloon, hotel and in season a place where you can try to get your money back. Squat."

Torrance moved to the rawhide-bottomed chair indicated, as though weary, and sat down with a long sigh. Murdo, who had been watching his every gesture and expression, spoke up then.

"Hello, Torrance," he said. "What are you doing up this way?"

"Hello, Murdo," said Torrance.

"Seems as though I'm gettin' a whale of a lot of comp'ny for this time of day on a snowy mornin'," observed the proprietor. "And so you two boys is acquainted, huh? That's nice. Me, I'm Andy Stock, an' though we ain't got around to breakfas' yet, I c'n give you a shot of licker right now an' a cup of cawfee in two shakes."

"I've been sort of thinking about coffee," said Torrance.

Andy Stock turned to the other man.

"How about a fire in the cook stove, Jake? It's cawfee time anyhow."

Jake downed what remained of his drink and moved off through a door at the side of the room, and almost immediately they heard him banging at a kitchen stove. Murdo stood twirling his glass, appeared about to speak, momentarily subdued his impulse, then let it go.

"Which way'd you come from, Torrance?" he asked, and sounded friendly and casual.

"Sundown," said Torrance.

"Sure. Of course. Up over the mountain or the round-about way through Tucker's Flats?"

"Would it make any difference to you which way I came?" asked Torrance. "And do you want to know why I dropped in and how long I'm staying and how old I'll be next birthday?"

Andy Stock laughed good-humoredly.

"Murdo just rid in himse'f," he said. "Kinda early ridin' for him, too. I reckon he's got something on his mind. He's lookin' for that girl that killed his pardner, Steve Bordereau. I reckon he thought maybe you had saw her somewheres. It ain't in Murdo, you know, to come straight forward with what he's hankerin' to find out; he's always beatin' around the bushes to get anywheres."

"You talk too much, Stock," growled Murdo.

"You think so, do you?" snapped Stock, suddenly angry. "Why, damn your eyes—"

"Forget it," said Murdo and stalked away to a window. He tried to peer out, but the windowpane was filmed over with snow. Coming back he said:

"Let me have some oats, Andy. There was nothing in

your shed but some dirty straw, and my horse needs a feed if he's going to carry me any more today."

Stock, still a trifle testy, snorted: "I'd say it's about time to think of feedin' your hoss. You been here half an hour already, swiggin' whisky, an' never thinkin' of the pore brute."

"Oh, hell, let's have the oats and less conversation," said Murdo impatiently.

Stock went off to his storeroom and returned with a dipper full of oats; Murdo took it and went out. Stock winked at Torrance.

"What'd I tell you, Stranger?" he demanded in triumph. "There he goes in his roundabout way to get him some place. He'd let his horse rest there a week 'thout feedin' the pore devil, but he's jus' figgered out he can take a look-see at the tracks you made gettin' here, an' can answer him his own question about whether you rid down over the mountains or come up from the south by way Tucker's Flats." He spat. "Hell take Clark Murdo an' all his pack," he said. "And you, too, if you're a friend of his."

Now Jim Torrance started asking questions, and asked them curtly and swiftly to have his answers before Murdo returned. He began.

"What was it he said about a girl killing Steve Bordereau?"

"A girl name of Sally Dawn Cannon. Hell, ever'body knows who she is; ol' King Cannon's daughter. She shot Bordereau at his place in Sundown. Kilt him dead, says Murdo. Then she hightailed out of there before they could grab her, though what they wanted to pester a girl like her for, for just beefin' a rat, me, I don't know. Likely he had drove her in a corner."

"Self-defense?"

"Murdo don't say so. Says just plain hate and meanness."

"Witnesses?"

"Murdo says him and four other Bordereau men seen it happen."

"And still they let the girl get away? What do they expect to do with her?"

"Lynch her, accordin' to Murdo. But, shucks, the country wouldn't let 'em get away with that. Or maybe, would it?" He grimaced. "The Bordereau gang of late has got a strangled hold on the country from th' other side Sundown to way up here."

"There'll be a big funeral, I suppose?"

"It's already been. Murdo must of been in a hurry to see the last of his pardner. They planted Steve Bordereau early next mornin' right after he was shot."

Just then Stock's roustabout stuck his head in through the kitchen door and bawled: "Cawfee! Come an' get it." And a moment later Clark Murdo came back from ministering to his horse and they all went to the kitchen together.

Torrance, from under those lazy eyelids of his, noted two things: Murdo on first entering looked relieved, and that meant that he had assured himself that Torrance had ridden up from the south and not over the mountain trail. Next, he saw that, as the four men chatted idly over their coffee, Murdo began to tighten up again, to grow restless and perhaps even anxious. He wondered about that until Murdo's own words gave him a clue. Again Murdo was asking questions, striving to be merely friendly and casual. He said, "Riding on north, Torrance?"

Torrance seemed thawed by his strong hot coffee. He answered carelessly, "Not in a hurry in all this weather." He turned to Stock, yawned and stretched and asked: "How about a shakedown for a few hours? I didn't get much sleep last night."

"Sure," said Stock. "Breakfast will be ready in a minute; then you can flop long's you like."

"Got a barn where I can put my horse up?"

The barn, Stock told him, was just back of the shed; he'd find hay there; help himself. So, while ham was frying and hot cakes were mixing, he went out to the stable. He unsaddled, gave his horse a rough-and-ready rubdown and returned for breakfast. Thereafter Stock led him to a little room, empty save for its bunk and a washstand with a lamp on it. At the door, as Stock was departing, Torrance called back to Murdo, who was standing watching from the kitchen doorway.

"Happen to know a gent who calls himself Jim Torrance, Murdo?" he asked.

Murdo said, "What?" and it wasn't because he hadn't heard; maybe he wanted to take a moment to think. Then Stock spoke up to say, mystified, "I thought you was Jim Torrance."

"I thought so too," said Torrance, "but it seem's there's some other man wearing the same name. Murdo might know him. How about it, Murdo?"

"No," said Murdo. "I don't know him."

"Well," said Torrance, "you might meet up with him some time. When you do just tell him I'm hoping to see him." And he closed the door.

He sat on the edge of his bed and slowly, with profound concentration on something else, started rolling a cigarette. For a little while he heard voices, Murdo's and Stock's, so clearly that he could catch some of the words. Suddenly Murdo's voice was lowered; then a door closed; then all sounds were gone. He kept on rolling his cigarette, his eyes the narrowest of slits, his face stern, his jaw set.

After a while, ten or fifteen minutes, he heard another door being closed; the sound was faint but distinct against the silence; he judged someone had gone out the back door. He went to his window and scraped at it with his fingernail. It was hard to see through the snow-filmed pane, but at last he found a spot in an upper corner through which the light filtered less dimly. A moment later he saw Clark Murdo riding around the corner of the house, headed back toward the mountain trail. He even made out that Murdo had some sort of bundle on the saddle before him; it looked like a full barley sack.

Torrance went back to Andy Stock then, finding him at the hot pot-bellied stove. Stock looked at him in mild surprise. Then he blurted out, "What the hell's going on here anyhow?"

"Guess I don't need a sleep after all," Torrance told him and went to the door to look out. Murdo was riding as rapidly as the snow would permit and was already close to the rim of the forest. He turned to stare the storekeeper in the eye, then to say thoughtfully, "Either you're an awful handy liar, Stock, or you haven't got any more use for Murdo than I have."

"Take your pick, Torrance," said Stock sharply. "What's it to you, anyhow?"

"Murdo's out to drag the Cannon girl down. Me, I helped her make her get-away."

Stock nodded. "Murdo told me."

"Well, I'll tell you something else; I was there when the shooting happened; I saw every bit of it. Until pretty recent I was taking it for granted, like a man does, that cards were being dealt off the top, and that things were what they looked like. Not now though. I don't believe the girl was the one that killed Bordereau. She shot him all right; he went down; we got out of there. Then what? Some other person, maybe Murdo himself, could have shot him again or popped a knife into him. Anyhow it was Murdo that got him buried so gosh-awful sudden."

Stock whistled, frowned and whistled again.

"What makes you think all that, man?"

"Two-three things. Maybe I'm right and maybe I'm wrong. Any way you look at it, Murdo's got no call to pull the kid down."

"I'm with you there," said Stock.

"All right. Now tell me a thing or two. Where did Murdo say he was going? And what did he have in his sack?"

"He said he was goin' up to see Pete Conroy. Conroy's an old prospector that lives back in the hills a ways. Murdo says Conroy hurt his leg and couldn't get out; that he's takin' him some grub. An' grub was in the sack."

"Murdo's a damn liar, but you don't have to tell him I said so. Now suppose you let me have a sack, too, and I'll put about a tenth as much stuff in it as Murdo has, and I'll stagger along too."

He laid in a small stock of provisions, making sure of coffee and sugar and tinned milk, all packed in a can in which the coffee was destined to come to a boil, and went for his horse. Andy Stock, from his door, watched him ride away through the swirling snow and tucked in the corners of his mouth. Jim Torrance rode mountainward in Clark Murdo's track.

"I'd sort of like to be on hand when it happens," said Stock.

CHAPTER VII

JIM TORRANCE was tempted up to the yielding point when he came to that spot on the mountain flank where a fresh track led deep into the dark ravine. For this far Clark Murdo had come up from Pocket, and here he had turned off to rejoin his companion of the earlier morning. And Torrance, so sorely tempted to follow him, kept saying to himself, "I'd know a lot if I overtook those two, and I've got the crazy hunch that at last I'd come up with a man I've been looking for, for a long, long time."

But there was that girl waiting for him high on the ridge. He couldn't quite make a go of just letting her wait. He couldn't quite get her face out of his mind's eye. She had stood pretty nearly all the punishment you could expect her to stand—alone up there for hours with only her own tragic thoughts for company. The kid must be nearly at her rope's end. In losing her mother it seemed that she had lost all she loved. On top of that there was a corroding horror in her soul; she'd be thinking over and over and endlessly over, "I killed a man." She'd be remembering the look on his face when he fell; she'd be thinking of him dead and soon to be dug under. With just those two to think of, her beloved mother and an ancient enemy, both dead so recently, she could no longer be left alone by any man who did not love torture for torture's sake.

So, though rage was in his eyes, Torrance rode on and let a chance slide by. Presently he got to thinking of other things: For one, Clark Murdo by now knew that he had been tricked into believing that Torrance had come up through the Flats in the south; he would have noted that another horse than his had recently traveled this way; he would have guessed mighty close to the truth. He could scarcely avoid being sure that Torrance, too, had stopped over last night at the old deserted mining camp. It was a simple step from that surmise to the next—that Sally Dawn Cannon had stopped there with him and was perhaps there now; that Torrance, like himself, had gone down to Pocket Valley seeking provisions for still another mouth than his own.

"And he may be showing up as soon as he carries the news along to his teammate," mused Torrance.

Further, he marked that it was no longer snowing so heavily; considering that this was the first storm of the season it might reasonably be expected to wear itself out soon. That fact would have its bearing on events.

When he came to the mountain cabin, there was Sally Dawn in the open doorway waiting for him, a pale and weary, tragic figure with eyes looking unnaturally large; he knew that in his absence she had broken down and wept miserably. But a flash of gladness came into her eyes on seeing him.

"I had no way of telling how long you were gone—I began to be afraid—"

"You began to wonder whether there was any breakfast coming up, I'll bet a man," he said lightly as he dismounted.

"Honestly, I forgot about breakfast!"

"You ought to be starved."

"Maybe I am!" She looked at his bundle in the barley sack. "I am starved!" Then her eyes traveled questioningly back to his. "Tell me what happened. What about Clark Murdo and the other man?"

He tethered his horse near the door and they went straightway to the fireplace where she had a small fire still burning. But she thought to ask, "Aren't you bringing your horse inside again?"

"No. We'll be riding right away, just as soon as you've

eaten. And I'll tell you about things while ham's frying and coffee coming to a boil."

"Coffee! I'd rather have a cup of hot coffee than a buckskin bag full of gold dust!"

"Sure," he grinned at her. "It's a lot more inviting this time of day."

Together they prepared her breakfast while he explained how first of all he had eaten down at the Pocket. "I'd have waited for you," he told her, "only I wanted things to look natural to Murdo." Then he told her briefly of his encounter with Murdo, of Murdo's having asked Andy Stock concerning her, of his general tall curiosity about Torrance's movements, about his having taken a sack of provisions to his somehow-mysterious side-kick.

"They're after me, of course," said Sally Dawn.

"That doesn't explain their hiding out in that canyon," he retorted. "But, yes, of course they're after you. So as soon as you've had all the coffee and hot cakes and ham you want—yes, I've got a couple of eggs, too—we'll fork our saddles and get out of here."

"But they'll be watching the trail, won't they? They'll see us on our way down into the Pocket."

"No they won't, because we're not headed down there. We're turning tail right here and drifting back to Sundown. We'll make an easier and quicker trip going down, and all by daylight too, than we made coming up. Even if they follow, I don't think they'll overtake us. And if they do come up with us— Well, that won't happen until it happens."

Round-eyed and puzzled she heard him out without an interruption; then she exclaimed:

"Sundown? You mean we're to go back there? After all this long ride, after we've almost got away? Back to Sundown?"

"Here's sugar for your coffee. Here's milk." He jabbed a hole in the can with his knife. "Yes, back to Sundown. It's exactly where they won't be expecting us to go; likewise, I'm beginning to think it's where you'll be safest. And it's where you belong; it's where your ranch is. Mine, too."

"Your ranch, yes. Mine?" She shook her head and

sighed. Time was when she had loved that ranch, King Cannon's and her mother's and hers, with all her heart. "Mine is as good as gone from me for good now."

"Maybe," said Torrance. "A man never knows."

"I'm not sure that I want to go back to Sundown," she said, and sounded altogether independent about it.

"Scared?" asked Torrance, and turned the sizzling ham with a stick. "Here's a hunk of bread and a dab of butter."

"Of course I am! Have you forgotten all the things you said to me about letting those men grab me?"

"While you finish eating, I'll saddle your horse," said Torrance, and rose from his squatting position on the hearth. Standing high above her, looking down on her tumbled brown tresses and then into her uplifted puzzled gray eyes, he added: "No, I haven't forgotten. I've sort of changed my mind, that's all."

A faint flush came into her cheeks and a flash as of fire into her smoky eyes. She could only surmise that he had had enough of their adventure together. She said swiftly:

"You can go back! I'm going on. I'm never going near Sundown again as long as I live."

Then she was treated again to the sound of that soft chuckle of his.

"If you don't go back, I don't go either," he said, and grinned down at her. "But as it happens, we're both going. Side by each, as the feller says."

Then he went and saddled her horse.

The return journey, as he had predicted, was much easier than had been their trip up into the high places. By the time they had dropped down two or three thousand feet there was but an inch or two of melting snow under foot. And all day long they had met no one and had caught no glimpse of Clark Murdo or any other following them.

In the early gray dusk she pointed, saying: "There's your ranch. We're almost there."

He seemed to come up out of a deep reverie.

"Know a funny little rooster named Sam Pepper?" he asked.

She looked at him wonderingly, he was so grave in his questioning.

"Of course I do! Everybody knows Sam Pepper. He *is* funny, but I like him. What put him into your mind?"

The gravity slowly faded from his face and in its place came a slow smile which in the end gave her the warm feeling of being enveloped by it.

"When a man needs a helping hand," he said, "he's got to think about a lot of folks he knows. Me, I've hit on Sam Pepper!"

"For help? Mercy! What sort of help? I never knew a more helpless creature."

"Is there by any chance a Mrs. Sam Pepper?"

"There is. She's a darling; everybody loves her, the most motherly—"

But something came to her throat at the last word and she broke off, averting her face. Torrance didn't say anything; he leaned outward from his saddle as though to pat her shoulder, but withdrew his hand without touching her and without her seeing.

When they came down along the road in front of his gate he reined in his horse and said quietly:

"I want you to stop here a little while. If the coast is as clear at my place as it looks, and as it ought to be, I'll poke over to have a word with Sam Pepper—"

"I'll go with you! Let's go straight on there first of all."

"Please!" It was the first time he had ever said that to her. "I've been thinking about this all day. I'll go alone to Pepper's first; I'll make sure no one else is there. You'll not be kept waiting more than a few minutes."

She nodded then and they rode on to his ranch house. The place was empty; there was no sign that any prowlers had been about. He hurried her into the house and her horse into the barn; it was nearly dark then. Less than ten minutes later he was leaning from the saddle to rap on Pepper's door with the loaded end of his quirt. The door was opened and a woman looked out, Mrs. Sam without a doubt. Sally Dawn's epithet "motherly" just fitted her. Middle-aged, apple-cheeked, comfortable and cozy looking, she greeted the stranger smilingly.

"Howdy, Mrs. Pepper," he said, and smiled back at her. "I'm your new neighbor, Jim Torrance. Is your husband here?"

"He ain't far," said Mrs. Sam, and stepped out in the yard to call her bugled notes. "Sam! Here's company."

She was calling and looking toward Sam Pepper's high hill, calling needlessly as it proved, for here already came Sam Pepper at a sort of dog-trot run.

"I seen you just riding home, Torrance," he said breathlessly as soon as he was within hailing distance. "You and somebody else. It was kinda dark and I couldn't quite make out for sure— You see, I just happened to be up on my hill and—"

"You two folks alone?" asked Torrance.

"Sure. Always alone. Better light down—"

"That was the Cannon girl with me," said Torrance. He speared the little man with a glance and, after a fashion, through a long silence, managed to keep him wriggling on the spear point. Then he added slowly and significantly, "In case you might be interested I can tell you several other things, things that a lot of folks are wondering about."

Mrs. Sam snorted. "If there's anything on earth Sam ain't interested in, I don't know what it is. When he was born they say he was tryin' to count how many toes he had. But if Sally Dawn, poor little thing, is over to your place—"

"Them Bordereau men will tear her to pieces if they find her!" burst out Sam Pepper.

"I'll go over and fetch her," said Torrance. "We'll be back right away. And then I want a good talk with you, Pepper."

When he brought Sally Dawn back with him she ran headlong into Mrs. Sam's mothering arms and put her head down on that deep, comforting bosom—and Torrance and Sam Pepper stepped along outside and sat on a log. That is, Torrance did; Sam Pepper couldn't sit still, couldn't even stand still.

"I aim to make a dicker with you, Pepper," said Torrance. "I need help and you're the one man can give it to me. And there are things you'd like to know about, and I'm the man can tell you things no other man can."

"What sort of help, neighbor?" asked Pepper, all eagerness.

"I want you to help me find out things, to nose out some facts that are keeping under cover."

"Like what?" asked Sam, growing excited. "What about?"

"Give me time and I'll tell you. Say, what's happened to Murdo?"

"Hanged if I know." He looked worried. "He's gone and nobody knows where! So's Doc Taylor! So was you and Sally until—"

"Who's Doc Taylor? What about him?"

"He was called in when Bordereau was shot. He went upstairs to look at Bordereau; I seen him. Next morning nobody could find him. I been asking folks; nary a one has seen hide nor hair of him."

Torrance stared at him through the growing dark for a long while, then whistled softly.

"I can tell you what Murdo's been up to all day and where he's been," he said crisply, and stood up. "And I can ask you this, Why did they bury Bordereau in such a hurry?"

If Pepper had been doing a sort of restrained dance before, now he fidgeted himself into something between an Apache war dance and an Irish jig. He was all but frothing at the mouth as he gasped out, "Mr. Torrance, I've been asking myself—"

"I know," said Torrance. "I can also tell you where the Cannon girl and I have been—I was on hand when Bordereau got shot, so I can tell you details about that—I can even tell you why I came up here looking for a man named Jim Torrance—"

"For God's sake!" pleaded the little man.

"Are you with me?" demanded Torrance sharply. "Will you throw in with me to find about everything? We'll be helping Sally Dawn Cannon, if that means anything to you. You'll learn one hell of a lot—but you'll keep your mouth shut about it all until I say the word or I'll chop you up into dog meat."

He looked as though he meant it. Sam Pepper shivered. Right now he clamped his mouth shut so tight that there were little puckers at the corners which Torrance, stooping so close to him, could see even in the fading light.

"It's a deal?" demanded Torrance.

Sam Pepper didn't open his mouth even then. But he nodded his head with a rapidity that made Torrance think of a woodpecker hammering on an oak.

"Go get your horse," said Jim Torrance. "We're riding into Sundown."

CHAPTER VIII

EARLY though the hour was, the Stag Horn was crowded. Excitement had run high in Sundown, and men clustered here where the current chain of events had seemed to have its inception; here, if anywhere, they could get the latest low-down on what it was all about.

Florinda, extravagantly attired, white-bosomed and sparkling with her "family jewels," strutted like a peacock. With Steve Bordereau away, with Murdo away too, she was more the tinsel queen than ever before. She disported herself as though it was she, Florinda de Valdez y Verdugo, who owned the place.

She saw Jim Torrance, travel-stained and somewhat hollow-eyed, come in with a furtive and apprehensive Sam Pepper at his heels, and stiffened.

Torrance's eyes were hunting her down. When they found her he came to her as straight as a string.

"Señorita!" he said to her in Spanish, and his tired eyes mocked her. "You are lovelier than a little white dove with pink feet; you are lovelier than a little dove sitting in the hollow of a man's hand. I am going to buy you some wine, and you are going to sit with me for three minutes and smile at me—and answer a question!"

Her teeth were like pearls, her loveliest and most genuine gems. Though she looked uncertain and frightened and ready to run, she smiled. She said, "Sí, Señor Jeem Torrance," and made her skirt billow above her slim ankles as she led the way in haste to a secluded corner table.

Sam Pepper, goggling wide-eyed in all directions, followed the two like a little dog with its tail tucked in. He had been upstairs in these rooms just once before in all his days; that was when Bordereau had opened for his first night, and Sam's insatiable curiosity got him admitted at a cost in dollars which he had never confessed to Mrs. Sam.

The three sat down. Florinda looked at Sam Pepper as at a bug. The waiter brought wine. When Torrance began to speak, Sam Pepper ceased goggling all over the room and distended his ears instead.

"Florinda," said Torrance, "we have met before, you and I."

She nodded.

"In Nacional," she whispered.

"So you remember?"

Her eyes became mysterious, unfathomable. She said almost inaudibly, "I am not going to forget; not ever, Señor."

"Bordereau was there that night?"

"Yes."

"A man was killed that night?"

"Yes! You know—"

"Who killed him?"

"But I do not know, Señor! It was— I thought it was—"

"I did not kill that man. Did Bordereau?"

"I thought—I thought you killed him! Bordereau? But I do not know, Señor! Not anything."

He stared at her a long while, trying to make out whether she lied. By this time there were hot spots of color in Sam Pepper's tanned cheeks. Abruptly Torrance switched to other matters.

"With Steve Bordereau dead," he said, "who takes over here? Who's the big gun now at the Stag Horn?"

"Murdo. He and Steve were somehow partners."

"Are you and Murdo good friends?"

Her velvet-black eyes unsheathed themselves in a flash.

"He is a pig. I hate him." Only she said, "He is a peeg."

"Did you see Doc Taylor come in the night after Bordereau was shot?"

"Yes. I followed into the room. Steve was not dead yet. Then Murdo t'row me out."

"And Doc Taylor?"

"I do not know, Señor. He was there when I go. Two-t'ree hour after that a man comes running, telling everybody his little boy baby is sick; he is crazy to find the doctor quick. He come back two, t'ree time. He come again to-day; he say he cannot find the doctor. I do not know, Señor."

Torrance slid some money across the table. "You can go now," he said.

She rose slowly with a queer, native dignity. The money she ignored absolutely, as though she had not seen it. Her eyes were a little brighter, her face hotter with color.

"I am your friend, if you will have it that way, Señor," she said, in a soft voice which trembled just a trifle and which was very earnest. Then she hurried away, almost running.

Sam Pepper, looking about to explode with all that pent-up curiosity seething within him, began babbling questions, but Torrance promptly shut him up, saying:

"Not now, Sam. You've got to wait, if it kills you. Right away I want you to help me. Remember that I'm a stranger here and that you ought to know everybody. We've got us a job of work to do tonight, and it might come in handy if we had a few other fellows, say four or five, to lend a hand. Men that are on the up-and-up and that we can trust. How about it?"

Sam Pepper's eyes started roving again. Then he shook his head.

"Not upstairs, Torrance. Downstairs in the bar I'd be sure to find some boys like that, that I know and that a man can tie to."

"Step down and round 'em up," said Torrance. "Make it lively. Friends of the Cannon girl if you can find them. I'll be with you in no time."

Sam slid out of his chair and hurried out of the room.

When Torrance went downstairs a few minutes later he had reason to congratulate himself on the choice of his ally. Pepper had already gathered half a dozen dependable looking men. Five of them, especially sought out by Pepper, were young stock men, and neighbors of the Cannons; the sixth, older and slightly bald, yet a man ready for anything, had not been invited but had horned in— and that man was Lying Bill Yarbo. Pepper looked at him accusingly; as for Jim Torrance, he was glad to have Yarbo of their number. At a nod from him they followed him outside.

"I'm playing a wild hunch tonight, boys," he told them. "I'll tell you all about it in a minute. First get this: If I'm wrong we're apt to have a fight on our hands, and if I'm right we'll be turning up to the light a pretty dirty trick that's been played and that's still in play."

One of the young fellows, lean and lanky Dave Drennen who had once worked for King Cannon and who now was running a small spread of his own, spoke up quietly.

"Somehow what you've got in mind is to help out Sally Cannon? You're a friend of hers and you know what's gone with her?"

"It's to help out the Cannon girl, and to help me out, too. Yes, I know where she is. So does Pepper."

"Sure I do," said Pepper. "Right now she—"

"Keep it under your hat a little longer," commanded Torrance. "Now if you boys will wander along with me we'll get busy. Likewise I'll tell you what I'm banking on."

He led the way and the others came along, walking swiftly down the sidewalk toward a hardware store which he had noted on his first day in Sundown. It was too early for a store to be closed and there were a couple of articles he wanted. But the little group of men hadn't gone over a block when Sam Pepper, who seemed to have eyes in the back of his head and whose ears were always registering sounds to which others gave no attention, came to a sudden halt.

"Say!" he exclaimed. "There's Clark Murdo! And there's someone with him! Say, he's got the girl! That's Sally Dawn he's yanking along after him!"

Three or four riders had drawn up in front of the Stag Horn; that was what Sam Pepper had heard first of all. They had dismounted; Clark Murdo had called out sharply, issuing some swift command. Then he and those with him passed into the Stag Horn.

"So," thought Torrance, "Murdo followed us after all, found the girl and has brought her here." He said aloud: "We'll go back, boys, but let Murdo show his hand first. Funny he has brought her back to Sundown; with so many folks around, he can't raise a finger against her. He—"

"You don't know what you're talking about!" snapped Sam Pepper. "He will hand her over to Rufe Biggs; Rufe's town marshal, as crooked and mean as a snake and a skunk —and belongs body and soul to Bordereau. Or did. With Bordereau dead, I guess he's in Murdo's pocket. He could jail her, couldn't he? After that, him and Murdo could do as they damned well pleased."

"Just the same, take it slow," muttered Torrance. "I've got something up my sleeve and we're going to know right soon whether it's an ace or a low card."

When they came back into the Stag Horn they saw that Pepper had things partly right if not entirely. There was Rufe Biggs, town marshal, tall and yellow-haired and pale-eyed, towering over Sally Dawn, who looked very small and helpless and weary. There was Murdo, doing a lot of talking; there was hot fury in his eyes, to be explained perhaps by a fresh gash on his cheek from which blood was still dribbling. He kept dabbing at it with his bandana.

"She's yours, Rufe," he said. "I caught her hiding out up at Sam Pepper's place. You ought to arrest him, too. You ought to go grab that damn wife of his; she threw a butcher knife at me. Anyhow here's this Cannon girl that murdered my pardner. Me, I say, woman or no woman, let the law take its course."

No one laughed at the thought of Sam Pepper's wife attacking Murdo with a butcher knife; that could be explained solely by the fact that nearly every man here was a follower of the team of Bordereau and Murdo. They would laugh later, when Murdo wasn't there.

Rufe Biggs, stepping closer to the girl, was just lifting his hand to put it on her shoulder, just opening his mouth to announce her arrest, when Jim Torrance's voice, sounding flat and toneless, made itself heard through the brief silence.

"Me, I'm a stranger here, but there are some things even a stranger might like to know about. One is, why did Murdo have to see to it that Steve Bordereau got buried in such a hurry?"

Sally Dawn, hearing him, whirled about, all eagerness and expectancy.

Murdo's black brows came down in a heavy frown.

"What the hell business is this of yours anyhow?" he demanded.

"Another thing," said Torrance in the same expressionless tone, "who killed Bordereau? This girl here? Well, how many times did she shoot him?"

"This ain't any trial court, brother," said Rufe Biggs.

"Of course it was the Cannon girl that killed him, and you know it," snapped Murdo. "She shot him twice, close up; once in the body, the second shot in the head. She—"

Sally Dawn's gasp was drowned by Torrance's reply to Murdo.

"You're a damned liar, Murdo," he said. "She shot him just once."

Murdo's hand went as quick as a flash to his low-slung gun. But Jim Torrance's two hands were already on his two guns, and there was a cold, deadly look in his low-lidded eyes which acted as a deterrent. Murdo shrugged.

"There's one more thing that a man might like to know about," Torrance went on after a little pause. "Where's Doc Taylor? Nobody seems to have seen him since he went up to take care of Bordereau."

A queer look came into Murdo's eyes at that; the color ran up into his swarthy cheeks, subsiding slowly.

"What the hell are you driving at anyhow?" he said thickly.

Torrance didn't answer him. Instead he said to Sally Dawn Cannon: "You'll be all right now; the marshal will hold you where you'll be safe for maybe an hour. Then we'll come back and see you home or wherever you want to go." He turned and went back to the door. "Come along, boys," he said, as the eyes of his new allies followed him. "We'll know damned quick what it's all about."

This time Sam Pepper was the last to follow. He hung back long enough to ask of the girl, "Is Molly all right, Sally?"

"They were brutes to her. They left her tied up, so she couldn't come along with us. Yes, she's all right, Sam—and she was wonderful!"

Sam Pepper then was sadly torn two ways. He wanted to rush back and free his wife and hear all details of what had happened; he wanted with all his heart to find out what Jim Torrance had up his sleeve, whether ace or deuce. In the end, hurrying after the men who were already hurrying after Torrance, he found a half-grown, gawky and open-mouthed youth whom he dispatched to set Mrs. Pepper free. Then at a run he came up with Jim Torrance.

"Where we going now, Torrance?" he asked. "What we going to do?"

"We want a couple of picks and shovels," said Torrance. "We're going out to the graveyard."

Sam Pepper's mouth came open for an exclamation and remained open with never a sound being made.

Together with the tools which Torrance had mentioned, they picked up a couple of lanterns. In the graveyard, companionably close to the edge of town, they shone the light of their lanterns on a freshly painted headboard. It advised that Here Lay Steve Bordereau, Gambler, Friend and Gentleman.

"Let's dig," said Torrance. "We might be interrupted, and there'd be sure to be some around here who'd say this sort of thing was against the law. Let's get busy."

Lying Bill Yarbo began swearing in his rich deep voice and was the first to wield a pick. Sam Pepper shivered delightfully from head to foot and was of no earthly use. A contagion of excitement spread over the others. In no time at all they brought the coffin up and pried the lid off.

Torrance, stooping to look closely, said only:

"This isn't Steve Bordereau. Who is it?"

A yell burst from Sam Pepper.

"It's Doc Taylor! Doc Taylor, by the powers! What's he doing dead here? Who done him in? And where's Steve Bordereau? And what'n hell's blazes does it all mean?"

"Let's pick up the box and carry it back to the Stag Horn, boys," said Torrance.

CHAPTER IX

JIM TORRANCE came stalking back into the Stag Horn. He had been away so short a time that he found things here pretty much as he had left them. Sally Dawn Cannon stood where he had seen her last and did not seem to have moved. Only a few paces from her, talking quietly into each other's attentive ears, were Clark Murdo and the marshal, Rufe Biggs, keeping their eyes on her all the time. The only change in grouping that Torrance could note was this: A dozen men, hard hombres he judged them, and Murdo men, had gathered just behind Murdo and Biggs; they looked ready at the drop of the hat for anything they might be called on to deliver.

As Torrance entered, the room grew hushed and every eye turned to him. He stepped to one side of the door and got his back to the wall before he spoke. Then it was the girl whom he addressed.

"Everything's all right now," he said. "You'll be free to go in about two minutes!"

"Like hell!" roared Murdo, tense and worried and truculent. "All you're doing is a lot of wild talking. You'd better fold up and blow before you get yourself dehorned. *Sabe, hombre?*"

Torrance ignored him. To Rufe Biggs he said:

"We stepped out to the graveyard. Somebody seems to have been digging out there. The boys are bringing you what we found. Here they come now."

They squeezed through the door, carrying the redwood box on their shoulders. It was Lying Bill Yarbo who set something down on the box when it had been deposited on the floor before Rufe Biggs.

"Here's the headboard that went with the coffin," said Yarbo. "Step up and read it, gents."

Neither Biggs nor Murdo moved or spoke; they looked swiftly at each other and looked away even more swiftly. Other men crowded close. One sang out: "Hell, they've dug Bordereau up! Can't they let a dead man lie in peace?"

"Maybe this dead man didn't want to lie in peace until he'd had his own funeral and not somebody else's," drawled Torrance, and kept watching Murdo. "Lift the lid off, boys."

A shout went up: "It's Doc Taylor! It ain't Steve at all! By the Lord, it's Doc Taylor in Steve's box!"

"You'll find he's had his head bashed in," said Torrance. "Whether that killed him outright or whether he smothered after his quick burial, I don't know. Maybe the coroner can find out. Anyhow, Biggs, he's yours now. And you might ask your friend Murdo what he did with Bordereau and why he put Taylor in his place!"

"Why, damn you!" yelled Murdo, and again went for his gun—and again he thought better of it.

"That's twice you've done that, Murdo," said Torrance. "Mean anything by it?"

Murdo, like Steve Bordereau in this, was a certain type of gambler, the cold-blooded, calculating type that will bet as high as any man—but only on a dead sure thing. Right now, though he had a hard, gun-slinging pack at his back, the odds for him personally did not appear to strike him as right. He got himself in hand, throttling down his anger, which he so seldom let sweep him away, and spoke coolly and with the affectation of a sneer.

"Seems like, for a stranger, you're getting around," he said.

"And at that I've still got quite some traveling to do," returned Torrance. To the roomful of silent, puzzled men he added: "Later on you boys can figure out just what happened, but one thing ought to be clear enough to the thickest skull right now: First, Bordereau isn't any more dead than you are; he wasn't even bad hurt. The Cannon girl shot him high up, in the right shoulder I think it must have been. He put his hand up as he fell back and got blood on it and got the blood smear on his forehead. Then he got him his hunch to play dead, and you can take it from me he had his reasons for wanting to do that! Then some busybody brought the doctor in, and some helping friend of Bordereau's cracked the doc over the head to keep him from going out and spilling the beans. That done, they have the funeral right away, Doc Taylor taking Bordereau's place while Bordereau goes off somewhere and holes up until his wound heals. I'd say Marshal Biggs would be inside his rights to gather Murdo in and hold him on suspicion."

A lean and foxy-faced young fellow, that same gimlet-eyed young hellion who had come out of Torrance's place looking for the vanished girl, began whispering in Murdo's ear. Murdo listened, then grinned.

"You're right, kid," he said, and then spoke his piece to all who cared to listen—and that meant all within earshot. "Torrance and some other boys go out and do some digging in the graveyard. They come back with Steve's head-board and a coffin! Who's to tell us it was Steve's coffin in the first place? And if it was, who's to say they didn't lift Steve out and put Taylor in? Who's here to say they didn't kill Taylor themselves?"

"That's right," said Biggs quickly. "Dammit, that's right!"

"Better watch your step, Echo Biggs," warned Torrance. "Anyhow get this straight: You can't arrest this girl for killing Bordereau when more than one of us knows Bordereau hasn't been killed. Now I'm going to tell you all a little story. About six years ago a pardner of mine and myself were down at a little border town called Las Lunas, sixty miles from Nacional. We had forty thousand dollars between us and were taking our time to sink it in a cow outfit. One day when Danny was alone at the cabin some gent stepped in, shot him in the back of the head and made off with our stake. And the gent that did that went to a good bit of trouble to make it look as though I had murdered my own pardner."

Murdo, though slow with his gun tonight, was quick with his tongue.

"A pardner-killer, huh?" he said. "So that's what you are!"

"The gent that killed Danny," Torrance continued imperturbably, "stepped right along. But he still kept up his play at getting me blamed for his night's work. Twenty miles farther along he wrapped a bandana about his face, held up two sheep men that everybody knew had been hoarding for a long time, robbed them, killed one, said to the other, 'Me, I'm Jim Torrance, and when you hear me coming you better hide,' and kept on going. And only a year ago the same gent, or I'm guessing wrong, plugged a man down in Nacional when I was in town, and tried to throw that on me. His game was and still is clear enough. He knows damned well I'll get him some day, if he can't fix it up so that some hot-headed party swings me to a cottonwood first."

"What the hell's this got to do with us?" demanded Rufe Biggs.

"Plenty. I came up this way looking for a man that calls himself Jim Torrance whenever he pulls a fast one. I've got a reason or two to bet any man of you a thousand dollars to a hundred that that gent is Steve Bordereau. And, if you want to know, that's why Bordereau is playing dead right now. He's the sort that shoots a man in the back, that tries to manhandle a girl, that sets his yellow dog onto smashing Doc Taylor over the head and burying him just to give him a chance to hide out. He means to make his final cleanup here, then drift along somewhere else where they don't know him, take a new name—and maybe get to be mayor or something like that."

"Got any proof of all this, Stranger?" demanded Biggs, beginning to look a trifle uncertain.

"Somebody's already said," Torrance told him, "that this place isn't any courthouse. Besides, I've talked myself out for one night." He turned to Sally Dawn Cannon. "If you're ready we'll step along."

She started forward eagerly. Rufe Biggs put out an involuntary hand to detain her, but Murdo moodily shook his head. Biggs dropped his hand and seemed relieved to do so, and Sally Dawn came swiftly to Torrance's side. She stepped around the grewsome thing lying there on the floor staring up at her, and shuddered; but once outside in the clean night air, with friends about her, shudders were forgotten and an ecstasy thrilled through her. She put her two hands impulsively on one of Jim Torrance's hard brown ones. She said with a catch in her voice:

"Some day when I can get a good dictionary I'm going to read it all the way through." He jerked up his black brows at her, as much as to ask: "Who's crazy now? You or me?" Then she ran on: "Maybe that way I can find the words to thank you! But for you, where'd I be now? But for you, I'd all my life go on thinking I'd killed a man."

He chuckled at last, the way she loved to hear him.

"Shucks," he said. "If you'd nailed Steve Bordereau proper, that wouldn't have been anything to keep you awake, and you'd have saved me a job."

Then they mounted, all of them, and rode out of town. For a few minutes Jim Torrance and Sally Dawn rode neck and neck. That was while he said to her a word or two he felt impelled to speak. He said:

"You've got good friends and unless I'm a liar you're going to have a lot more real soon. You can go back to your ranch when you want to. Why not stay with the Peppers tonight? And when you go back home, why not have them come along, and Bill Yarbo and a couple of the other boys? And keep this in mind: You haven't lost your ranch yet; you can bet your sweet life that Bordereau pulled a crooked trick or two getting you folks out on a limb; stick to it and you'll beat him yet."

At the edge of town they rode into the deep dark under a thick grove of big pines; when she said something to Torrance, still thinking him at her side, it was Lying Bill Yarbo who answered.

"Where's Jim Torrance?" she asked.

He didn't exactly know. No one else knew. They called for Torrance and got no answer.

He had dropped back, cut into a side trail and was already well ahead of them hurrying to his own place. He said to his horse, with whom he grew conversational at times when they had it all to themselves: "Here we've been putting in a lot of time messing around in a girl's affairs and letting our own slide. Let's change all that."

At his ranch he went out to the barn and threw down a plentiful lot of hay into the mangers; the stock would be finding short browsing and feeling the want of warm shelter. He pulled his saddle and bridle, gave his horse a good rubdown and a here's-thanks-old-boy slap on the rump, went out into the corral and tossed a skilful noose over his liveliest black mare's neck. This one he saddled and left in readiness; thereafter he went into his house for a shave, a bite, and ten minutes' relaxation flat on his back.

And then the thing happened which he might have expected, had he had all his wits about him. For of course he had lighted a lamp, and he had not covered his south window—and here came Sam Pepper on the run.

And Sam's words, as he bounced into the house, ran even faster than a spry Sam Pepper could travel. There was a gleam in his eye, there were red spots in his cheeks, there was something akin to venom on his ready tongue. From the doorway he cussed Jim Torrance up hill and down dale.

"What's eating you?" demanded Torrance, leaning on his elbow.

"You—you—you—" There Sam bogged down. But he grew vocal instantly. "You wanted me to help you, and I done it. You was going to let me in on a lot of secret doings —and, instead, you run out on me! What's more, you only set me wondering about a lot of other things! I got a notion to cut your gizzard out and fry it in hawg fat and make you eat it!"

Torrance stood up. Of a sudden Sam Pepper, thinking himself about to be attacked by a man to whom killing was just a chore, leaped back out through the door, which, perhaps subconsciously, he had kept open against retreat.

"Don't shoot, Jim. Don't shoot!" he pleaded. "I was just funning. Shore I was, Jim."

Torrance laughed at him and sat back on the edge of his bed. Pepper sidled back into the room. And then, brushing him aside, Lying Bill Yarbo came barging in.

"What the merry hell's going on here?" shouted Bill Yarbo, comporting himself like a storm wind blowing its heartiest. "You'd run out on me, would you? And connive with this tricky, lying Sam Pepper? The truth ain't in him and you ought to know it; and still you let him come in and powwow with you unbeknownst to others. Torrance, are you a damn' fool on top of other things?"

Here was another cue for a laugh from Jim Torrance that started low down somewhere in his anatomy and rose into a glorious crescendo. He got to thinking, "If I went out gunning for a couple of boys to keep me from going to sleep on my feet, I couldn't do better than S. Pepper and L. B. Yarbo." But all that he said to them about all this was said in that laugh of his. He was a man with a tight smile, with now and again a mellow chuckle—with a laugh like that maybe once a year.

Sam Pepper stared, pop-eyed; Lying Bill glared. It was Lying Bill Yarbo who spoke.

"What'n merry hell are you talking about?" he demanded, and his big burly fists were doubled into young parboiled hams at his sides.

"Since you ask," said Torrance, "I'm going for a chat with Steve Bordereau."

"You do know then where he's at?" gasped Sam Pepper, goggling.

"I've got a notion. My horse is saddled. I'm riding right away."

"I'm going along," said Yarbo heavily.

"Don't you let him, Jim!" stuttered Sam Pepper. "There's like to be trouble when you find Bordereau. Me, I'm your man. Yarbo here, he'd let you down—he's the damnedest coward in seven states and—"

Lying Bill made a lunge at him but with almost incredible alacrity Sam Pepper scuttled across the room and established himself behind the headboard of Torrance's bed.

"Pepper's such a damn little liar," snorted Lying Bill.

This time Torrance didn't laugh; he was no longer in the mood for any light comedy. He saw what ailed them both, each man hating the hide the other walked in, each wishing his own subconsciously acknowledged failing upon the other. He said curtly:

"You boys stood in with me tonight and I'm obliged. I'll be glad any time to do the same for both of you. Now I've got me a job that belongs to me and I'd better take it on single-handed."

"Dammit, you ain't got no gratitude!" yipped Sam Pepper. "If you had, you'd ask me along. You made a deal with me, remember; me, I done my part and you ain't done yours!"

"Oh, hell, come along if you want to," grunted Torrance. He got up and jammed on his hat. "You've got a ride ahead of you though."

"Me, too!" boomed Bill Yarbo. "If there's apt to be a showdown with Steve Bordereau, I've got a right to be in it. Hell's bells, man, I'm the best friend Sally Dawn's got; me and her old man, King Cannon, was boys together and—"

"He never seen King Cannon but once," cried Pepper, "and then Cannon booted him clean off'n his ranch."

Yarbo made a dive at him and Pepper slid up close behind Torrance's back. Torrance sang out sharply:

"Look here, you two horn toads! You're both welcome to trail along if you're fools enough to do it, but I can't bother with you if you can't keep your damn mouths shut about each other. If you want to start something, better stay here and do it. I've got something else to do than trying to stand betwixt you."

"I'll leave him alone if he'll leave me alone," muttered Sam Pepper.

"Me too," grumbled Lying Bill, though with reluctance.

"Only," added Sam, "it would be a heap sight better if he went back home and stayed there!"

"You—!" shouted Yarbo.

But under that cold, low-lidded look that they got from Jim Torrance they grew silent. And in the end, not over ten minutes later, the three mismated musketeers rode out together—toward a meeting with Steve Bordereau.

CHAPTER X

THEY had made their packs—blankets, bacon and beans, coffee, frying pan and coffee pot—and headed up into the mountains, riding the same trails Torrance and Sally Dawn had so recently traveled. They camped that night at the same deserted shack that had sheltered him and the girl on the first leg of their journey, and were up and riding at the first glint of a pale gray daybreak. No snow fell that day; by midforenoon tattered streaks of clear sky were like pale blue banners above the far ridges. And when they came to the old mining camp high above Pocket Valley, the mountains as far as they could see swam in a diaphanous purple mist, and the western horizon was aflame with a red-and-gold sunset.

"Now I'll tell you boys all I know," said Torrance, and hooked a leg over the saddle horn while he reached for the makings. "Murdo and somebody else camped here night before last. I could see Murdo through the window; the other man was on a bunk in the corner and I couldn't see him. And I couldn't hear what they were talking about. But I could tell that the other man was giving orders and that Murdo was taking them. So it's a fair bet it was Bordereau."

"Where'd they go to?" demanded Sam Pepper.

"Down trail toward Pocket. But they swung off where there's a narrow canyon. Then Murdo went down alone to Pocket, filled his grub bag and went back up the canyon. So it's my bet that that's where Bordereau is now, hiding out where nobody'd look for him, the same time he gets well of a bullet hole somewhere in his carcass."

"Me, I know that canyon like I know my hat," said Bill Yarbo. "And I know right where we'll find Bordereau, sure. You see, Torrance, about thirty years ago there was all hell to pay about the mines up here. And Sally Dawn's old gent, though he was a stock man first, last and all the time, took an interest. He was in the money in them days. He come up here; he bought up some mining properties; and he likewise grabbed off a little valley all his own for a summer range. What's more, he built him a house, and he'd come up here when he felt like loafing, and go hunting and fishing. That house stands there yet, quite a place, and it's up that canyon—and you couldn't find a likelier place for a man to hide out and lick his wounds."

"And for once he ain't lying!" said Sam Pepper, in a tone of awe.

"Far from here?" asked Torrance.

Bill Yarbo, having glared at Pepper, said, "Hell, no. If we poke right along we'll get there before it's too dark to see the whites of their eyes. Bordereau won't be all alone, you know."

"No," admittd Torrance. "He'd have someone—"

"I know!" exclaimed Sam Pepper. "He's got anyhow three-four, maybe more men with him! There's Hen Billings and Varny Slack and that half-breed, Joe Tortillas; that's three of 'em anyhow! And—let's see—"

"How would you know?" snorted Bill Yarbo.

"Me, I sort of notice things," snapped Pepper. "When I go places, I look around. Now since the night Bordereau got hurt I ain't seen hide nor hair of any one of them three, and they're always hanging around where Steve Bordereau is! Yep. And— Say, I ain't seen Turkey-trot Smith or Andy Pollack, and they was both in Sundown when Bordereau got shot! I'll bet he's got the whole gang up there!"

Torrance shrugged.

"There's just one way to find out," he said, and unhooked his leg from the saddle horn.

"Hey, wait!" said Sam Pepper, and looked worried. "It'll be dark—we better camp here overnight, anyhow. And maybe—maybe—"

Bill Yarbo glared at him scornfully, then pretended spontaneous laughter. Sam Pepper went red to the gills.

"I ain't scared!" he sputtered. "I'm just using my brains. If only three of us go jumping a crowd like Bordereau's got—"

"There's only two of us that counts," said Yarbo. "Come ahead, Jim, let's get along."

"There's something else," said Pepper hastily. "You can bet your boots that Bordereau'll be ready for us! Don't you suppose Murdo got word across to him in a hurry? Them two are playing this game close together."

"If Murdo or a messenger had passed us—"

"He wouldn't have to. He could have come up by the Flats. Or he could have sent some sort of signal. Me, I noticed some smoke standing up in the sky back yonder over High Man's Ridge; I wondered about it, too."

"You would wonder," guffawed Lying Bill Yarbo. "Come ahead, Jim. Let the little rooster stick here or run back home to his old woman." Then he grinned very broadly, "Maybe Murdo and a bunch of cutthroats are following along behind us now, Jim; maybe Mr. Sam Pepper, scooting back home, will run smackkerdab into them!"

Sam Pepper, from red, turned a pasty white, and his eyeballs rolled. Then, when Torrance pushed on again and Lying Bill Yarbo fell in behind, Sam Pepper knew a moment of dreadful doubt. It was soon going to be dark. A timber wolf, perhaps the same hungry old fellow that Sally Dawn and Jim Torrance had heard, howled after a fashion to make the white solitudes seem ten thousand times more dreary and lonely. It wasn't that Sam was afraid of the wolf; a man in a haunted house wouldn't be afraid of the creak of a floor board; such sounds, however, didn't perk a man up. He shivered and spurred hastily along after Torrance and Yarbo.

The old house that so long ago had been a sort of vacation home and hunting lodge to that great-hearted gentleman, King Cannon, when first glimpsed by Jim Torrance gave him a flick of surprise, despite what Bill Yarbo had hinted of it. There was a small upland valley with a round bit of a lake like a dusky mirror in its center; there was a rushing stream pouring down into the lake; on a narrow bit of bench land stood the building, massive and four-square, honest granite for foundation, no less honest and rugged spruce logs for the rest of it. Candlelight glimmered out through two or three windows.

There came a hushed bleat from Sam Pepper alternately holding back and pressing up close to their heels.

"Listen!" he pleaded. "You damfools listen to me! Ain't you got any sense? Look how the place is lighted up! Say, there's apt to be forty men there! If we go running into that mess—well, we might's well cut us our own throats and save 'em the trouble!"

"Don't listen to him, Jim," muttered Bill Yarbo. And then in a confidential tone, yet one raised loud enough to make sure Pepper caught it, he demanded as though in wonder, "Why'd you bring him along anyhow?"

"Funny they've got the place lighted up like that," said Torrance. "If it's Bordereau, and he's in hiding, you'd think—"

"Shucks," said Yarbo. "He ain't got the faintest idea that there's anyone on his trail. Up here, why a man might hang out all winter and never have a nose poked in on him. We'll take him clean by surprise."

"You're c-crazy!" stuttered Pepper. "Murdo's sure warned him."

"Come ahead, Jim," said Yarbo.

The two started on again.

Sam Pepper stopped where he was.

"Me, I'll guard the trail," he said faintly. "In case anyone's following us, I'll head him off."

Yarbo laughed and Torrance grunted. Sam Pepper watched them ride on, but himself sat where he was in the trail and shivered from head to foot. He saw his two companions draw on closer to the house, then turn off the trail into a grove, then emerge on foot, moving on guardedly. He was tempted then to turn and scurry back the way he had come, at least as far as the mining camp, but the thought of being in that lonely place all night—and of perhaps having some most unwelcome callers drop in on him—gave him a fresh set of jitters. He dallied with the thought of going back only as far as the main trail, then down to Pocket Valley. But suppose he should meet

Murdo and his gang coming up from Sundown by way of the Flats?

He just shivered and stuck tight where he was.

Yet he'd have given anyhow a good left hand to know what was ahead of Torrance and Yarbo, what they were going to find out and just how things would happen to them.

"Maybe they'll be dead inside ten minutes," his dry lips whispered. His spare shoulders twitched as he added: "Me, too, maybe. Why'n thunder did I ever come along with two such crazy fools?"

Again Torrance led the way, watchful for some guard who might well enough be posted outside. It appeared however that Bordereau, as Yarbo had predicted, was confident that no one was likely to look in on him here. For when the two men came stealthily up onto the front porch of the old King Cannon mountain place and looked in at a window, they saw that the men inside had no thought of anything but of their own affair. There was Steve Bordereau on his feet and moving about restlessly, carrying one shoulder stiffly yet beyond that seeming whole and unharmed. With him were five other men.

"What'n hell are they doing?" whispered Lying Bill Yarbo. "Tearing the house down?"

"Who are they?" asked Torrance. "Know them?"

"Sure. That little weasel Sam Pepper guessed it; somehow he's apt to guess right once in a while. They're the fellers he said we'd run into. And take it from me, Torrance, they're tougher'n saddle leather. If it comes along to a scrimmage, you better shoot damn fast and twice as straight—or that little egg-sucking Pepper'll have the laugh on both of us."

Bordereau's men, under his orders, were making a wreck of the big rude-timbered living room. With pick and crowbar and hand ax, they were tearing up floor boards now, and had already demolished a considerable section of one wall in a corner near the fireplace. One man, down on his knees, was prying up stones from the hearth.

"There's six of 'em altogether, and maybe more hanging around," said Yarbo. "There's only two of you and me—"

"Better go back with your little friend Pepper," said Torrance.

"Why, damn you!" growled Yarbo. "Me, I can handle that crowd alone and single-handed. I was just going to say—"

"Sh! What do they think they're doing in there? What are they looking for?"

Sam Pepper could have told him, nailing the fact on the head; and Sam would have been in an ecstasy of interest to mark whether they found it or not. When this country had been filled years before with old free-lance miners, when King Cannon had come up here and looked around and made him this place, he had grubstaked many a man, he had been a friend to nearly all of them—and a lot of gold, both raw and minted, had passed through his hands. Sam Pepper would have explained: "Why he kept a lot of gold, King Cannon did, and he put it somewhere, didn't he? Here in this house, wasn't it? And it's never been found in all these years. Somehow, Steve Bordereau's got a hunch at last that he can find it."

But Sam Pepper, missing all this, wasn't on hand to explain, and Bill Yarbo didn't know. He relieved himself of a ponderous, thick-shouldered shrug.

"After all," he suggested, "we come up here to gather Bordereau in, didn't we? Me, for a long while, I've wanted to see that bull dehorned. Now while he's busy, no matter what he's looking for—"

"The door'll be locked," said Torrance. "If we start anything through the window, they'll scatter six ways, douse the glim and have us guessing. Let's slip around back and see if we can get in."

"Fair enough," agreed Yarbo, and they started to withdraw. Just then however they were riveted in their tracks by a mighty uproar exploding in the room on which they had only now turned their backs. There was an excited yell in a high tenor voice, that of Joe Tortillas; there was a triumphant, bellowing shout that came from an exultant

Steve Bordereau. And then a half dozen men were shouting like schoolboys.

Torrance and Yarbo whirled and ran back and peered in again. They saw what the excitement was all about. Joe Tortillas was the man who had been ripping up boards near the fireplace; he had come upon a small wooden box, pretty well rotted away, and from it dumped on the floor several rusted old tobacco cans—and thus proved that in old rumors there could be a lot of truth. What gushed forth was gold, some of it dust and knobby nuggets, some in minted coins.

"Looks like a million dollars!" gasped Bill Yarbo. "—And, oh, Sam Pepper, where were you then?"

"Looks like Bordereau's got it for keeps," snapped Jim Torrance, "unless— Come ahead, Bill! Now's our chance! At the back door. They won't be thinking of anything but that King Cannon gold."

He leaped down from the porch and ran, breaking through a deep snowdrift at the corner of the house, and after him like a lumbering plow horse came Lying Bill Yarbo.

They found the back door locked. They tried a window; it, too, was fastened. They hunted farther, hoping to enter without any splintering of wood or crash of glass. It was Yarbo who found a narrow door in a corner and got it open. He was aquiver from stem to stern—just as Sam Pepper shook through icy fear, so did Yarbo tremble with rage. He muttered in his throat:

"Damn him, Jim! That belongs to Sally by rights. It might get her in the clear again. And if Bordereau thinks for a split second—"

Again a stone-cold Jim Torrance gave him a soft "Sh!" to bring him back to some degree of caution. It would be like Bill Yarbo to go bounding in like a roaring lion.

"We ought to get the drop on them, Bill, but watch your step. Walk light and have your gun ready."

They entered directly into what had once been a large kitchen, the sort of place where you'd expect to have the ox roasted whole, the sort of kitchen a man like King Cannon was sure to dream into being. They saw strips of light under two doors, both giving entrance to the living room where Bordereau and his exultant followers were. Jim Torrance jerked his thumb toward one of these doors, then pointed to the other, and Bill Yarbo nodded. They'd burst in simultaneously from two points of vantage upon seven unexpecting, loot-excited men.

Torrance stepped softly, tiptoeing, toward one of the doors. Bill Yarbo went his lumbering way like an old bear toward the other. They had enough light to guide them and to see each other by, due to the two glass panels set over the two doors Torrance began a slow opening of the door to which he had stepped, drawing it inward toward himself. Bill Yarbo turned a knob, had trouble because of a warped jamb, gave an impatient tug, found that his door opened the other way, shoved at it and—

Then of a sudden, as he remarked later, on regaining consciousness, it seemed like all hell broke loose. Certainly these three things happened simultaneously: The door flew open with a crack and a bang of a heavy panel striking against a wall; the toe of Bill Yarbo's boot caught on the threshold and Bill plunged headlong, sprawling on all fours into the living room—and from somewhere outside and near by there came the rapid-fire explosions of gunfire. If every energy had been bent toward giving Bordereau full warning that an attack was bearing down on him, the thing couldn't have been better done.

Bordereau experienced his instant of consternation; so did Torrance and Bill Yarbo; not one of them had the least certainty of what those shots outside meant.

But Sam Pepper knew!

Sam Pepper kept twisting his head this way and that like a little owl sitting on a post; he wanted to watch for happenings at the old house, and at the same time in desperate apprehension he kept watching the trail along which they had ridden. When all of a sudden he saw two men bulking big as they rode toward him, his heart pounded, fluttered, threatened to stop for good and all, and the bones within him seemed to melt. He had been scared many a time in his life but never like this! He knew these oncomers for what they were—killers who'd make no more of Sam Pepper than a cat would make of a mouse at breakfast time.

He wanted to scurry along to the house where Torrance and Yarbo were, but he couldn't move. He saw the two men closer; there was enough light reflected from the white expanse to show him their bulky forms and, even more clearly, the horses they rode. They were Barty Evans and Butch Vorich, as sure as he was born, and if there were two more merciless brutes within a hundred miles of Sundown, he didn't know them. He began to wilt and slide down out of his sadlde. As he slid he reached automatically for his belt gun, just as it is said that a man will grasp at a straw.

Sam Pepper wore an old Colt forty-four that hadn't been fired for years; he wasn't even dead sure that it was loaded! It was a wonder that the thing could still shoot. Scared stiff and rigid as he was, there were certain uncontrollable, spasmodic jerkings of his spare frame. A voice yelled at him; a gun roared and spat orange-yellow flame; he was sure that he felt a lock of hair cut away.

His hands, despite the cold, were sweaty. That old gun of his got itself into his grip, he never quite knew how. A slippery finger slipped on the trigger. And, a wonder again, the bullet went on its way as from a fresh cartridge. Finally, a thing that cannot altogether be explained, an act of fate if you like—just one of those things—that wild bullet took a man, none other than Barty Evans, square between the small crafty eyes.

And Sam's slippery finger kept on slipping. His gun, blazing away as of its own accord, emptied itself—and a howl of pain shrilled through the air as the man riding neck and neck with Barty Evans pitched headlong from his saddle into the snow and lay there moaning and writhing and trying to get up and falling back and lying where he fell, a black formless blot on the white of the snow.

The gun slid out of Sam Pepper's hand. Sam himself balanced drunkenly as though he too had been shot, then melted from the saddle and slowly settled down into a snow bank. He didn't faint exactly, but for a few moments he didn't quite know what it was all about or where he was or why. He felt sick.

He was only vaguely conscious of other shots being fired within the house, of wild yells and scurryings. He heard more clearly a man shouting, and recognized Steve Bordereau's voice: "Get the hell out of here! There's a mob after us!" He heard a roar from Bill Yarbo, a roar cut short off; he heard pistol shots until the world seemed to rock with them; he heard Steve Bordereau shout again: "The gold, dammit! Get the gold, Joe! Let's get the hell out of here!"

And here came men rushing toward him on horseback, a hundred men he would have sworn, though there were but half a dozen of them in all. He cowered deeper in the snow and watched them race past; he saw Barty Evans' body trampled, saw stricken Butch Vorich try to wriggle out of the way, screaming, and saw him too trampled, then lying a still black spot emphasizing the whiteness around him. They were gone, gone with a rush as they had come. And Sam Pepper, feeling more dead than alive, was alone.

After a while he picked himself up and slunk into deeper shadows. His brain began functioning again in its own peculiar way. He began wondering just what had happened there at the house—what about Jim Torrance? And Bill Yarbo? After Yarbo's shout there hadn't been a sound from them.

So once again Sam Pepper was torn two ways. He wanted to scramble up on his horse and get out of here on the dead run, get out and stay out for good. Also he did want with all his heart and soul to know what had happened at the house.

He began inching back into the trail.

CHAPTER XI

THREE men lay sprawled in the house from which Bordereau had fled so precipitately, all three looking to be dead. In fact one of them was beyond ever stirring again; that one chanced to be Turkey-trot Smith, shot close under the heart.

When, after no little reconnoitering, after many hesitancies and withdrawals, little Sam Pepper at last came inching into the room still lighted by three or four candle ends and also by a flickering light which came from an adjoining room, he saw Bill Yarbo lying on his face across a threshold, his gun near his lax hand, and saw Jim Torrance lying half in and half out of another door, as still as the already dead Turkey-trot Smith. Sam Pepper thought in agony, "Oh, my God, they're both dead—and me, me, I'm all alone up here!"

That flickering light from the next room impressed itself on him. He went tiptoeing to make out what it was, who was there. It was a lively young fire just getting well under way. Bordereau, as he ran out, had thrown a burning candle onto a heap of rubbish in a corner, meaning to let the house burn down behind him and thus to leave no definite evidence to the nosy ones, whose bodies, burnt to cinders, lay on the living room floor, nor when and how they had expired. Sam Pepper, just in time, began stamping out the flames. He ran to the kitchen, found two buckets of water, doused the fire with them and so put it out. Then, slack-jawed in awe, he came back gingerly to the scene of the indoor battle.

Two minutes later he and his kind fate were crowning him hero. His emotions were like those of a proud conquering monarch to his coronal, or like those of a young girl being crowned Queen of the May. Most definitely little Sam Pepper was "Aces."

And he had his audience. For Jim Torrance reared up and took stock of things, and presently Bill Yarbo rolled over and groaned and made it emphatic that he too was still alive. Both men had been shot, Torrance once and Yarbo twice, yet neither was in any grave danger. Sam Pepper saw that immediately. Lying Bill, falling, had struck his head against the door jamb and was for some few moments out cold. Torrance, taking a bullet groovingly along his skull, had been within a hair's breadth of reaching the end of his earthly trail, yet would be as good as new in a few hours. He had lost blood, he had suffered shock, but otherwise he was unimpaired.

Both men, pulling themselves up into a sitting position, groped for their guns, then looked in a dazed and questioning way at Sam Pepper. Bill Yarbo, as soon as he was able to speak, began to curse the little man. That was because, most of all, he knew that it was his own awkward blundering that had precipitated disaster, and the words were sweet on his tongue that strove to put all blame on Sam Pepper.

Bill Yarbo said:

"Here me and Jim Torrance has been fighting, doing men's work, and you—you little runaway rat! If you'd stuck with us, if you'd done your part— Go get out of my sight! You make me sick."

"Here's a dead man," said Sam Pepper. "It's old Turkeytrot. He's been shot square through the heart, looks like. Must of shot himself, huh?"

"Why, damn you!" roared Bill Yarbo in weak thunder. "It was me that plugged him—else it was Jim— It was me, that's who. And you! Sticking your head in a snow bank!"

Sam Pepper inflated himself.

"If you two boys," he told them pompously, "had did your part as well as I done mine, you wouldn't be laying here now for me to have to tend to. I guarded the trail, like I promised. When two fellers come storming in, Barty Evans and Butch Vorich they was, why I stopped 'em!"

"You stopped 'em? Oh, my eye!" groaned Yarbo. "You—"

"Sure," said Sam Pepper vaingloriously "I kilt 'em.

Both of 'em. They're laying out there in the trail; you can go see for yourself."

"Of all the liars I ever knew!" growled Bill Yarbo in disgust.

He managed to get to his feet and then would have toppled over in a dead faint if Sam Pepper hadn't run to him and helped ease his big bulky body down onto a bench before the fireplace. Jim Torrance looked at Pepper strangely; he had heard those shots outside and had wondered about them. He too pulled himself up, retrieved his fallen gun, and went staggering across the room and out through the front door. He went weaving along the porch, lurching down the steps, stumbling along the trail beaten through the snow by several running horses, and came presently to the spot where Sam Pepper had experienced his great adventure. There, black blots on the pure white of the snow, lay two men. It was as Sam Pepper had said, and Jim Torrance, still swaying slightly though the clear cold outside night air was beginning to steady him, swore softly under his breath.

He stood there a while, leaning against a pine, breathing deep, getting his head clear and his unwilling muscles under control. Then he went on a few steps, just to make assurance doubly sure about Bordereau's departure. The trampled snow told the story; Bordereau and those with him had ridden on their spurs, going somewhere else.

It was Sam Pepper who stabled the horses in a wreck of a shed behind the house, and who brought their packs in and spread blankets before the fireplace and made a roaring fire of splintered boards that cluttered up the place. And it was Sam who made a sort of broth out of scraps from their provision stock, bacon mostly with beans mashed up in the concoction; and it was Sam who, despite his patient's curses, did the major job of binding up Lying Bill Yarbo's wounds. Yarbo hadn't said much until then; he had looked his questions at Jim Torrance and had said a bleak:

"Well! He was lying as usual, I suppose?"

Torrance leaned against the chimney and stared a long

while at Sam Pepper, then shifted a penetrating gaze to Yarbo.

"It's the way Sam says, Bill," he said. "He shot the two men, one square between the eyes, the other close to the throat. Damn straight shooting, if you ask me, with what little light there was. I found his gun in the trail." He tossed it to Sam. "Looks like, after he'd emptied it, he'd thrown it in somebody's face. If he'd had another gun, likely he'd have got Bordereau and the whole crowd."

Sam Pepper blushed. Bill Yarbo began turning red; he had swallowed some unwanted pills in his life but never one harder to get down than this.

"What was happening in here, while I was heading the others off?" asked Sam, brisk again. He looked all about him cheerfully and wonderingly.

Torrance told him. Wider and wider did Pepper's eyes stretch open.

"With all the noise outside," Torrance concluded, "Bordereau thought there was a posse bearing down on him. I guess he thought he'd done for Yarbo and me anyhow; he was burning down the house to make sure. And he got away with Sally Dawn's gold, enough of it, from the looks, to put her up on easy street again."

"Gosh, I'm a sick turkey," muttered Yarbo. "Bring me a bed and let me die in peace. After what's happened tonight—" His roaming eyes rested for an instant on Sam's perky face; then he shut them tight. "After what's just happened," he said faintly, "me, I'd ruther be dead anyhow."

They holed up there at the old King Cannon mountain house, and were grateful for its shelter. Sam Pepper was nurse, kitchen hand and general roustabout. He went down to Pocket Valley for more provisions and for odds and ends; he kept the fires burning; he ministered to Lying Bill Yarbo when that bull of a man was delirious and threatened to tear the house down. Torrance came and helped when Bill was at his worst, and gave Pepper a hand with his labors. The two of them at times talked, Sam doing most of the speculating, as they wondered whether Bordereau and his men were clean gone for good, King Cannon's gold along with him.

From Pocket Valley they sent a man secretly, Andy Stock's helper, to carry word to Mrs. Sam, who would pass it along to Sally Dawn, that all was well and that they would be showing up before very long. The women were to keep their mouths shut if possible; if Steve Bordereau liked to consider both Torrance and Yarbo wiped out of the picture, let him.

"He tried to play dead on us," said Jim Torrance. "If we sort of do the same for him, maybe he won't hurry out of the country. Maybe we can meet up with him again."

"How much in gold do you suppose there was?" asked Sam, on edge. "A thousand? Ten thousand? Maybe a hundred thousand?"

It was Torrance who, when he could, went out and scooped shallow graves for Turkey-trot Smith and the two men Sam Pepper had brought to the end of their trails; Sam wouldn't go near them. Torrance got the job done of a windy afternoon with a storm threatening; it did snow that night but by morning cleared and a glorious blue sky hung over them. The sunlight, warm and golden, fell across Bill Yarbo's bed and heartened him.

"Hell's bells," he said. "I'll be up and around tomorrow sure." Then he glared at Sam who just then was departing in his chipper fashion toward the kitchen. "That is," he said confidentially to Torrance, but loud enough to make sure that Sam heard him, "I would if I was fed right instead of being shoveled out the stingy messes that lying little lizard feeds me."

"I've been thinking about things," said Torrance.

The three had made themselves as comfortable in the big living room as circumstances permitted. There was a genial fire going on the hearth, windows had been blanketed, some of the splintered floor boards replaced. Bill Yarbo lay in a corner on the bed they had laid down for him; Sam Pepper squatted on the wreck of an old chair, and Torrance had humped over on the bench at the side of the fireplace.

"Me, too, I been thinking!" spoke up Sam. "Gosh, if I only knew—"

"There are some things we do know," said Torrance. "Steve Bordereau came here by night, went out in the dark and hasn't come poking back; it's clear enough he's still playing dead and doesn't want it generally known that he was ever up this way. We know, too, that he's got quite a gang with him; and that seems sort of funny when you first think of it, since he is playing dead; and men do talk. Another thing is this: Those two men that Sam stopped out in the trail were coming straight here; they were Bordereau men; it's a ten to one bet Murdo sent 'em racing with word and warning for Bordereau, and—"

"Sure," said Sam, and rubbed his hands, "that's why I kilt the son-a-guns!"

Bill Yarbo, who had given no sign of life, groaned. Torrance ignored both the little man's boastfulness and the big man's pain at having to swallow it.

"And so," Torrance continued, "even yet there's a chance Bordereau is pretty much in the dark about what's happened around Sundown while he was up here. He's not apt to know about his grave being opened and about the stir that made at the Stag Horn."

"That's likely, Jim," agreed Sam, and could not help adding, "Good thing I did stop them two messengers of Murdo's."

"What I'm getting at is this," said Torrance, frowning into the fire and speaking to himself as much as to the others, "what is Bordereau up to now? And why those several men with him? He's got King Cannon's gold, and it looked like a sizable pot. Is he running out with it, skipping the country while the going is good?"

"No, he ain't," said Sam, and sounded cocksure. "For one thing, you said you thought you nicked him last night before they downed you; well, that's two pretty fresh wounds he's carting around. Another thing is, like you say, he's got all those hard hombres along with him; it means that he plans still playing dead and so playing safe, to do a bit more hell-raising before he drifts and, when he goes, to go with all his pockets full. He's been down in Mexico before; well, likely he's headed back there when he's made things too hot to hold him up here. Likely he'll buy him half the damn country and set himself up like a king. That's the sort Steve Bordereau is. One thing about him, Jim he don't shoot nickels."

Torrance nodded.

"That's sort of the way I've been figuring it, Sam," he said. "But there's this: When he does find out about Doc Taylor being found in his grave, what then? It's going to look to most folks like Bordereau had a hand in that, huh? And I gather that Doc Taylor was pretty well liked. Bordereau might do some lively stepping out of here if a lot of the doc's friends started looking for him."

Yes, there were a good many things to think about, and in the silence which shut down—broken only by the faint crackle of the fire and a dull, rhythmic thumping of a board loose somewhere and flapping in the night wind— they were thoughtful and uncertain. Presently Sam, who could never be silent for long, started to say something; but he hadn't gotten out the first half dozen words when he leaped to his feet, his eyes goggling, and scurried into a shadowy corner of the chimney behind Torrance's bench.

"Oh, my gosh!" he gasped. "What's that?"

Bill Yarbo strove to rear up on an elbow in order to glare at him. He was in a good bit of pain and his voice was thick and faint, yet he managed to mutter scathingly:

"The brave little fighter and man-killer is scared out of his britches by the wind blowing! Of all the—"

"Shut up!" commanded Torrance in a whisper. "There is something—"

All Sam's terrors, which had left him in peace for a few hours while he had gloated over his heroism of last night, came back to clutch him by the throat so that he could scarcely get the whispered words out:

"It's s-somebody trying to break in! Somebody at the back door—t-trying to get in through the k-k-kitchen—"

Jim Torrance heard it too now and knew that Sam was right. He rose and, gun in hand, stepped softly toward the kitchen door.

CHAPTER XII

WHOEVER it was trying to get in at the rear door suddenly desisted; Sam Pepper had gone to infinite pains to make sure that all doors were barred, all windows fastened. There was a brief silence while Torrance cocked an ear against the slightest sound. Then he heard quiet voices, though he could not make out the words, and after that there came a sharp rapping.

"Well?" demanded Torrance then. "Who's there?"

A voice answered quickly, "That you, Torrance?" And then another voice spoke up, giving him a start, saying eagerly: "Oh, Jim! Let us in!"

Sally Dawn's voice! And she should be safely out of all this, many a mile away. He unbarred the door and jerked it open, and Sally Dawn hurried in, and with her came a young fellow, lean and lanky, whom Torrance didn't recognize at first but presently, in a better light, remembered as Dave Drennen, that upstanding young rancher who was neighbor and friend of the Cannons and, if the look in his eye meant anything, a pretty warm admirer of Sally Dawn.

"Jim!" she exclaimed. "Oh, I'm so glad! You're all right then?"

"Anyone else with you two?" he asked, and when she said, "No, just Dave and me," he shut and barred the door and led the way toward the other room. On his way he demanded, "What in thunder brings you here?"

"We got the message that Sam sent; that you and Bill Yarbo had been hurt. And did you think for one minute that I wouldn't come to try to help?"

"Why should you?" he asked curtly.

"After all you had done for me—did you think—"

"Here's company, boys," said Torrance.

Sam had already popped out of his corner and came hurrying, the most relieved looking man imaginable, and Bill

100

Yarbo, also looking glad, though his face was drawn with pain, again made his attempt to come up on his elbow.

"Howdy, Sally! Howdy!" cried Sam. And then, "Howdy, Dave! Say, this is great!"

Bill Yarbo muttered something. Sally Dawn, standing in the middle of the room, her hair wind-blown, her cheeks bright with the nip of the night air, her eyes shining, looked them all over. Longest of all did she study Jim Torrance; she saw that his dark lean face looked haggard; she saw that his eyes looked hard between their narrowed lids; but she saw too that he was not as badly hurt as she had feared. Then she hurried to Bill Yarbo and went down on her knees beside him.

"Poor old Bill," she said gently. "I'm here to doctor you, Bill."

"For which thank God!" said Bill Yarbo fervently. "Sam Pepper's been trying his damnedest to kill me."

She laughed at him and patted his hand and then held it tightly in her two. Bill Yarbo settled back with a long sigh.

Torrance turned to Dave Drennen.

"Well, what's it all about?" he asked bluntly. "What are you two doing up here? What did you let this girl come for?"

Drennen grinned.

"You try to stop her when she makes up her mind about anything she's got her heart set on. Try it sometime, Torrance."

"There's no sense she should go sticking her nose into any more danger than she has to."

"I'm safer right here than I'd be anywhere around Sundown," said Sally Dawn, and sounded triumphant.

"You are not," said Torrance angrily. "Steve Bordereau—"

"We know where Steve Bordereau is at this minute, Dave and I!" she said exultantly; and, by way of telling Mr. Jim Torrance what she thought of him for the sort of welcome he had given her, she wrinkled up her nose and put out the tip of her tongue at him. "Don't we, Dave?" She fairly drenched young Drennen with a smile; let Jim Torrance take stock of that, too!

"What's all this?" cried Sam Pepper, electrified. "What do you know about Bordereau? How do you know where he is? And does he know—"

"Let's have it," said Torrance.

"And," said Sally Dawn, still exultant and meaning to let Mr. Jim Torrance learn that she knew a thing or two that might interest him, "Steve Bordereau and the men with him have a lot of gold—some looking like it had just been dug out of the ground, some in what looked like a lot of twenty dollar pieces! And I hope they get to quarreling over it—"

"Why, Sally Dawn!" yipped Sam Pepper. "That's your gold, every ounce of it! They—"

"What!" cried Sally Dawn, her eyes seeming to grow as big and round and bright as any of those twenty dollar gold pieces.

"We're not getting ahead very fast with anything," grunted Torrance. "Seems as though the more there is to be explained, the more words get poured out and the less gets said. Suppose, young lady, that you or Dave Drennen here tells us what you know about Bordereau and where he is."

She drew a deep breath and pulled off her hat and pushed the tumbled hair back from her face. Then between them she and Drennen got their story told.

Immediately on getting word of a part of what had happened up here, of both Torrance and Yarbo being wounded, she had insisted on coming to do her part; if they were hurt it was in her quarrel, wasn't it? Drennen had done all that any mere man could do to deter her, and that was nothing at all, so he had come along. They had taken the longer but more open way coming up through the Flats. It grew dark when they were several miles south of Pocket Valley. About a mile from the old abandoned mine road they had glimpsed a light through the trees; Dave Drennen knew the ranch with its clutter of tumble-down buildings and corrals—

"Turkey-trot Smith's place, I'll bet a hat!" put in Sam

Pepper, and slapped his bony thigh. "It would be just the place—"

"We didn't see Turkey-trot, though," said Drennen.

"You wouldn't!" said Sam. "Jim shot him, and thereby saved Bill Yarbo's life!"

"Liar!" snorted Bill Yarbo, weak but not too weak to refute Sam's libel. "Me, I shot him and—"

"Dave told me about the place," Sally Dawn hurried on, "and how Turkey-trot was suspected of hiding stolen stock there, and how he and Steve Bordereau had been thick as thieves—and we stopped and looked at the light and got to wondering. And just then we heard somebody coming up the trail behind us, riding hard, and we ducked into the timber and watched for him to go by. Only he didn't go by! He was coming up from Sundown-way the same as we were; at a dead run he swung into the side trail and went straight on to Turkey-trot's ranch. And we followed him!"

Torrance withdrew his eyes from her to glance accusingly at young Drennen. Drennen heaved up his shoulders.

"Me, I couldn't stop her," he muttered. "And anyhow, the way things worked out, it was all right."

The man whom they followed at a respectful distance, themselves making a cautious arc through the timber, proved to be a certain fox-faced, narrow-eyed youth whom Torrance remembered, a man named Brill, and he went straight to Bordereau. It seemed that Murdo had sent out two men the day before to warn Bordereau that trouble was afoot, to tell him of the discovery in the Sundown graveyard and all the rest of that night's events. When no report had come back to Murdo, he had sent Brill out, and Brill, taking the old road through the Flats, had seen the light at Turkey-trot Smith's and judged he'd get the latest word of Bordereau there.

He had scarcely called out at the house and swung down and got himself admitted when Sally Dawn and Dave Drennen, their own horses hidden among the trees behind the barn, crept up to the rear of the house. They could peek through a crack in a warped old shutter, could see quite clearly what was going on inside, and could even catch a few words.

"And we saw the gold," said Sally Dawn. "It was in a heap on a table. I think Steve Bordereau was keeping nearly all of it for himself, but doling a little bit out to the others. What did Sam mean by saying it belonged to me?"

They told her and she said thoughtfully: "Daddy used to keep a good bit of gold on hand; he lost a lot in a bank that failed once, and after that he wouldn't have anything to do with banks. But we always thought he kept it down at home, on the ranch. And so now Steve Bordereau has that, too! Oh!"

"You say you heard part of what they were saying tonight?" Torrance prompted her.

"Yes. That was just after Pete Brill burst in on them. He was telling them that Murdo had sent him; he told them about you and me coming back to Sundown and how you knew he was alive and how you brought the body of Doc Taylor back to the Stag Horn and accused either him or Murdo or both of the murder. Steve Bordereau was limping up and down—he seemed to have been hurt in the thigh or side—and I never saw a man look so furious! He began yelling your name, Jim. And he seemed to blame me, too; he swore he'd get everything I had on earth and"—she shuddered—"and that he'd get me, too."

"And then?" asked Torrance coldly.

"That was about all we got to hear, wasn't it, Dave? The men were all excited and stirring about and one of them started toward a door and we ran back to our horses and hurried on here."

Torrance, who had been leaning against the chimney, moved toward the kitchen.

"Come ahead, Drennen," he said. "Let's take care of your horses."

"We brought some grain for them," said Sally Dawn. "And for your horses too. And we brought some food and some bandages and a bottle of whisky—"

Torrance kept on going and Dave Drennen followed him out. A few minutes later Drennen returned bringing the things Sally Dawn had mentioned. She was already busy with Bill Yarbo; she gave him a big shot of whisky and in return he gave her such a look of gratitude as one doesn't see often. Drennen then went out again to lend further help to Torrance with the stock.

"He pretends his hurt don't amount to anything," he said from the door, "but it sort of looks to me he's riding on his nerve. He oughtn't to be out in the cold."

"Make him hurry back in, Dave," pleaded Sally Dawn.

But when again the door opened, it was to admit Drennen, returning alone.

"Torrance says to tell you, Sally, you better get back to your own home soon's you can, and you better stay there, being as after this you'll be safer near Sundown than anywhere else. And he says you get some friends of yours, men like Sam and Bill and me, about half a dozen good men, he says, to stick close night and day. And he says put 'em all on your pay roll and you can pay 'em out of that gold when you get it back, and if you can't, he'll pay 'em himself. And he says—"

She sprang to her feet, exclaiming: "Dave Drennen! What are you talking about? Why doesn't Jim—"

"He's gone," said Drennen. "Gone hell-for-leather!"

"Gone! Where?"

"How do I know? He didn't say. He just went."

"Why didn't you stop him?" she wailed.

"There you go," muttered Drennen. He wiped his brow with the back of his hand. "Torrance says why didn't I stop you—you say why didn't I stop him! You two just try stopping each other, once, will you?"

Because the night was clear and frosty, glittering stars, and because there were patches of snow where the side road turned off, Jim Torrance was enabled to hit upon the trampled trail of many horses leading through the woods to the Turkey-trot Smith place. Otherwise he must have passed it, since there was no light in the house to guide him.

He rode, as Sally Dawn and young Drennen had ridden, in a wide arc through the timber and to a place behind the old barn. Like them still, he went forward on foot, but he did his first bit of reconnoitering at the barn itself; it was dead still, with never the sound of a stamping horse. He moved on to the house and stood listening; the silence remained unbroken save for the faint rustle of wind through the tree tops.

He went up the back steps and found the door open. After that he knew that already Steve Bordereau, perhaps because of a new slant at things afforded by the news brought by Murdo's messenger, had led his men elsewhere. Still, to be dead sure, he stepped in through the open door. Again, after he had waited a long minute and heard never a sound, he moved forward; he didn't immediately strike a match because he thought: "If any of them are here, the dark's all in my favor. They won't dare indulge in any wild shooting, and there are no friends of mine here to stop a bullet!"

At last, however, he did strike a match; he had been on the verge of retreating without doing so, but knew he'd never be quite satisfied that way. As the match flared up, his first thought was, "Not a man here." And then he saw something, and whipped his gun over and thought, "There's one of 'em, sleeping on the floor."

The man's sleep was one that nothing on earth could ever break. Torrance stooped over him; he lay on his back, his arms outflung, his eyes glittering ceilingward in the flare of the match. Torrance didn't know the man by name but remembered his face well enough, one of Bordereau's followers, a burly, beetle-browed, heavy-jawed fellow who looked stubborn and sullen even in death. He had been shot through the head.

Torrance's match burnt out and he did not strike another. When he left the room he at least closed the door behind him, a thing that Bordereau hadn't troubled to do. He didn't worry himself greatly trying to figure out why this man had been killed. Bordereau's work no doubt, since Bordereau was undisputed leader over his wolf pack. Maybe Sally Dawn had been right when she sensed the likelihood of a quarrel over the division of King Cannon's gold; this man had the look of one who would speak up for himself. And if Bordereau had shot him in cold blood— Well, those others who still clung to him would be apt to watch their steps.

In the saddle again he rode slowly, trying to pick up the trail of the riders who had so recently departed. He found it with little difficulty. They had cut straight back into the old road, then had turned south. That meant back down toward the Flats, toward Sundown.

But within three or four mile all tracks faded out, because down here there had been little snow, which had melted already, and there were many rocky ridges and slopes on which it would be hard to find tracks even by day. Bordereau might have ridden straight on, hammering out the miles to Sundown or to some hideout near town, or just as conceivably could have turned aside somewhere along the way.

Jim Torrance didn't waste time looking for signs which he had such scant hope of finding, but pressed on toward his own place, which he reached at that bright moment when all along the crests of the ridges creating the broken line of the eastern horizon, gleaming strips of red and gold were being spread as for a carpet for the advent of the new day. As the rim of a red sun came up he was rapping at Sam Pepper's door. Mrs. Sam, already up and dressed, came bustling to open for him.

"You!" she exclaimed. "But—"

A couple of men, two of the party who had officiated with him at the graveyard, both staunch friends of the Peppers as well as of Sally Dawn, pushed back chairs in an adjoining room and came to the door, as eager as Mrs. Sam. Torrance got a delectable whiff of breakfast, bacon and coffee floating out their fragrance on the sweet morning air.

After breaking off with a "But—" suspended in mid-air, Mrs. Sam invited warmly: "But come in, Mr. Torrance. Breakfast is ready, and you can tell us over a cup of coffee. I'll bet you haven't had one yet!"

"Thank you, ma'am," said Jim Torrance.

Over the table he brought them the latest news. They heard him out in utter silence, their faces tense and earnest. At the end, he said:

"Me, I've got a little of my own business to tend to. It would be a good idea if several of the boys went straight up to where Sam and Bill and Sally Dawn and Drennen are, just to be on hand. We've had one storm, we might get another, and it would be tough on them, the way they are, if they got snowbound. I don't think you can drag Bill Yarbo out inside a week. I'll see you later."

He went back to his own place and attended to his stock. . . .

A couple of hours later the two men, with Mrs. Sam insisting on going along, left for King Cannon's old mountain home. When they arrived, about the first thing Sally Dawn said was,

"Where's Jim Torrance?"

They didn't know.

They had stopped at his house; they found a man there he had sent out from Sundown to care for the place. Mrs. Sam just shook her head and said, "Gone."

CHAPTER XIII

"GONE," was all that any one of them could say of Jim Torrance, and "Gone," was all that they were to know of him for many a day. Speculation was rife: He had met up with Bordereau somewhere in the wilderness. Bordereau had killed him and there was an end of him. Or, he had decided that he had tackled too stiff a job, going up against Bordereau and his gang, and had ducked out, going fast and far to save his hide. Or, he still lurked somewhere near Sundown, playing his lone hand, still hunting down the man he so long had hunted. Or, after all—for what did anyone really know about him? —he was just one of those wandering, restless figures always moving across the great Southwest, and had merely shown up here and passed as he doubtless had in so many other places, like a comet.

Sally Dawn returned to the King Cannon ranch, to the sprawling old home under the oaks, and did not want for company on the way nor friends about her when she got there. It had been a week before they made the journey down from the mountains above Pocket Valley, for it was that long before they dared move Lying Bill Yarbo. Now he reposed in pampered ease in a bright bedroom at the ranch house and even began to stir about a little, and there was always Sally Dawn or Mrs. Sam to make him sort of glad he had been shot up. There was also, a thorn in his side, Sam Pepper, for the Peppers had closed up their house and moved over to Sally's. And further there were other friends, always two or three of them within calling distance, sometimes six or eight. Two foot-loose young cowboys, Smudge Talbot and Curly Redmond, well known to Drennen, had been put on the Cannon pay roll and, after two days, were taking full advantage of every opportunity to make eyes at their fair employer; Dick Pardee, one of the three brothers who owned Cold Spring Ranch, could generally be found here when wanted; and Andy Forsythe, Art Simmons and Blackie Webb, Cannon friends from nearby outfits, were always coming and going when they weren't just lingering. Sally Dawn felt something rise up in her throat and had her eyes go wet many and many a time when she saw how old friends rallied about her as word went to them of what had happened and of the threat that a vanished Steve Bordereau still constituted.

For Bordereau, like Jim Torrance, had somehow passed over the horizon and into a desert of silence, leaving no sign of his whereabouts or of his intent. About him, too, was much speculation; most men began to contend that he had played his last card here and was gone for good. And a good thing that would be—but what about Sally Dawn's gold, her last hope, that had gone with him?

The Stag Horn still flourished, in fact did a bigger business than ever before, for there was always the chance that Steve Bordereau's bravado would bring him back, that the game was not yet played out; and an intensely interested community, splitting itself fairly in half on the rock of the Sally Dawn-Steve Bordereau situation, wanted to be on hand when anything further happened. Murdo, denying all knowledge of the substitution of Doc Taylor's dead body for Bordereau's, still operated the two bars and the gambling rooms; Florinda's still plied her trade and fished for suckers' dollars with her exotic lure.

Despite existent conditions, on the King Cannon ranch Sally Dawn found herself living a more normal, a brighter life than had been hers for many a weary day. That smoldering, smoky, sullen look was less in her eyes now, and something of the infectious gayety came back into her rippling laughter, and she could again tease a romantically inclined cowboy in the same playful spirit that had been hers when she was sixteen. A source of unfailing glee for her existed in the residence here, cheek by jowl, of Lying Bill Yarbo and Sam Pepper.

"Don't you love the two old humbugs?" she laughed to Mrs. Sam. "They have to try so hard to hate each other."

Carrying Bill Yarbo his mid-afternoon nourishment of soup and pie and strong coffee—he was out on the porch in the mellow sunshine now, for, with the first storm vanished and the skies blue again, a last mild period of Indian summer claimed the land—she also bore an olive branch. She was fully determined to be an intriguing little dove of peace until she had her way with these two and made them in all things the staunch friends that she suspected deep down in her wise little heart that they were—and Sally Dawn Cannon, once she made up her mind about a thing, was as stubborn as Barney, the old pensioner mule out in the pasture.

"Sam Pepper was asking about you, Bill," she said cheerily. "Do you know that, if anything happened to you, Sam would be lost! He says—"

"Don't tell me what Sam Pepper says!" growled Bill Yarbo. "He's a man I don't want to think about. I can stomach some of his cussedness, but leastways a man oughtn't to lie like he does all the time."

That tickled her so, it started her laughing so merrily, that Bill got red in the face. From him she went, as soon as she had a chance, to speak to Sam of his old friend Bill Yarbo.

Sam sniffed.

"Him! Pampering him, Sally, is just like feeding a rattle-snake. He ain't the kind you can tie to; he ain't got no courage and he ain't got no stamina. I never knowed a bigger coward and quitter, and once I knowed a man that set a trap for a bear and caught a rabbit instead and was scared to take his game out'n the trap lest it bite him! Look how Bill Yarbo let Jim Torrance down in that mite of a scrimmage up in the hills! Shucks!"

Sally Dawn made a good story of all this when she carried it to Mrs. Sam, but at the end of her recital she asked wonderingly, "Do you suppose they both actually believe what they say about each other?"

It was not that sorrow and mistrust of the future did not visit the girl during these days. On her return here, had it not been that so many a true-hearted friend came along to chase shadows away, she must have wept her heart out. She slipped away as soon as she could and crept through the dusk to her mother's grave, that pitiful grave so hurriedly dug, so unceremoniously filled. She threw herself face down and hugged the earth to her tortured breast; she shoved herself back from it and beat the earth with her small clenched fists. . . .

But a pair of shrewd and kind eyes had been upon her, and after a little while Mrs. Sam came out to her and took her into her arms and let her cry. The very next day a fence was built around the grave, and Mrs. Sam said to Sam: "It looks mighty pretty out there now, Sam; kind of bright and gay and cozy. I don't know where she could get so many flowers this time of year."

Also Sally Dawn knew her times of black depression superinduced by the vague yet still ominous threat of some further act of a lawless and desperate Steve Bordereau, by the mess of money affairs which seemed to make it impossible for her to hold on here much longer—and by a troubling uncertainty concerning the missing Jim Torrance.

"Shucks, Sally," said Mrs. Sam, her hands in biscuit dough and her round arms floury, "you just get your mind off that roving rascal. Fellers like him take care of themselves all right; it's here-they-come and there-they-go, and you've got enough on your mind without pestering yourself with a lone wolf like Jim Torrance." She brushed the hair out of her eyes with a forearm that left a snowy streak on her placid brow and looked sharply into the girl's troubled eyes with her shrewd ones. "I'd say you're just as well off if you never see hide nor hair of that man again. Run outside and make Davy Drennen happy."

Sally Dawn shook her head.

"I keep worrying about him," she said. And then she added thoughtfully: "He's no wolf either. He was mighty kind and gentle with me. I'll never forget. Why, that first night—"

Mrs. Sam sighed.

"I know, child. Well, don't you fret any; after all, most likely he'll come riding back any minute."

"Do you think so?" asked Sally Dawn. She idled around the kitchen aimlessly a few minutes, then drifted out on the porch and stood there a long while, looking up the long wavering white road, stretching lonely and empty into the blue hills that were just now turning misty in the sunset.

She was still standing there, day-dreaming, when suddenly she became aware of something that looked like a small blue-gray cloud forming against the tenderly flushed horizon. There had been no rains for a week, the roads were dry and that faint blue-gray cloud was a cloud of dust. For a single instant she tingled from head to foot; then she relaxed against the pillar supporting the roof over the porch and sighed. It was Thursday afternoon and time for Hank Webber to bring the stage, rocking and rumbling, down from Bridgewater to Sundown. There had been the time when the stage itself—with its speeding horses, with the mystery it always was, what with its unknown passengers and mail and, perhaps, money box—had fascinated her. Today she had not the least interest in stagecoaches. But then she did not know that Hank Webber was bringing to Sundown word that would put Jim Torrance's name on many a tongue that night and keep it rolling there with one implication or another for days.

"All hell's busted loose up around Mountain City," said

Hank as he booted his brake on in front of the Sundown House. "Three stick-ups in three days, the Mountain City Bank, the Rock Valley Mine and the Yellow Pine Lumber Company. Four men killed already, two-three more bad hurt, and nary a one of the raiders gathered in. It's a gang's work, six or eight or ten of 'em riding masked and shooting fast and straight; they've got away with some says fifty thousand and some says a hundred thousand dollars—and everybody says the man that's leading 'em is Jim Torrance."

The news inundated Sundown in a swelling tidal wave of excitement. Bridgewater was but sixty miles away; Mountain City lay but a score of miles southeast of Bridgewater; both the Rock Valley Mine and the Yellow Pine Lumber outfit were within less than a half day's ride on horseback from Mountain City. The result was that many men hereabouts had friends and acquaintances in the newly raided districts, and presently the names of those who had been ruthlessly shot down were added to the news which Hank Webber and Will Banks, the guard who rode with him, had brought.

By the time word of this back-tracked along the stage road to reach the King Cannon ranch, Sundown was eddying into a turmoil. There were hard-eyed, angry men vowing that this was all the work of Steve Bordereau and that Jim Torrance had nothing to do with it; there were other men, those who had come to group strongly about Clark Murdo, who lifted voices no less strong and challenging in placing the onus of the whole affair where the first rumors had already put it, at Jim Torrance's door.

"There'll be fights over it tonight," said Curly Redmond, who had raced back to the ranch with the news, "and it'll be lucky for them that mixes in 'em if they're only fist fights!"

"How do they dare say it was Jim Torrance?" cried Sally Dawn hotly. "As if anybody knew! If the men were all masked and all got away—"

"That's what I wanted to know," answered Curly, "and I asked all over, and at first nobody could guess at it any better'n I could; and then a feller told me that he heard Phil Moody say that Hank Webber said—"

"Just about what I expected!" sniffed Sally Dawn sarcastically. "What nice straight proof of anything!"

"Hold on, Sally," cut in Dave Drennen. "Anyhow let's get what Curly was going to say. Go ahead, Curly."

"Well, I don't know anything about it, but they say Hank said that at the bank hold-up, the bandana that the leader of the raiders was wearing slipped, and a man that was standing in the bank and skipped into a corner saw the robber's face, and he said it was a man he used to know. He said it was Jim Torrance."

Sally Dawn flared out. "It's a lie!" Save for that single exclamation from her the little group which had gathered in the yard was hushed.

"Then there's something else that they're saying in town," Curly went on. "At the Rock Valley Mine there was a sheet of paper stuck with a knife to a door. One of the big shots at the mine was killed; his name was Connoly; and on the paper it said, 'Connoly did me dirt once, and this is what he gets for it.' And it was signed with Jim Torrance's name."

Mrs. Sam patted Sally Dawn's shoulder.

"I reckon that ought to let our Jim out," she said drily. "He might be a robber all right, but he ain't fool enough to do a thing like that." And Sally Dawn caught her roughened hand and squeezed it with all her might.

But when she slipped away to be all alone and sat in a place that had been a favorite dreaming and brooding spot since childhood, where a big flat rock stood up commandingly from the hillside back of the house and when she let her eyes traffic with the faraway stars, and the hush of night over the wide range lands was over her, she asked herself, "What do I really know about Jim Torrance?" She clung to the fact that he had been good to her. But how many and many a time had she been afraid of him? His face seemed to take form between her eyes and the sky and to come closer and to grow clearer; she could see again those hard, dark eyes which gave glimpses of mystery and perhaps of menace through the narrowed lids, and his mouth that at times frightened her, it could become so cruel and savage.

She jumped up and hurried back to the house, eager for companionship.

Rumors, rumors and rumors—they flew as swift and erratic and dark and elusive as night hawks. Sometimes they dealt with Steve Bordereau; they had him everywhere, on both sides of the international border. For the greatest part they bruited Jim Torrance's name about. Again, he had fought with Bordereau and had been shot to death; he had been seen gambling for high stakes at High Crest; he had had a run-in with a sheriff of Morongo County and had been gathered in and had escaped; he was leading a bandit band, all killers, down near Nacional; he was headed back toward Sundown. Those were the tales a-wing, and there were many more of their sort—until at last a cleancut and definite word was brought of him.

It was Sam Pepper this time who brought the news out to the ranch from Sundown, Sam Pepper wild with excitement, thumping his heels into his horse's flanks, beginning to shout through the dusk long before a word could be made out. So by the time he scrambled up onto the porch to his swiftly gathering audience, he was so out of breath he could hardly gasp out what he had to say.

"Now, Sam," said Mrs. Sam sharply, "you go easy a minute and get your breath, else you're going to bust a boiler, and I'll be a handsome young widder woman and will up and marry Bill Yarbo. We ain't going to run away, and whatever you've got to say will most likely keep."

"J-Jim T-Torrance!" stammered Sam. "He—he—"

Sally Dawn, not in the least patient like Mrs. Sam, pounced on him and caught him by an arm and began to shake him. Then Sam got his story out.

"There's been another hold-up, the biggest of the lot. Over to Canyon City. The biggest bank in seven counties. Cleaned out. I don't know how many men was killed—but they say they nailed the boss robber this time. They say it sure was Jim Torrance. They say he's shot all to hell and was left behind for dead—that he's dying now—most likely dead by this time. And down in Sundown, Clark Murdo is serving free drinks and—"

He stopped for air. For a long, still moment no one said

a word, but eyes went from Sam's puckered face to other eyes and they were all alike in their expressions, all alike in that they stared out from under frowning brows. All, that is, saving Sally Dawn's alone.

Hers were wide with horror. Her lips were parted; she had started to say something but had not spoken. The color seeped out of her cheeks until they were white.

"Sally—" said Mrs. Sam.

The girl whirled and ran into the house; they heard the door slam.

"Better go look after her, old lady," Sam said to his wife. "Seems as though she's hit hard; seems as though she's sort of took a liking to this Jim Torrance."

"Leave her alone," snapped Mrs. Sam. "She's all right, that girl is."

Very swiftly Sally Dawn showed them just how all right she was. She came back, out onto the porch, pulling on a pair of gauntlets. In this short time she had jerked off her house dress and gotten into riding breeches and boots; she had a sweater over her arm and a little hat jammed down emphatically over her curls. The color had come back into her cheeks; there were twin hot spots in them and her eyes were shining.

"Sally!"

"Saddle me a horse, will you, Dave?" said Sally Dawn, as cool as "Good morning."

"But where on earth—" began Mrs. Sam, only to be cut short with Sally Dawn's counter question. "Where do you suppose?"

"But—"

"Will you saddle me a horse, Dave? Or will you, Curly? Or shall I?"

"It's fifty mile—" expostulated Mrs. Sam.

"I don't care if it's five hundred!"

"And it's almost dark—"

"Oh!"

Sally Dawn made a dart for the steps. Both Dave Drennen and Curly Redmond were galvanized; both sped away to the corrals. And what was more, when her horse was saddled, their two horses were saddled along with it.

CHAPTER XIV

JIM TORRANCE lay flat on his back in bed—and he didn't know in what bed or in what house—and he didn't even know that he was in any bed at all. He opened his eyes and looked about him dully, puzzled yet not greatly concerned. Then he strove to move slightly and was so wrenched with pain that an involuntary groan parted his pallid lips.

A face bent over him. He saw it only vaguely, the unfamiliar face of a middle-aged woman, one that looked above all other things capable. Old Doc Kibbee, of Canyon City, whenever he had a patient who had demanded the best to be had in nursing, sent for Nancy Hamilton. And Nancy Hamilton now leaned over Torrance and put a calm, steady hand on his forehead and said gently yet in the tone of one who commands:

"There now, just you lay still, Mr. Torrance. You're doing fine."

"I don't know who you are—I don't know where I am," he muttered, and closed his eyes and let his head loll to one side. She stepped to a table for a bottle and spoon and glass, but a glance over her shoulder showed her that his eyes were closed, that he was either asleep again from sheer exhaustion and weakness and the shock of pain, or was dying. Efficient and practiced as she was, there were times when she couldn't tell. She went back to her rocking chair and dropped down heavily into it; she herself was haggard, worn out, her eyes thumbed deep into their sockets from all she had gone through since she had been sent for.

The man in bed lay still a long while, existence become for him a sort of gray haze twisting into a thousand misty labyrinths. He had moments of semi-consciousness but nothing mattered, nothing that had happened or that they did with him. He swallowed the liquids that were forced

117

between his teeth and lay inert for long periods, neither awake nor asleep. The doctor came and went, and he knew of the visits but was not greatly concerned. Doc Kibbee talked aside with the nurse; he did not even try to listen.

He went to sleep and slept deeply for two solid hours; Nancy Hamilton sank gratefully deep down into her big chair and relaxed. She too slept. But when he awoke, there she was standing over him, saying: "Just you lay still, Mr. Torrance. You're doing fine."

He nodded this time. Either something they had given him or his rest made him feel stronger; his head was clearer, he thought.

Again he slept. Again he woke. This time he stared up in puzzled fashion, a heavy frown of concentration dragging his black brows down. He began to grow confused; he guessed his head hadn't cleared after all. For the nurse had changed miraculously. Just now she had been a capable looking middle-aged woman. And here she was young and flushed and very bright-eyed and incredibly pretty, and she looked just exactly like Sally Dawn Cannon.

He closed his eyes an instant. Sally Dawn was as still as a mouse. He opened them quickly as though to catch the nurse at her tricks if she was trying any funny business on him.

"Sally Dawn!"

"Sh! You're not to talk." She stooped closer and for a fleeting second her cheek was against his on the pillow, her curls making him intensely aware of their softly brushing caress. "Jim!" she whispered.

"But look here—"

She stood erect, rosier than ever, and put a finger ever so softly on his lips.

"Your nurse is resting; she said I could sit with you a little while if I promised to call her if you wouldn't just be quiet and rest."

She always thought of his eyes as being narrowed, as though he were forever on guard, watchful and suspicious and hard. Now she saw them open up wide, quite as though they had to do that to take her all in, and she discovered that they were not absolutely night-black, but that there was a hint of warm brown in them. She smiled at him and patted his hand; his fingers curled slowly and with the gentlest pressure about hers. . . .

Sally Dawn had already had a talk with Doc Kibbee, a chubby, pink-cheeked, hearty old fellow with snow-white mustache and imperial and sharp, wise eyes. She had commanded anxiously, "Tell me about him!"

He had hunched up his thick, round shoulders.

"How should I know? Me, I'm not much of a doctor anyhow. He's been shot close-up and lost some blood; he was hammered over the head from behind by a club or a gun barrel, and first I thought he might have a fractured skull. 'Tain't so though. That's what I'm always doing with patients of mine until they up and die on me—making mistakes and—"

"Doctor Kibbee! Don't I know all about you? You're the finest doctor that ever was! You—"

"What do you know about me? I never saw you before!"

"But you did! You were a friend of King Cannon's, weren't you? For years and years? Well, I'm his daughter."

"My, my!" he said. "You, King Cannon's kid!"

"Now tell me! And tell me the truth about him."

"Hm." He stared at her and appeared to consider. Then, very gruff about it, he shot his own question at her: "What are you all warmed up about it for? Happen to know this Torrance?"

"Of course I do! That's why I'm here. He—he's the finest friend I ever had!"

Her words didn't please him. He snorted at her.

"You're a little fool, that's what you are. All you young pretty girls seem to be infernal damn fools sooner or later about some no 'count, and most generally it's sooner. Know who and what he is—and how come he's shot up the way he is?"

"I've heard a lot of crazy rumors—"

"Rumors, my eye! He's one of the gang that held up the bank right here in Canyon City, that killed Phil Gates, the cashier, that's made off with Bill Hasbrook, the bank president, and has probably cut his throat long before now and thrown him down in a gully somewhere. That's who your friend Torrance is."

"Why, Doctor Kibbee!" she gasped at him. "If anybody's an old fool—"

"If you call him a friend," he cut in bruskly, "you just go and get down on your knees and pray he dies in bed. Most likely he will anyhow, being that he's a patient of mine. That's what happens with me right along. Just as sure as he gets well enough to stand the shock, the boys are going to hang him good and high."

"They won't! They mustn't! Oh, can't you see it's all just a horrible mistake?"

After her visit with Torrance, which lasted two hours, with him sleeping most of that time, she had a few words with Dave Drennen and Curly Redmond whom she found waiting for her outside the little house in which Jim Torrance was hospitalized. They looked unhappy, both of them, and uncertain; they shifted their boots in the dust of the road and looked furtively at each other rather than at her. Her little chin, which was emphatic enough at times despite its lack of ruggedness and square lines, came up.

"I know," she said tartly. "You've been over at the saloon having a drink—and you got to talking and asking questions and getting answers—and you believe all they tell you. Oh, you make me sick!"

"It's tough, Sally, and sorta hard to take," said Dave doggedly. "But there's no use trying to dodge facts. There was a hold-up, there were men killed and a bank robbed— and he'd been off and away with his crowd only he got dropped and left behind. He'd have swung for it before now, only the boys up here can't see anything in hanging a man while he's unconscious first and so damn near dead next. They're just giving him time. You better come home."

She pointed to the squat, sturdy building next door.

"That's the jail, I suppose?"

"Yes, it is, Sally; and he'd be in there now, only the sheriff—"

Sally Dawn smiled at the two boys very sweetly, so sweetly indeed that both began shifting uneasily again.

"Thank you, boys, for having brought me over," she said. "You can go home now if you want to."

"Oh, hell," said Curly Redmond, and Dave silently concurred as Sally Dawn headed straight to the jail.

"Drink, Curly?" suggested Dave Drennen.

"It's an idea," admitted Curly gloomily.

In an untidy little office cozily close to the strongly barred room which served Canyon City as its jail, Sally Dawn found the county sheriff. He was a man of equal vintage with Doc Kibbee, which is to say somewhere around sixty, and looked like something carelessly hacked out of mahogany. He was mahogany-colored and wore habitually a perfectly wooden lack of expression; he had enormous black eyebrows which looked artificial, great tufts that might have been stuck on for a masquerade, a heavy, uptwisted, black and impossible mustache and a clean-shaven, ruthless, square chin. Even his eyes looked false, they were so steady, and bright and expressionless as shoe buttons.

His boots were cocked up on top of a table littered with papers, which gave her the impression of having gathered there undisturbed for years; and along with the litter were an empty ink bottle, a couple of rusty pens, an ancient Colt forty-four, with neither hammer nor trigger, which served as a paper weight, an old long-roweled Mexican spur and a serviceable Winchester thirty-thirty. A good bit of this detail so forced itself on her that she took it in with one flick of her eager eyes; after that she saw only the man.

"You are Sheriff Evans?" she asked.

She smiled at him as at an old friend.

He remained utterly motionless, not so much as a ripple stirring him; she couldn't even see that he breathed. Certainly he did not take his feet down from his table, nor did he remove the broad black hat that was already pushed as far back on his head as it would go, nor for a long moment did he speak. He was looking toward her, whether at her or not, and was perhaps continuing a chain of thought her entrance had interrupted—provided of course he was even thinking.

At last he said in a quiet, low-toned voice, "Yes."

"I came to talk to you about Jim Torrance. He—he is a friend of mine."

She waited for him to speak; he didn't. He didn't have anything to say; in his turn he waited for her to speak.

"He's not a bad man," she said with a passionate fervor that put a quiver into her voice. "He's not a robber. He didn't have anything to do with that bank hold-up; I know he didn't!"

Sheriff Evans didn't say anything one way or the other. Sally Dawn, already so overwrought with anxiety, flared up with anger. "Do you hear me?" she cried hotly. "Do you hear me? Why don't you say something?"

"What'll I say?" he asked.

"Say—say anything! Don't just sit there like a—like a— Say that you don't believe me, if that's what you think."

"I don't believe you. Jim Torrance is as guilty as hell. I'd have him here in jail right now only I'm hoping, give him the best of care, to do two things. One is, get him to talk. The other is, hang him."

"How do you know that he is guilty?"

"He was one of the gang that robbed the Canyon City Bank. One of 'em that killed Phil Gates, the cashier. One of 'em that made away with Will Hasbrook, the bank president. One of the gang that got away with thirty thousand dollars that day—only he didn't happen to get away."

"You were there? You saw it all? You saw him—"

"Nope. I wasn't there. Tom Long was, though; Tom's a deputy of mine. He got shot, Tom did, and's a right sick man now. But he shot Jim Torrance before he went dark."

Sally Dawn whirled about and went to a dingy window and made pretense of looking out, an utter impossibility, considering the unwashed state of the windowpane and the watery blur that came into her eyes. She stood with a small fist clenched, gnawing at her knuckles, biting at them to keep the tears back, to keep from bursting out hysterically. Presently in a very small voice, without turning, she said, "You're not very sympathetic, are you, Mr. Walt Evans?"

"No. Not with any friend of this man's. Happens Phil Gates was a friend of mine. Happens it's the same with Will Hasbrook. Happens—"

"Happens you ever had any other friends? Happens you ever knew a man named King Cannon?"

"Hell's bells!" said Sheriff Evans and sounded almost, not quite, human. "What about King Cannon? He's been dead years now."

Sally Dawn turned slowly and looked him in the eye.

"Happens I'm his daughter," she said coolly. "Happens, when I was a little tyke, you and Doc Kibbee and Daddy—"

Walt Evans' feet came down off the desk then like something hurled by an explosion, and he surged to his feet as quick as any boy, and his battered old black hat came off his head with something next door to a flourish—all this pretty much in one gesture.

"Sally Dawn Cannon!" he exclaimed, and sounded altogether and warmly human. "Well, I'm damned!" He looked at her with new eyes; he put out a big leathery paw and caught her hand and came close to breaking the bones in it. "And at that I might have known! I always said you'd grow up into the prettiest girl that ever sprung a dimple. Why, you little devil! Come here to me!"

He gathered her into his arms, lifted her clean off the floor and kissed her.

"Will you offer me a chair now, Mr. Evans? And will you let us talk together?" It was a flushed, breathless, and very eager Sally Dawn speaking.

"I heard about your good mother—"

"Don't! I can't talk about that. Not yet! And there are other things that happened down at Sundown—"

"Yes; I heard about some of them, too. Just garbled gossip, that's all I got. I was going down to see you— Dammit, I haven't been down that way since your old man died, have I? I ought to be kicked— Want to tell me about all these happenings?"

"Yes! That way I'll be telling you about Jim Torrance, all I know about him, and then— Well, you'll see!"

Long before she had finished, old Walt Evans was frowning and tugging at a lower lip, and his eyes, from being merely bleak, grew wintery, the sort of winter that now and again lights up to a flash of lightning.

"You're one hell-of-a-lot like your old man, Sally Dawn," he said soberly. "He was a man you could tie to, and somehow, kid that you are, I'd like to string all my chips along with you. Maybe you're right as rain—and maybe, just being a girl and having a man like Jim Torrance look at you, you've got your heart, God bless it, all mixed up with your brains."

"No!" said Sally Dawn, knowing what he meant. "No! I tell you this is all Steve Bordereau's work, and that Jim Torrance is out with all he's got to break Bordereau down, and somehow he's got caught wrong in the thing that Bordereau has just pulled off."

"Maybe," said the sheriff. "Maybe. Only it looks bad. It looks so bad that, while I'd rather cut off a thumb than go against you, I'm as sure as Billy-be-damned that this Torrance has made a sucker of you. Here; look at this. Nobody but you and me knows a thing about it; I'll ask you to take a look at it and then forget it. That means, keep your mouth shut."

She nodded, he thought, just the way old King Cannon used to do, and a nod from that old boy was worth as much as reams of legal phrasings with signatures and seals and notaries' stamps affixed.

From the pocket of an open, sagging vest he pulled a folded sheet of paper. He gave it to her and stood back, watching her read the few lines:

Dear Walt: They've got me, and it's going to be up to you whether I get out alive or not. They'd cut my throat in a minute. So, Walt, hold your hand. It's ransom, of course. I'll be sending you another note in a day or so. Don't try to follow the man who brings it; don't do anything. Just wait. They hold the cards, and I'd rather pay than kick off. This is damned serious, Walt.

Yours,

Bill Hasbrook.

P.S. They left one of their men behind, pretty badly hurt, I think, a man named Jim Torrance. Hold on to him; give him the best of care; I guess they'll want him sent back to them along with some money; he's the boss of the gang. If anything happens to him, they say the same thing will happen to me. Watch your step, Walt.

Bill.

When she had finished reading, "Now what?" said Sheriff Evans.

"I—I don't understand," said Sally Dawn in a small voice.

He put his big hand very lightly and sympathetically on her shoulder.

"It's kind of easy to understand, Sally," he said gravely. "This Torrance sort of stands out; he's not the common run; he's born to be a leader. What he is is the head of this gang. You can't get away from it."

"He isn't! I know he isn't! He—he is fine, Walt Evans!"

And in answer Sheriff Walt Evans leaned comfortably on those two good old Western crutches, saying, "Sure, Sally Dawn, sure." But nonetheless he had his mind made up, and she knew it. And her own mind was terribly unsettled. This letter from Hasbrook, president of the bank, a captive of the bank robbers, a man being held for ransom, seemed to come straight from the shoulder; and he said, "He's the boss of the gang."

She didn't know what to think—but she did know what to do. She was going to stick by Jim Torrance through thick and thin, as he had stuck by her when her need was sorest. She went straight back to his bedside and there she meant to stay.

Sheriff Walt Evans went back to his chair, hoisted his boots up on top of his untidy table and read Hasbrook's letter all over again. Sally Dawn would have been greatly surprised if she could have known just how that shrewd old brain of his was ticking. He started wriggling the toes in his boots; it must have been to them that he spoke when he said softly: "He called me 'Walt' four times in this damfool letter. And he signed himself 'Bill.'"

CHAPTER XV

"GOOD morning, Mr. Torrance," said Sally Dawn.

"Good morning, Miss Cannon," said Jim Torrance.

"It's a lovely morning. And you're looking just fine."

"It's more than a lovely morning. And you're lovelier than any round dozen of lovely mornings. And—"

"You're feeling—"

"Like being on top of the world. Ready to jump up and go prowling. Like singing you a song. It goes like this:

" 'Oh, hand me down my high-heeled boots,
    And hand me down my hat;
    And hand me down my long-tailed coat,
    Likewise my silk cravat.' "

She laughed at him and wrinkled up her nose in the way she had, and he grinned at her and, for about two minutes, the world was a mighty nice place to live in. Then he started frowning.

"Pain?" she asked solicitously.

"Yes. The worst one I've had yet."

"Where, Jim?"

"In my conscience. You've been doing too much for me. You've come all this distance and you've stuck here until you're worn out. I want you to go home and get years of rest. I'll ride down and see you later; I'll bring you all my thanks then and—and a pinto pony."

So she laughed at him again. His frown went away and his grin came back, but behind the grin, lurking in the dark depths of his eyes, was a sober thought. He said, looking at her steadily:

"I've been sort of sick. I've heard things said while I lay here, and they didn't matter and most of the time didn't

126

even make sense. But now I've got to think 'em over, and—"

"Convalescents are not supposed to think," said Sally Dawn. "It's against the law."

"Tell me this: In Canyon City, who are the two best friends?"

His hand had stirred slightly; hers sped to a meeting with it like a little dove coming home.

"We are, of course."

"Right. And as I remember it, a friend can bank on a friend. Now tell me this: What's wrong?"

"Wrong? Why—why, just that you've been hurt—"

"No. The way Doc Kibbee looks at me, the way the sheriff digs into me with those old fish-eyes of his—even the way Nancy Hamilton handles herself—dammit, the way that even Sally Dawn Cannon does sometimes!—all this has got me wondering about something."

"About what, Jim?" she asked, getting ready to be brave.

"We'll forget it. But there is something you can tell me: Why hasn't Hasbrook dropped in?"

"Hasbrook?"

"Yes. Bill Hasbrook, the bank president. He hasn't been in at all, has he?"

"I haven't seen him."

"Why? Where is he?" She started tucking her chin down, as though she could hide behind it, and he demanded sharply, "Well? Where's Bill Hasbrook?"

"I've heard that he isn't here. That he had to go away somewhere."

His eyes grew more penetrating, began to grow suspicious.

"What about Gates? The cashier, Phil Gates?"

"Jim! They told me that you weren't really to talk; not about anything that mattered, anything that might possibly upset you. And if I let you talk, Mrs. Hamilton will come in and send me away."

"I hear tell they've got a sheriff up here in Coconambo County, that is a sheriff," said Jim. "You, up and around, maybe might know? It would be kind of nice if he would drop in on me and say hello. Think he might?"

She didn't want to say yes and she didn't want to say no. She had never endured such a troublesome moment in all her life. But she had to look him in the eyes, so did his eyes insist on it, and at last she said:

"Yes. He will come to see you right away."

He squeezed her hand.

"Thank you a lot, Sally Dawn," he said.

Then, when she had darted out, with little delay Sheriff Walt Evans came stalking in. He said, as crisp as a new-baked biscuit:

"Well, Torrance? I hear you want to see me."

"Squat, Sheriff," said Torrance. "And tell me."

"What's on your chest, Stranger?" asked the sheriff, having drawn up a chair.

"Where's Hasbrook? Why hasn't he dropped in to ask me whether I was dead or alive?"

"Hasbrook? He ain't here right now."

"What about Phil Gates?"

"He ain't here either. Happens he's dead."

Jim Torrance thought that over. Phil Gates had been very much alive not so long ago, and to be dead now meant that he was out of luck when the bank hold-up was pulled off and bullets got to roving wild. He didn't have to ask Sheriff Evans. But he did have to swing back to Hasbrook, the bank president, and ask about him.

"What about Hasbrook?" he asked. "Let's have it all, Evans."

"Maybe you don't know?" said the sheriff.

"No. I don't know much of anything. Somebody hammered me over the head—"

"And a good job, too! That was a deputy of mine, a feller named—"

"Hell with his name! It ought to be John W. Jackass. Tell me about Hasbrook. They didn't kill him too, did they?"

"You wouldn't know, would you?"

"If I knew I wouldn't be asking. Let's have it. Is Hasbrook alive or dead?"

"Pretty much alive," snapped the sheriff.

The man in bed filled his lungs; for a moment he had pretty well stopped breathing.

"Tell him I want him," he said. "Tell him to get a move on. I've waited long enough. Get him here on the run."

"No can do, Torrance. They've nabbed him. That gang of yours is holding him for ransom. Maybe you didn't know that, huh?"

Torrance stared at him.

"Say it again. What gang of mine? What in hell are you talking about?"

"You'll be telling me that you didn't have anything to do with the hold-up? Just an innocent bystander when the job was pulled off?"

"You think I had a hand in that? That I was one of the crowd that stuck the bank up, killed Phil Gates and grabbed Hasbrook?"

"There's not a man in Canyon City who doesn't know it. What do you take us for anyhow? Blind men or just plain fools?"

"Both!" growled Torrance, and sounded downright disgusted. "Good Lord, man, I went to Hasbrook and told him to watch out for this very thing; I had a hunch that this was going to happen and—"

"I guess you did," said Evans drily.

"And now Gates is dead and Hasbrook is gone—and your crazy deputy plugs me—and you figure me for one of that crowd of rats! Haven't you got the sense of a little gray seed tick?"

"Maybe you know who the stick-up gents were?" said Evans, very sarcastic.

"Of course I know! It's a gang of Sundown killers led by Steve Bordereau."

"And you knew ahead of time that they were going to pull off this job?"

"No, I didn't know. But I know Bordereau, I have an idea of what's in his head, and it was an easy guess he'd strike here. His crowd is the same one that stuck up the Yellow Pine, Rock Valley and the Mountain City Bank. They're out to make a big killing before they blow; and it was my guess that Canyon City would be next."

"Just a wild guess on your part then, huh?"

"It wasn't so wild, was it? And now you're doctoring me, working to get me on my feet again, just to throw me in jail? That it?"

"There are a good many boys around here," said Evans, "friends of Hasbrook's and Gates', that don't think much of the jail idea. Maybe I'm going to have my job cut out, as soon's you're able to get around, to keep them from taking you off my hands."

"Little hanging party?" grunted Torrance.

"Your guesses keep right on being good."

Torrance lay still a while and stared at the ceiling.

"You think I'm lying to you, do you?"

Evans shrugged heavily.

"I just wish I knew, brother," he said sourly.

That was about as far as they got at that time. But a couple of days later the sheriff dropped in again. This time he found Torrance dressed, sitting on the edge of his bed, looking gaunt and weak but with a clear, bold eye.

"Let's talk, Torrance."

"Shoot. What's new?"

From his pocket the sheriff drew a couple of folded sheets of paper. One was that communication from Hasbrook which he had already shown to Sally Dawn. Jim Torrance read it carefully, then read the second note which Evans handed to him with the remark: "This one just got to me today. I don't know who brought it; it was shoved under my door last night."

When Torrance had finished reading it also there were spots of color in his cheeks showing a dull angry red through the dark stubble of beard, and his eyes were bright and hard. The words that Hasbrook had penciled were:

Dear Walt: You'll have one more letter from me in another few days, inside the week anyhow. Meantime I want you to raise fifty thousand dollars in cash and have it ready against demand. That's my ransom money. Instructions for delivery will come in my last note to you. And there is one other thing and, Walt, I'm depending on you for this. The boys who are holding me have learned that Jim Torrance is alive and getting well, and they insist that he be returned to them the same time the money is sent. As I wrote you before, he is one of the crowd and their leader. I know you won't want to let him go, but if you don't send him back to his men they swear they'll do me in even if they lose the ransom. I feel sure I can depend on you, Walt. So long.

Bill Hasbrook.

Jim Torrance didn't speak immediately; he rolled a cigarette first and lighted it and sat there, staring for a while at the floor, then into Sheriff Evans' gimleting eyes.

"Bill Hasbrook," said Torrance at last, "is a dirty rat. On top of that he is a—"

"Never mind all that," cut in Evans. "Hasbrook's a friend of mine; he's the squarest man you ever heard a man tell about."

"Is that so? Why, a skunk wouldn't come near him! He's two things I hate, a sneaking cur of a coward and a double crossing sidewinder. After I went to him and put him wise, after I chipped in with him and damn near got myself killed in the mixup, look what the yellow louse is doing to me! Just to save his own dirty hide, he'll be tickled pink to have me slaughtered. And I thought—"

"Easy, Stranger! What's he doing to you, after all, but just save you from jail or hanging here, and send you back to your own men?"

"He knows better than that, and you'd know too, if you had sense enough to pound sand through a knot hole!" said Torrance hotly. "I tell you, that's Steve Bordereau's gang. Bordereau wants to have the fun of butchering me, and Hasbrook knows it."

Evans made himself a cigarette, yet did not for an instant withdraw that penetrating gaze of his from Jim Torrance's angry face.

"Take it from me, Torrance," he said evenly, "Will Hasbrook is no coward, and he's no crook; he's known over a good many miles as a man you can tie to."

A queer, puzzled look came into Torrance's eyes.

"That's what I thought," he muttered. "I'd heard his

reputation; I had a few good talks with him. Dammit, I'd have bet my life on that man—and I guess that's what I did."

"Yes, a man could bet his life on Hasbrook playing square," said Evans.

Torrance got up and stirred about the room restlessly; then he came back and leaned on the head of the bed and looked down curiously at the sheriff's hard-bitten face.

"You've got the name of being a square shooter too, Evans," he said thoughtfully. "And I'd say you are. Suppose you tell me the truth about this bank president; how long have you known him?"

"Not very long," said Evans. "Only about forty years."

"And he's neither a coward nor a crook?"

"The squarest. An old friend of King Cannon's, if that means anything to you. And not afraid of all hell on wheels."

"That's how I made him out. And here he is, caving in to those bums, paying a ransom and letting them make a monkey out of him."

"Well, maybe he figures he'd rather be alive than save that fifty thousand."

"And you feel kind of sure that he isn't the sort of man to save his own hide by letting another man take his place? A man who he knows played square with him?"

"Is this a cigarette I'm smoking? Might be a pipe, might be I'm not smoking at all but eating a watermelon! I'm just that sure."

"Damn it then! He didn't write these letters at all! They're forgeries! I tell you there's something phony about them!"

"He wrote 'em all right. I know Will's hand-of-write; know it as well as I know my own hat."

"Then—"

"I'll tell you one thing," said Evans sharply. He stood up and tapped Torrance on the shoulder. "Will Hasbrook wrote these letters, and just the same you're right; there is something damn phony about them. It's a little thing, but it's something that hit me in the eye right off, and that stands out a mile after a feller does notice it. Here, squat;

you're looking white around the gills. I'm going to tell you something."

Torrance came back to the bed and sat down. It was Evans' turn to walk up and down for a while; his brows were dragged down in tangled thought and he was taking his last moment to consider all angles of a puzzle before he committed himself. Then he shrugged and stood in front of Torrance and spoke his piece.

"Look here, Torrance, maybe I'm the idiot you've called me, but I believe every word you've said to me. That's partly because of what Sally Dawn Cannon told me; partly from sizing you up for myself; partly now for something in Hasbrook's letters that makes me hunt around for just the sort of a queer set-up you've told me about. Like you said, there's something phony here, and Hasbrook's been to a lot of trouble to tell me so, and he's figured it was up to me to find out about things."

He put the two letters, spread out, on the bed.

"Look at this first one," he said. "He calls me 'Walt' four times in it! And Will Hasbrook never called me 'Walt' in his life. Everybody else does, but since we were kids he's always called me Walter. And I've always called him Will —and I guess I'm the only man in the county that ever called him anything but Bill Hasbrook. And now look at the second one. He's got three 'Walts' in that. And both of 'em he's signed 'Bill.' And if he's not trying to fly some sort of signal for me I'm all that you've called me."

By the time Sheriff Walt Evans left, Jim Torrance was ready to crawl back into bed and just lie there and try to be patient about getting stronger. They had gone into a conference, planning ways and means, that had lasted a solid two hours.

What was more, they had cooked up their plan that had enough hazard in it to have claimed all Torrance's thoughts as long as he lay awake. But, as a matter of record, he wasn't thinking of this present problem at all but a vastly more pleasant one. He was wondering when Sally Dawn would pop in again.

CHAPTER XVI

THE third letter reached Sheriff Walt Evans four days later. He found it, like the two others, stuck under his door. He brought it straightway to Jim Torrance, whom he found, early in the morning, up and about and devouring a man-sized breakfast. He tossed the fresh news onto Jim's table and started prowling up and down the room.

Torrance read it to the neglect of a sort of Tower of Pisa made of rich brown buckwheat cakes.

Dear Walt: Be sure you get these details straight: You are to hand Jim Torrance over to his friends tomorrow night. They don't want you to let him know what you're doing with him; the boys want to have their fun and give him a surprise. So you'll put him on horseback after dark; you'll have him tied down to the saddle; you'll tell him you're taking him to some other jail to make sure his gang doesn't pour down and get him free. Also, you're to stuff the fifty thousand into his pockets. Got all that, Walt?

Next: You and Torrance, alone, ride out on the Bear Creek road about seven miles, to where the trail cuts up over the mountain to the old Sun Dodgers' place. When you get up to the mouth of the pass you'll tie Torrance's horse to a tree, make sure he's tied down hard in the saddle, and you'll back off down trail. Got that straight, Walt?

You'll wait there for me. I'll be with you right away. I've fixed things with these boys so that I know I'll be all right if you just do what I say—Walt, old man, my life depends on you and I don't want to die. Walt, for God's sake, do as you're told.

This whole thing is getting me down.

Bill Hasbrook.

Evans, watching Torrance read, said curtly: "Well, you'd take Will Hasbrook for a yellow skunk, wouldn't you? And that's just what he ain't! They couldn't get him down if they took out their pocket knives and started to skin him. And here again he calls me 'Walt' all over the map."

"And I'm to be tied up good and tight," said Torrance. "No gun on me, of course. As Hasbrook puts it, 'The boys want to have their fun and give him a surprise!'"

"He says for tomorrow night," said Evans. "Going to be strong enough for that sort of ride by then? Anyhow ten miles."

"Sure," said Torrance. "That part of it's all right. But do you think it's possible that Hasbrook has tried to write in anything else between the lines? And that you've missed it?"

"I've read every one of his notes forty times," growled Evans. "I know damn well that his 'Walts' and 'Bills' are stuck in to give me a high sign. Beyond that I can't get an inch. He might mean I'm just to stall along and pay no attention to anything. Or—maybe—"

"He might mean that you're to talk things over with me, just as you have done. That business of having me tied down in the saddle, just for fun, makes you pretty sure what Bordereau's game is, I guess!"

"We start out a little before midnight, Torrance," said Evans. "That's for tomorrow night. You better take things easy today. Will says we're to wait for him up at the mouth of the pass; we'll do that."

"There's the chance, of course, that they'll be hid in the brush and burn us down—"

"Nope. If he hadn't been sure on that point, Will wouldn't have written the way he did."

"I'll be ready," said Torrance.

That afternoon Doc Kibbee, who had had a good talk with the sheriff, came in, looked Torrance over, grunted and went out. Later Sally Dawn ran in.

"Jim Torrance," she said, "you look as good as brand-new again. You're about ready to ride, aren't you? You're to come back home with me, you know, and get a good rest there. Mrs. Sam will feed you and—"

"Sally Dawn," said Torrance, "you just travel along back home today, and you tell Mrs. Sam to start in roasting chickens, baking cakes and making pies, for just as sure as you're alive I'll be dropping in on you mighty soon. I've got a thing or two to tend to here first, and—"

Sally Dawn looked at him sharply.

"If you had said you'd promise to come 'Just as sure as you're alive' it would sound more like you meant it," she said unhappily. She put an impulsive hand on his arm. "Jim Torrance, you and Walt Evans are cooking something up. You're back on Steve Bordereau's trail, aren't you? Why can't you just forget he ever existed? He'll be up and away, out of the country for good after this." She pleaded; her eyes and her softened voice were beseeching. "Please, Jim."

"Take that back, Sally Dawn," said Torrance gravely. "I don't want you to ask me, ever, anything I can't do for you. Take it back, Sally Dawn!"

Sally Dawn turned abruptly and went to the window, giving him her back to look at. He looked at it and waited. Then she turned again and came back to him, and somehow it struck him that she was marching like a little soldier with drums beating and flags flying.

"I understand, Jim," she said very softly, and there was only the vaguest hint of a quiver upon her red lips, though no tremor came into her steady voice. "I don't blame you, Jim. I'll go home now. There'll be roast chicken and cakes and pies and—and I'll be waiting, Jim Torrance."

She darted out of the room then, as swift as a swallow, and it was not ten minutes later that Jim Torrance, out on the porch in the weak October sunshine, saw her and Curly Redmond and Dave Drennen swoop by, riding out of Canyon City, headed south. She didn't wave good-by, she didn't even turn in the saddle. He pulled off his hat and stood with it turning slowly in his hands until the three riders were out of sight.

The next night between eleven o'clock and midnight Torrance and Walt Evans rode out of Canyon City headed toward Indian Mountain and the old Sun Dodgers place and the high pass across the ridge. There was a packet tied to Torrance's saddle strings; in it, in gold and bank notes, was fifty thousand dollars. Torrance's hands were on his saddle horn and there was a rope about his wrists. Also there was a rope about his ankles and under his horse's belly. You would have said that he was bound hand and foot; that he was unarmed; that he was still the helpless prisoner of the sheriff of Coconambo County.

It was a clear night and there was a moon, and the mountain ridges stood up sharply defined against a star-strewn sky. It was a fair bet, both men agreed, that from the time they rode out of the dark alley behind the livery stable they were being watched. They were equally aware of the fact, as they left Canyon City behind them and struck into the road that was like a long winding slash through thick timber, that a rifle might crack at any minute and a storm of bullets knock them out of their saddles. They were at Steve Bordereau's mercy, and Bordereau was merciless. Just the same, they banked on Will Hasbrook.

"I know damn well," said Evans, "that Will wouldn't have let us in for this without somehow being pretty sure we'd make out. I don't see how he figures it, but a man can gamble on Will Hasbrook and on his keeping his head. Just the same— Look here, Torrance, if you want to back out while you've got the chance I can't say I'll blame you. If I've got you right, if you haven't lied me blind, this may be the last night you ever get a good look at the stars."

"We'll play out our string, Evans," said Torrance.

Before they were a mile on their way, a rider, coming on after them from Canyon City, overtook them and passed on. He called out, "Hello, Jim! We'll be waitin' for you and glad to have you with us again." They could make nothing of his face, lost in the shadow of his hat.

For an instant the sheriff's hand hardened to the butt of his old walnut-gripped Colt; then he sighed and relaxed in the saddle.

"Nothing we can do about anything until we get to the rendyvoo," he said disgustedly, "and most likely damn little we can do then. Looks like they had us with our noses shoved down in the dirt."

"They've got the edge on us," conceded Torrance coolly.

"They've got us guessing more or less, and they've got the odds on us. That's all they've got."

"Good Lord, man! Ain't that a-plenty?"

"Just the same," Torrance went on, "you never quit on a proposition just because it was an uphill pull, did you?"

Sheriff Walt Evans of Coconambo County swore fluently. At the end he said:

"Damn if I don't sort of like your style, Torrance. And if they get your hide tonight I'll do my level damnedest to sort of even things up with them later on."

"Fair enough," said Torrance.

They rode on in silence. The road under their horses' scampering hoofs started abruptly climbing up Indian Mountain, winding in and out of graded ravines, and they had to pull down to a swinging walk. Torrance said: "That hombre took a look-see to make out whether I was tied up or not. They'll have some more spies posted along the road, sure as shooting. And I'm here to bet you we meet up with them quite a spell before we get to the place where Hasbrook said we were to come."

High up on the flank of the mountain they struck into a road that ran almost level in a high valley, and here they rode hard and were watchful and suspicious. Every shadow might be a man with a rifle at his shoulder; the place was lonesome enough for that sort of thing. But they shot across this bit of mountain meadow without anything happening, dipped into another canyon and climbed steeply again. Then, startling them, with their nerves already at stretch, a voice shouted: "Hello, Jim! Like old times come again, huh?"

"Damn 'em, they make my flesh creep," snorted the old sheriff.

"They're having them their fun," said Torrance.

"We ought to be there in ten-fifteen minutes now, Kid," said the sheriff, and for the first time sounded uncertain and uneasy. "If I was you— Dammit, Kid, if I was you— Oh, hell, I dunno! But if you want to turn tail right now and get the hell out of here, headed back where we just came from, me I wouldn't blame you."

"We called for cards; let's play the hand out," said Torrance. And after that, if he was ever going to have need of a friend, all he'd have to do would be send word to the sheriff of Coconambo County.

Then it wasn't long before they saw what they recognized as a signal to halt. In the middle of the trail where there was an opening through trees, and where the moon and stars made the place bright, a freshly skinned pole stood upright, based in a nest of stones, and from the top of the pole a scrap of white cloth drooped and fluttered in the draft of night air down through a cut in the mountains. They reined in when they first saw this mast and flag, something like fifty yards, before they came to it. Beyond, so straight-as-a-string was the trail right here, they could see an open distance of perhaps twice fifty yards.

"If it comes to fighting it out, Kid," said Evans in an undertone, "I'm with you."

"No," said Torrance, and though he too spoke almost under his breath his tone sounded savage. "No change of plans now, Evans. You get Hasbrook out of this if you can; all I want is Bordereau."

Then they saw three mounted men moving slowly out of the timber ahead of them and coming toward them down trail. Evans called out sharply:

"That you, Will?"

"Yes, it's me, Walter," answered the banker.

"You're to come ahead alone," the sheriff called back. "Those coyotes with you know they can take your word, and I know they're a pack of liars whose word is no better than rotten eggs."

Another voice spoke up. Jim Torrance felt a tingle run through his blood as he heard it; he recognized it beyond a doubt as Steve Bordereau's.

"You, Evans!" the voice called. "You'll do as you're damn well told, or the gun I've got jammed between Hasbrook's shoulder blades is going off; and there's a rifle trained on you now that will zip you into kingdom come."

"No, by the lord!" yelled back an angry sheriff. "You'll do as I say now. Send Hasbrook down alone to me and let the two of us ride out of this, and you've got my word for it your money is tied to Jim Torrance's saddle strings. If you don't like that, kill Hasbrook and try to kill me and be damned to you."

"Is that Torrance with you?"

The three oncoming riders had stopped.

"Yes. It's Jim Torrance. I've done my part; you do yours and do it the way I say, or else."

Then one of the three horsemen came on alone, and Torrance and Sheriff Evans made out that it was banker Hasbrook. Bordereau called out again, not waiting for Hasbrook to reach the sheriff's side:

"Evans! You give me your word you've got the money with you?"

"Yes."

"Is Torrance tied or free?"

"As if you didn't know already! He's got ropes on his wrists and on his legs, if you call that being tied. The money's on his saddle; I'll drop it into the trail or leave it there. But you're to let me and Hasbrook get down trail to the bend before you come on. If you boys had rather prove yourselves the bunch of liars I've called you and would rather shoot it out, hop to it."

"Leave the money where it is," said Bordereau. "Tie Torrance's horse to a tree like I said. Then get to hell out of here."

"Here goes," said Evans.

Hasbrook came on. By the time he had reached them, Sheriff Evans had used the tie rope on Torrance's saddle, an end of which was already around the horse's neck; the other end he tied and drew tight with a jerk around a young tree. Then for a moment or two Torrance and Evans and Will Hasbrook were together, no Bordereau man in sight but the two uptrail, and they a good seventy-five yards away. Hasbrook, grasping Evans' arm, said sharply:

"Dammit, Walter! Haven't you and Torrance talked? Hasn't he told you—"

Torrance in a savage undertone cut in:

"We've made our plans, Hasbrook. You do what Evans says. What Bordereau says, too. Get the hell out of here."

"I'll do nothing of the kind! Leaving you tied like this? They'll murder you in two minutes!"

"Hey, there!" shouted Steve Bordereau. "What are you birds talking about? Break it up and scatter for home—or else, like Evans says."

Evans muttered, his voice in Hasbrook's ear: "He means business. I've done all I could with my eyes shut, Will. Now you do as I say. We're on our way."

Hasbrook called softly to Jim Torrance: "I don't get this. Until hell freezes solid I'm with you, Kid."

"Ride then," snapped Torrance. "Now."

Their hushed conference was so short that when Evans sang out to Bordereau, "All right; me and Hasbrook are on our way," it was before Bordereau even called a second command. Evans whirled his horse and spurred down trail, gone at a run, and with him went a reluctant Hasbrook. The two vanished around the bend in the trail.

Bordereau and the man with him came on then, riding at a slow trot; Torrance could see the metallic gleam of the rifles they carried. He saw also something else, for those narrowed and watchful eyes of his were everywhere at once, as they had to be, did he mean to go on living even a few minutes. He saw a third member of Bordereau's party; this man stepped out from under the trees almost at his side. He carried his belt gun in his hand and was not six paces away when Torrance heard his soft tread and made him out, close enough to assure himself that Evans had done a good job of tying the free end of Torrance's tie rope about the tree; close enough to see the rope about Torrance's wrists. He called out, laughing:

"Come ahead, boys. He's tied up tighter'n a drum."

A shout and a big booming laugh broke from Steve Bordereau then, and he and the man with him came on at a swinging gallop.

"Now!" thought Jim Torrance. "Now!"

CHAPTER XVII

AS SHERIFF EVANS and Banker Hasbrook rode down trail and around the bend, Evans slipped a hand under his coat, dragged out two hefty forty-fours and slid them into Hasbrook's eager hands.

"I hope you get a chance to use 'em tonight, that's all," growled an unusually disgruntled sheriff.

"Me too, dammit," growled Hasbrook.

Just then two men rode out into the trail in front of them, and one of the two called sullenly as Evans and Hasbrook pulled their horses down:

"You're to keep on going, and go like hell. Got it?"

"Got you," snapped Evans, and started to ride on.

But already Jim Torrance had muttered to himself, "Now!" That was uptrail and around the bend, and they couldn't see him for the trees. Nor could they see Steve Bordereau and the man riding with him, nor the other man who had just stepped out so close to Torrance.

Torrance, having said "Now!" meant "*Now!*" Bordereau and the man with him wore big bandanas over their faces, for masks; they'd kept their faces hidden all the while from Will Hasbrook. But as they pulled in close to where Torrance waited for them, Steve Bordereau jerked the cloth away from his face. Already he saw Torrance's hands on the saddle horn, and saw too the rope about them.

But there was something he didn't see. The rope about Torrance's horse's neck went just so far and was pieced out with a bit of cotton string; the ropes about Torrance's legs were pieced out in the same way, as was the rope about his wrists. One jerk, no more emphatic than that with which Steve Bordereau snatched his handkerchief away, was all he needed to set him free.

"Got you at last, damn you!" exulted Bordereau. He reached in leisurely fashion for his gun. "You're a dead man in ten seconds, Torrance. You'll live just exactly long enough to know who burned you down. Take this—and like it!"

"Hold it, Bordereau," said Torrance quietly. "Me, I want to tell you something too. I felt sure down to my boots that it was you and your gang pulling off these jobs, bank robbing, murder and such. Now I know from seeing you and listening to you. Here's a tip for you. I don't think you'll live through the night; if you do you'll be where you put Doc Taylor before your whiskers grow long enough to shave two-three times."

Bordereau hardly heard him out before he started shooting, and not ten paces away. But Torrance, whom circumstances forced to make his final, revised plans in a hurry, wasn't in the saddle when Bordereau's finger hardened to the trigger. Knowing that he could never hope to go free on horseback, he spilled out of his saddle, breaking the little cotton strings that bound him, throwing himself against the fellow who had just stepped from the wood, knocking him endwise. Torrance's frightened horse leaped and reared and lunged, and in the narrow trail caromed flank to flank against Steve Bordereau's mount.

By that time Bordereau was firing as fast as he could, not caring in the least if he knocked over his own man, tangled there on the ground with Jim Torrance, not caring much about anything, just so Torrance was one man he killed. But in his excitement and rage he had the poorest of luck; Torrance was firing back with less excitement, with more precision. As he threw himself from his horse's back his gun was in his hand; he brought it down smashingly on the head of the man against whom he catapulted himself; thereafter he did his level best to make an end of Bordereau. But three horses were rearing and snorting their fear, and trying to run away, and, close as the men were to each other, it was hard to make sure with any single shot.

But he came mighty close to making sure with the first bullet he winged on its way; it carried Steve Bordereau's hat away and left a bloody groove along Bordereau's scalp. The gambler, emulating his enemy, went down out of the saddle in a hurry, keeping the reins in one hand, getting behind his horse, and he kept on firing from behind his restless barricade as fast as he could pull a trigger.

He did kill his own man, the one whom Torrance had downed; Torrance heard the thud of the impact in the lax body, thanked his stars for the eight or ten inches between them, and leaped into the dark of the wood bordering the trail. Bullets were singing all about him, the other bandit slamming lead at him as fast as did Steve Bordereau.

Bordereau too sprang nimbly out of the open trail, ducking behind a tree. The fellow with him was slower of wit or of bolder mettle; in any case he stopped one of Torrance's bullets and went to the ground headlong. By that time, above the crash and thunder and clamorous reverberations of gunfire, rose Bordereau's voice, choking with anger, yelling savage commands:

"Varny! Billings! Where the hell are you? Get into it or—"

Varny Slack and Hen Billings were the two men he had set on guard lower down the trail, to make sure that the sheriff and Hasbrook were on their way; for at the time of cooking up his plans Bordereau hadn't counted on Torrance bursting his bonds like this. And just now it happened that Varny and Billings had other matters to attend to beyond listening to their leader's commands. For the instant Walt Evans heard the start of a duello of gunfire, he chose to consider that his contract with these rats was fulfilled and that he was a free man to do just what he damn well pleased. He grabbed a gun up out of its holster where it rested so loosely, yelled downright joyously, "Stick 'em up, you two, or go for your guns!" and cut loose. For he saw they were doing what they had to do; they were going for their guns.

If there was one thing and there were several—that Walt Evans could do pretty close up to the fine edge of perfection, it was shoot on the draw true to the mark. He unlimbered before either of his two opponents got their guns up six inches from their holsters; they should have shot from the hip and taken their chances that way, for no other chance was to be granted them. He shot one man through the throat, the other man through the gun elbow. And

Will Hasbrook by that time was in action; he drilled with a lucky shot the fellow whom Evans had merely wounded.

Then the two went storming back uptrail.

"Hey there, Jim!" and, "Torrance! Torrance! We're with you!" yelled Evans and Hasbrook. And Bordereau, hearing and understanding what must have happened when he heard the shooting around the bend, got into the edge of the forest, dragging his horse along, and got up into his saddle and left behind him only the faint sound of his cursing and the livelier racket of brush crackling under his precipitate flight.

Out in the clearing was a rock some five or six feet high. Torrance with a single leap seemed somehow to be on top of it. From there he shouted so that his vociferations were like the challenge of a crowing cock. That was because already he tried to see into that thing that they call the future—into happenings which, yet unborn, might come out this way or that.

"Bordereau!" he shouted, inviting a bullet and feeling in his heart, standing high just then, that he could dodge it! "Bordereau! You've run off and left your fifty thousand! And I've scared you out of the country, me, Jim Torrance! Hell with you—since I know after this you'll never come back! Me, I'll own this whole damn country a year from now; and you—you'll be down below the border with the rest of the half-breeds, sucking eggs for supper, hungry and dirty and lousy and down and out. And it was me, Jim Torrance, that ran you out."

And for full measure he simulated rollicking spontaneous laughter.

That extravagance of his nearly cost him his life—but since it was merely a case of nearly but not quite, he didn't in the least mind. Steve Bordereau heard his taunts and stopped and shot at him through the uncertain region of twigs and shadows and moonlight, and his shots whistled close but left Torrance unscathed. Nor, after having fired his verbal volley, did Torrance choose to linger on the rock. He spilled down again, almost under the running hoofs of the horses bringing Evans and Hasbrook.

"There'll be sure to be more of the rats hid in the brush,"

he sang out warningly. "Better duck for cover among the trees."

"I don't see you ducking," snorted the sheriff.

Torrance's horse had run but a short distance uptrail and stood there stamping and whirling and jerking its head high, making a lively jingle of bridle chains. Torrance ran forward, caught up the reins and went up into the saddle. Then there was a crashing in the underbrush where he had vanished, going after the already vanished Bordereau. Close behind him came both the sheriff and Hasbrook. And now Hasbrook, though he was not going to hang back when the others led, called out a warning:

"You'll never get him at night in this rough country—he knows every step of it—look out or he'll let you have it before you ever see him."

Torrance didn't stop and didn't bother to answer. He knew that Bordereau still fled on somewhere ahead, for he heard the drumming of speeding hoofs. But he had to swing this way and that among the trees; his horse balked once where a big fallen tree lay across the way; he had to draw back and ride around it—and then all sounds of the horse ahead of him died away. He stopped and listened; the trample of Evans' and Hasbrook's horses, coming closer, was all he heard.

"Let him go, Torrance," said Evans brusquely. "You're no sorrier than I am to have him slide out on us—but we've saved Will's fifty thousand dollars for him—and we've done what we could to square things for Phil Gates, potting two of the devils. And tomorrow I'll come back up here with a posse and comb these mountains—"

"You got two of them?" said Torrance. "Well, Bordereau himself got a third man, plugging wild at me. If we haven't busted up his gang, at least we've thinned it. And I guess you're right; it's about all we can do for tonight."

Evans said to Hasbrook: "This man Jim Torrance is barely up out of bed; he got himself shot up a bit in the scrap when they grabbed you. It's time we rode home with him and tucked him into bed again. Let's catch up these horses running free, and be on our way."

"Torrance," said the banker warmly, "if it hadn't been for you—"

"Let's ride," said Torrance.

No posse went out the next morning, but just a couple of men with a buckboard to haul back into town the three dead bandits. That was because the sheriff and Will Hasbrook had had a good long talk with Jim Torrance.

"It's a funny thing," said Hasbrook, "how Jim here seems to sort of know what Bordereau's apt to do next, what he's thinking even. He came to me and told me to look out for this raid, and I did—well, half-heartedly maybe, still I did feel in my bones that he knew what he was talking about."

"How come?" demanded Evans. "You and this Bordereau bird had lots of heart-to-heart talks, Jim?"

"Nary a talk, Walt. But you see, I know the sort of things Steve Bordereau has been pulling off for years; I've done a lot of thinking about him; I've got a hunch I know what he's like inside and how he figures things."

"I heard you yelling after him when you stood up there on that rock last night. You figured he was on his way at last, clean out of the country."

"That was just my way of inviting him to hang around a little longer," grinned Torrance, and looked vastly good-natured and hopeful. "After my reminding him that we still had his fifty thousand, and after my doing a bit of big-mouth bragging, there's no more chance of his running out on us than there is of the world falling apart. If he never does another thing, he's going to have a try at me." His grin passed swiftly and his eyes darkened and grew low-lidded and moody. "You see," he said thoughtfully, "Steve Bordereau is three things by nature. He's a crook and a killer—and a gambler. He's sure by now that his luck is running high."

"After last night?" said Hasbrook, puzzled.

"He's got a gang with him, hasn't he? And he's raked in several sizable jack pots already, hasnt he, grabbing King Cannon's gold, sticking up the Yellow Pine and the Mountain City Bank and the Mines? Last night he lost a trick, yes; but at the same time he had the good luck to have three of his followers put out of the running; he'll grab their share, won't he? But then you don't know Bordereau."

As it happened, both men did know him, though but slightly; both had sat in at a poker table with him. They understood.

"And what next?" demanded Evans.

"First, there's Bordereau on the run in the mountains. You know damn well you could hunt him until the next snowstorm and never catch a glimpse of him, not up there in the rough country. And after snow flies, what then? He'll be well provisioned; he'll have a snug hide-out; it'll be in a place where one man can hold off fifty. And he'll still have a few men with him."

"And you think he won't do what you said, duck out for south of the border?"

"Not if I know him. He'll count noses of what's left of his party, pick up another three or four of the same kind, and try his luck again while he still thinks that luck is running high."

"And you've got a notion where he'll strike next time?"

"Sure I have," said Jim Torrance.

They talked the thing out for hours. Then, when Torrance headed back toward Sundown, Sheriff Evans and Banker Hasbrook rode with him. And, to meet them at Sundown, went another old-timer of Canyon City, Doc Kibbee, traveling by stage. Those three, Evans and Hasbrook and Kibbee, just about ran Coconambo County in those days and had done so for many years. True, Sundown was over their county border and, rightly speaking, they had nothing to say about how little Sundown behaved or misbehaved itself; yet it remained that the influence which these three hearty old mountain lions could exert extended through many channels and to considerable distances.

"We'll come swooping down on Sundown like the wolf on the fold," said Doc Kibbee.

The three horsemen came abreast of the main gate to the King Cannon ranch just about sunset. Both Evans and Hasbrook cocked an eye at Torrance; his face was without expression and he was staring straight on ahead, giving no sign that he knew where he was.

"How about turning in here for a while?" said Evans. "The folks might even feed us. Me, I'm getting hungry and sort of thirsty too."

"It's an idea, Walter," said Hasbrook.

So they turned in at the ranch wagon road, and rode up to the house on its knoll among the trees. Sam Pepper, loafing out by the chicken yard, saw them and came with all due haste to meet them.

"Say, it's you, Jim Torrance!" he exclaimed. "Say, here I been wondering— Wipe my eyes if it ain't Walt Evans! And Bill Hasbrook with you! Say!"

Then Mrs. Sam, hearing them, came bustling out of the house, dough on her hands and her arms all floury—and, while they were all just shaking hands and saying the first howdys, Sally Dawn made her appearance, sweet and fresh in a pink dress and with pink in her cheeks and violet in her eyes.

The visitors were pressed to have a snack and something cold to drink and remained for a hot supper. There came a time when by chance Jim Torrance and Sally Dawn were alone in the early dark on the porch. They strolled down into the yard.

"There's so much left over yet that you haven't told me, Jim," said the girl.

And he said: "Instead of saying a whole lot more, I'd like to ask you something. Between my ranch and the upper end of your ranch there's only the old Harper place, and the Harpers have been dead ten years and the ranch is pretty well going to the dogs. What would you say if I bought the place in? We'd be neighbors then."

"Lovely! Only—only, Jim, I'm not sure that I'll be here much longer. The ranch is so badly crippled—and what with the mortgage on it and with Steve Bordereau making all the trouble he can—and—"

"Shucks, those things are bound to get ironed out smooth, give 'em time. And don't forget Bordereau owes you a hatful of money, all that free gold he dug out of your father's old house up in the mountains. When you get that back—"

"When I get it back!" she said ruefully, and shook her head.

"You're going to get it back. You're going to keep your ranch, too; all clear and cleaned up. Steve Bordereau thinks he's riding high, wide and handsome right now, but don't let him fool you."

"And you, Jim? Do you know, sometimes I think if you just forgot all about him, if you just settled down to your ranch, your horses—"

"That's what I aim to do," said Torrance. "Right here close to Sundown. I kind of like it here."

"I'm glad," said Sally Dawn.

Then he said, almost rough about it: "Look here! You came all the way up to Canyon City when I was hurt. You—"

"Hi, Jim!" called Sam Pepper. "That you?" He came along hastily. "Are you sure it was Bordereau stuck up Canyon City? Think he's skipped the country or's coming back? And what's brought all those Canyon City big bugs, Evans and Kibbee and Hasbrook, down here so far off their stamping grounds? And—"

"I wonder why somebody hasn't killed Sam Pepper long ago," said Jim Torrance to the girl.

That made her laugh, and she said, "He makes me wonder, too!" But she gave Jim's hand, so lingeringly withdrawing, a good tight squeeze.

Supper done, the Canyon City big bugs rode on into Sundown, Jim Torrance with them, and they did not go unaccompanied. Sam Pepper was on hand to ride neck and neck with the first of them; Bill Yarbo showed up and went along; Curly Redmond and Dick Pardee and Dave Drennen were also of the party.

Within twenty-four hours that hard, tight nucleus of determined men turned a new page in Sundown's history. They looked up old friends; they talked cold turkey. The second night some four or five score of the squarest-shooting, hardest riding men of the community met in the "Hall." The yellow light of their coal oil lamps shone on grim-jawed faces. They sent out for the man they wanted, and Biggs was brought in before them, Rufe Biggs, the town marshal.

Seth Hathaway, an old stock man of the King Cannon type, spoke to him.

"Rufe," he said, "there's two kinds o' folks in an' around Sundown. There's folks like us men here; there's folks like Steve Bordereau and Clark Murdo and their crowd. Steve Bordereau put you where you are and our crowd ain't got any more use for you than a grizzly's got use for feathers in his tail. Bordereau's a killer, a crook, a stick-up gent, and he's on the run. Clark Murdo's just as bad and won't be here always. If you, Rufe, have got as much sense as a bedbug, which I doubt, you'll resign right here and right now. Sabe?"

Rufe Biggs bristled and did his small amount of unconvincing blustering, but he looked frightened, and in the end he slammed his badge of office down on the floor and kicked at it.

"Hell! I quit," he said, and got out of the room the quickest way.

Then the men gathered in the hall took it upon themselves to name their new town marshal to fill the vacancy voluntarily made by Rufe Biggs. Someone picked up the fallen badge and handed it to their new law enforcement officer.

Jim Torrance's hands just naturally slid down to the guns at his hips.

"I'm naming myself two deputies right now," he said. "Later maybe I'm going to ask two-three more to kick in with me—that is, if it comes to a clean-up. You, Sam Pepper; you, Bill Yarbo. You're both sworn in to lend a hand. Pop out and get me an ax and a crowbar."

Only a block from the hall was the Sundown jail. Torrance knew that Biggs had the key, hence the ax and crowbar.

He got the battered door off its hinges and stood it against the side of the squat, square building.

"You come out, you fellows in there," he called. And out came three untidy men, one swaggering, two cowering, all scared. For they didn't like this sort of an exit, and they didn't like the tone of the voice commanding them—and the grim-faced crowd that had followed Torrance looked as much like a lynching party as anything else.

"We're not going to need a jail in Sundown any more, boys," said the new marshal of Sundown. "If you're the right kind of men, you don't have to go into jail. If you're not the kind that Sundown hankers for—well, that's going to be your hard luck. Now you three—and I don't know a damn thing about you—just get the hell out of here as fast as you can, and keep on going. You don't have to come back unless you think it's healthy here. Just spread the news as you go. That's all, boys. Good luck."

The suddenly released three vanished in the dark.

Somebody laughed.

A cheer went up.

Jim Torrance hitched up his guns, rolled a cigarette, pushed his hat pretty far back—and strolled over to the Stag Horn saloon.

CHAPTER XVIII

JIM TORRANCE didn't stop in the barroom downstairs; he looked in at the door, saw that Murdo wasn't there, and went on upstairs. On his way he was thinking: "I came to Sundown for two reasons—to get to ranching again and to find Steve Bordereau. I hardly know what my ranch looks like; I've scarcely more than clapped my eyes on Bordereau, though we've tried to shoot it out twice."

He entered the main gambling room on the second story and went up to the bar. The place was pretty well filled; men were drinking and games were going full blast. But again he failed to see Clark Murdo.

His thumbs were hooked into his belt as he leaned against the bar. He was about to call for a drink when he saw Florinda. She was across the room, standing stock still and looking at him, her eyes enormous, her face pale, her lips vivid red, her jewels flaming. She made a queer little gesture, her beringed hands going up to her bosom. But it was not that that called him; it was the look in her eyes. He went across the room to a small table and sat down. Instantly she hurried to him; she gave him a smile which was all too patently made for the occasion, for he saw that she looked frightened.

"Sit down, Señorita?" he invited. "We might have something to drink."

"*Gracias, Señor!* Oh, yes, I will be glad "

She sat down; a bottle and glasses were brought them; Torrance sat idly twisting his glass between hard brown fingers while she looked deep into his eyes in a queer, troubling sort of way.

"You have come back, Jim Torrance?" Only she called him "Jeem" and put so many r's into his name, Torrance, that it sounded like water rippling over smooth stones. "I have heard so many things, such wild tales about you! You were hurt, no?"

He shrugged. "Nothing to matter." And then he asked abruptly: "Did you want to see me? You've got something to tell me?"

She snatched up her glass and drank thirstily. She said, as though he had accused her of something and she were defending herself, "Me, with something to tell you?" Then she laughed at that. "What could I have to tell you, Señor Jeem?"

"I imagine there are a good many things you get to hear about here that I wouldn't mind knowing," he said bluntly. And then he asked: "Where's Murdo?" I don't see him here anywhere tonight."

"He has not come yet. Maybe he won't come tonight."

"Once you said you were a friend of mine."

"I am!" Dramatically she pressed both hands to her breast. "With all my heart, Señor Jeem!"

"You are a friend of Murdo's, too?"

Those lusciously full red lips of hers hardened and thinned.

"Clark Murdo to me is the same as Steve Bordereau. They are the two men I hate!"

"Why?"

"There are ten million reasons. Do not ask me, Señor; to talk about it would make me want to stick a knife in them."

"The two are good friends, Murdo and Bordereau? They're on the level with each other?"

She laughed in his face, and her laugh was a sneer.

"Are you a great big fool, then? Do you think either one of two men like those could be square with any other man? They are two cheats, always cheating each other."

"I thought so," said Jim Torrance.

"Murdo hates you," she said, and, whispering, her whisper was almost a hiss, "for what you did when you brought the dead man here from the graveyard, and maybe for other things. I do not know, but he hates you. And he is the kind of man, like Steve Bordereau, who would come up behind you and kill."

He nodded. "I generally keep my back to the wall," he said.

She gave him an elaborate Southern shrug. About to rise and go, for it was seldom that she tarried long at any one table, a moment she held poised, uncertain, undecided. Then she said with a quick, savage flash of her deep black eyes:

"Yes! Maybe I will have something to tell you! Vamos a ver! Oh, but we are going to see!" She rose then, yet finished her thought: "Men are such fools! They think when they go in a room and shut a door, no one can listen!"

"Florinda! Tell me this. Has Bordereau been here lately to see Murdo?"

But she didn't stop to answer. He watched her go, an enigma now as ever; he saw her stop hoveringly like a butterfly at another table where three men were.

He saw that Charlie, the bartender with the bull neck, was watching him. He was conscious too that two other men—men he didn't know, yet whose faces he had seen here before, Bordereau's men or Clark Murdo's without a doubt—were watching him even more narrowly than the man behind the bar. Presently one of them got up and went out, passing around the end of the bar and through the door which Torrance knew led into the hallway that gave upon the private rooms.

"Gone looking for Murdo," thought Torrance.

After that he didn't lose sight of the door, but nevertheless out of the corner of his eye saw the several men who came into the room together, having just come up the stairs from the street. They were Hasbrook and Kibbee and Evans, leading the way, with Curly Redmond, Dick Pardee, Dave Drennen, Bill Yarbo and Sam Pepper. Their eyes sought and found him; when he gave no sign of having seen them, they proceeded to ignore him after his own fashion. Hasbrook, Kibbee and Evans went straight to the faro layout and into action, three old stagers who, when they made their bets, bet 'em high. The others, with the exception of Sam Pepper, stepped over to a long table where dice were tumbling and rolling, while, as for Sam, he just hovered. He was so tensely alert, trying to take in everything, that his eyes looked to be on fire and his ears seemed actually to quiver like a nervous horse's.

Then the narrow door opened and Clark Murdo entered. He stopped and ran his eyes swiftly over the room. Jim Torrance pushed his chair back and stood up, and Murdo's eyes hardened to a meeting with his. Torrance went across the room to him.

"Murdo," he said crisply, "I want to talk with you."

"Yes? Well, I'll listen if you make it snappy," said Murdo. "What's on your mind?"

"Two-three things. First, maybe you've heard that Rufe Biggs has decided to quit being town marshal?"

Murdo stepped back through the still open door.

"Come into a room where we'll be alone," he said.

Torrance followed him, not saying anything. They went into one of the small poker rooms. Murdo flung open the door and said, "Come in."

"After you," said Torrance, very polite.

Murdo shrugged and went in first. Torrance, following him, saw that the room was already occupied by two men; one was the fellow who without doubt had just come to warn Murdo of Torrance's presence in the main gambling room, and who looked like a cross between a seedy fox and a gaunt bulldog, and the other was that gangling, ferret-eyed man so nearly always at Murdo's beck and call whom Torrance remembered having encountered at least twice already. Their eyes were like snakes' eyes, just that cold and void of expression—snakes' eyes or bright hard-polished shoe buttons.

"Sure, let's talk!" said Murdo, and, having spoken, his jaws suddenly clamped hard, his lips squeezed together in a bloodless line of hate and menace; his mouth was then like a frog's mouth.

Torrance shut the door; there was a key in the lock and he turned it and drew it out and dropped it into his pocket.

"We won't want to be disturbed," he said, and took a single sidewise step which put him snugly in a corner, his back to the wall. His two thumbs had again hooked themselves into his belt.

The three pairs of eyes bent so steadily and balefully upon him flickered then. It had been in Murdo's mind to lock the door, but Torrance had been too quick for him; somehow the thing upset him.

"Well, what's it all about?" he demanded. "Put a name to it."

"Rufe Biggs has quit, like I told you. I think he was wise at that, don't you, Murdo?"

"Biggs is a yellow dog," said Murdo. "It makes no difference to me what he does."

"He told you who the new town marshal is?"

"You won't last long at it, Torrance. You can take that from me."

"No, I won't last long. That's the way I want it."

"What the hell? Are you driving at anything or ain't you?"

"Me, I'm a rancher, not a nursemaid for a sick town. Me, I want to get my job done and go back to my stock. That's why I won't last long here as marshal."

Murdo laughed at him, but it wasn't much of a laugh. Torrance went on quietly:

"You, Murdo, are not to last here even as long as I am.

One way or another you are getting out of here now, to-night. One way or another you're going fast and far. And you're not to come back."

Murdo, his mind made up, was temporizing, waiting for a break, and Jim Torrance was no such fool as not to know it. Murdo, affecting a sneering sort of manner, said:

"So I'm to just roll my bundle and vamoose, am I? Just let the shop here run itself—"

"That needn't worry you. It's not your joint anyhow; it's Steve Bordereau, and Bordereau's on the run, maybe already streaking for the border, wanted for robbery and murder. You don't think he'd be fool enough to ever come back here for an accounting, do you?"

He saw that, while Murdo was watching him like a hawk, Murdo's two killers now had their eyes bent on their boss, watching for a sign.

"So I'm invited just to step along and let the place run itself?" said Murdo. "Maybe you're thinking of taking it over yourself?"

"The girl out there, Florinda, can run it. Between her and Charlie, your barkeep, they'll do well enough."

Murdo strove for a sort of bantering, good-natured laugh —and Jim Torrance, knowing full well that there was no laughter in the man's heart, grew a notch more tense and alert than before.

"Stop your bluffing, Torrance," said Murdo, trying to be genial. "Come on out and I'll stand you a drink. Why, man alive—"

Somehow Murdo had given the signal, and Jim Torrance knew it, though he didn't quite know how. At the same split second Murdo and his two gunmen went for their guns.

Into the gambling room the noise of a sudden crash of gunfire burst like rolling thunder through the comparative silence. The first men to run out of the room and into the hallway were Dick Pardee and Curly Redmond; close behind them, a sturdy and compact mass of determined men, came Evans and Hasbrook and Doc Kibbee, with Dave Drennen and Sam Pepper and Lying Bill Yarbo crowding one another for elbow room, each striving to get a leap in advance of the others. They came to the door of the poker room and found it locked; they yelled their demands for ingress and hurled their weights on the door. Before they could batter it down, they heard a key shoot the bolt back, the door was opened and they looked into the small room through a blue haze of powder smoke.

Clark Murdo leaned back, white-faced, against a wall, his left hand clutching his right shoulder; his gun lay on the floor at his feet. One of his men, the gangling youngster with the furtive eyes and rabbit teeth, crouched down, his gun arm broken, blood dripping from his finger tips. The other of the Murdo men lay on his side, doubled up in agony.

It was therefore Jim Torrance who had opened the door. There was not a scratch on him. Already he had slid his guns back into their holsters. He was finishing the cigarette he had been smoking.

"Boys," he said as they came in, "can you scare me up a wagon and a man to drive it? I want these gents hauled out of town. They're not supposed to come back any more. Cart 'em out to the graveyard and dump 'em there. If they're alive in the morning, they can move on; if they're dead by then, we'll dig 'em under."

"I'm damned!" said old Doc Kibbee. "All three of 'em had their guns in their hands—and not a one of 'em fired a shot! Is this man Torrance fast? Or is he just chain lightning?"

After that for a time Sundown called its new marshal Lightning. But that was too direct and obvious, and also they grew to like him, and so after a while Marshal Jim Torrance of Sundown was familiarly and affectionately known as Slow Jim.

CHAPTER XIX

AND days passed, as days have a way of doing. That fine old trio from Canyon City, Evans and Hasbrook and Kibbee, had returned home well content after seeing the sign nailed to the tree in front of the Stag Horn. It was painted in big black letters on a pine board; you could read it across the street:

NOTICE

1. Steve Bordereau is on the run, wanted for murder and robbery.
2. Clark Murdo has been kicked out of town.
3. Men like them are invited to clear out of Sundown.
4. The jail door is busted: So no arrests will be made.

The town marshal was no longer in town. He went back straightway to his new ranch; he hired a couple of extra men and was busy from daylight to dark making improvements, building for the future, digging in for the winter. He said:

"I like this country. I've moved around enough. I'm here as long as I live."

He looked over the old Harper ranch, one panhandle end of which cut in between his own place and the King Cannon spread, and found it utterly to his liking, with its rolling hills, its valley land and meadows, its water in plenty supplied by Sundown Creek weaving a glinting, laughing way across it. He opened negotiations with the absent owner, now enjoying the sunset of his life under a shade tree down in Yuma. And at times Jim Torrance, riding over these half-wild, half-tamed acres, met a slim, sweet, eager girl also riding, and they rode together through sunlight and shadow of days which were crisp and clean with October merging into November, and which were days never to be forgotten, subtly touched with green magic.

The Sam Peppers had returned home. Bill Yarbo had gone back to his own ragged mountain ranch. At the King Cannon ranch Sally Dawn, with an Indian woman as housekeeper and chaperon, had launched herself upon a brave campaign of starting life over. She knew that the chances were all against her; she dreaded the day when the old home would be hers no longer, gone, through the trickery of Steve Bordereau, into his hands or those of some consignee of his—anyhow, irretrievably gone from hers. Still, since she loved the place so and was so young and vital, there were times when her hopes were as strong and gay as a flock of bluebirds. Because of their insistence, she kept on a purely theoretical pay roll Curly Redmond and Dick Pardee and Dave Drennen. They, like Jim Torrance and his men, were rebuilding.

Days shortened; flurries of rain came and were blown away, leaving the freshly washed sky a wonderful blue; storms gathered and rumbled over the mountains and painted the heights a dazzling white which was to last until May, a good five or six months or longer, then the storm clouds went where all things go, and there were again still, chill, gloriously bright days, and nights that were velvet-black but sprinkled with frosty brilliants.

The Stag Horn still ran full blast. A young man, bloodless looking and thin and with the stamp of towns on him, came in one day and took the place over. He had bought it, lock, stock and barrel, from Steve Bordereau. Jim Torrance, news of this brought him by that carrier pigeon of a gossip, Sam Pepper, rode into Sundown and in his official capacity of town marshal had a heart-to-heart talk with Art Pilgrim, the new owner.

"Where'd you see Bordereau?" asked Torrance.

Art Pilgrim's slim white hands went up to his hollow chest, his thumbs into the armholes of his flowered vest.

"Didn't ever see him, Mr. Town Marshal," he said.

"How come?" asked Torrance.

"Any business of yours?"

"Yes. You're a new man here; if you're on the up and up, you'll last. If you're a Bordereau kind of man, and if you're kicking in with him, you won't last."

"I don't know Bordereau. I never saw him. I don't know anything about him except that he owned this place and made it pay big money. He knew about me the same way; I had my own saloon at Alamogordo. I had a chance to sell and sold. My business with Bordereau was done through a lawyer over there. That's all I know."

"Fair enough," said Torrance, and got up to go. Over his shoulder he said: "If you've got a good strong safe here, you better keep your money in it. And you better go dig a hole somewhere and stick the safe in it and cover it over."

"Now, what's that mean?"

"So long," said Torrance.

Sam Pepper, living so near Torrance, was in and out at all hours, his ear to the ground, his nose twitching to any breeze that might bear even a hint of something. A queer sort of friendship sprang up between the two; and a friendship also between Torrance and Lying Bill Yarbo who, like Sam, dropped in frequently. The three were sitting on Jim's porch one evening, sampling fresh cider out of a jug that had been sent over that day from the King Cannon apple orchard, when Sam blurted out:

"Looky here, Jim! You keep hanging on to the idea that we ain't seen the last of Steve Bordereau. What in tarnation makes you so sure?"

Torrance said promptly, "Bordereau is a gambler first, last and all the time, isn't he?"

"Sure. He's a lot of other things, killer and highwayman and all round crook, but the bottom of everything with him is that he's a gambler. But what about it?"

"A gambler always loses," said Torrance. "Ever notice?"

Both Sam and Bill thought that over in a silence broken only by gurglings now and then from the jug. They had known many a gambler in their time, and had known many a big-time gambler to get into big money.

"A gambler always loses," said Torrance. "I've noticed. I've never known one of the breed yet to have enough money left to bury him when he died. It's like this with

Steve Bordereau. He's made himself a bit of a stake, and when a gambler makes a stake, right away he's got to double it; he can't quit any more than a booze hound can stop lapping up his booze. He's got Sally Dawn's gold; he's got what he made from his stick-ups at the Yellow Pine, the Mountain City and the Rocky. On top of that he got something out of Canyon City—but he's not forgetting that that night I had fifty thousand dollars tied to my saddle strings, and it was his money—and he lost it. Think he's going to let that go? Having played in luck all this time, as he's got to figure it, think he's going to quit? Give a man like that a winning streak at poker or faro or at the wheel, is he going to stop? The answer is, Hell no!"

"What about Murdo?" demanded Sam.

"That, I don't know. I wanted him to get out of here alive, and he did. I hoped he'd know where to find Bordereau and would kick in with him. I hoped that they'd feel like maybe I owed 'em something, and that they'd drop in some time to collect. And, talking about gambling, I'll bet either one of you two gents, or both of you, a forty dollar Stetson against a bottle of beer that inside of ten days or two weeks we have 'em, or anyhow Bordereau, with us. Maybe tonight or tomorrow night or the next."

"Got a notion where he's holing up, I suppose?" said Sam.

"No. Might be anywhere. Could be up in the hills yet; there's not too much snow. Could be within half a dozen miles of Sundown all the time; could be a day's ride away. Not any further than that, Sambo."

"And you figure him to come down looking for you?" Sam sat back tighter against the wall, and stared off in all directions into the gathering dark and began rubbing his hands together as though to get them warm; well, the evenings did grow cold now.

"That's the way I figure it," said Torrance.

"How many men you suppose he's got with him by now, Jim?" asked Bill Yarbo.

"Sam can tell you, Bill."

"Me?" exclaimed Sam.

Torrance's face looked stern in the flare of the match he

lifted to his cigarette, yet there was a humorous quirk coming and going at the corner of his mouth.

"Sure," he said. "You told me only a couple of days ago."

"Me?" said Sam again. "You're crazy, Jim."

"You were saying how Sundown had been losing part of its population the last few weeks. You mentioned the names of several men who used to hang around the Stag Horn and who've gone on somewhere else lately—and you said 'Good riddance, anyhow,' seeing the sort they were!"

"Why, shoot me down!" gasped Sam. "I never thought of that! You mean all them boys has kicked in with Steve? Why say! If you're right he must have eight or ten or a dozen boys with him altogether."

Torrance stood up to go inside. "Getting cold out here," he said.

"But listen!" said Sam. "If Steve Bordereau's got all those hell twisters with him— Say, it's quite a crowd! And what would he want so many for?"

"Maybe he's figuring on a good sized job of work," said Torrance. "Maybe he's figuring on making his last play up here, then riding hell-for-leather somewhere else. Anyhow there's not a bank inside a hundred miles that I haven't sent word to that they better sleep with one eye open; and whenever the stage carries a fat money box they're carrying two extra guards inside."

Bill Yarbo said ponderously, "If you're halfway right in your guess work, Jim, here's this to chaw on: Steve can still dodge around in the mountains, what with the way the weather's been, where a man's as hard to find as a flea on a long-haired pup. But come one good storm that might blow along any day now, and he'd get himself plugged up where it would take some getting out. What I mean is, if he's set, like you say you think he is, for another play, he'll be making it right soon. It'll be right soon or not any this year, Jim."

"Right soon, Bill," said Jim.

A new trail, weaving among the little hills, threading through the pines, came into being across the panhandle of the Harper place and connected Jim Torrance's ranch with Sally Dawn's. Tonight, since it was early when first Sam and then Bill rode away, Torrance rode that trail. He said to himself: "That was mighty good cider. I'll just ride by and say thanks."

But, about midway between his place and Sally Dawn's, where the winding trail went over a gentle knoll among both pines and big oaks, he saw another rider coming to meet him. Wondering who it might be, he eased himself sideways in the saddle, his right hand on the cantle close to his hip. He was getting so he watched shadows of late; he had a feeling in his bones it might pay to do so.

It was Sally Dawn, riding alone.

"Right here," said Torrance where they met on the top of the knoll, "I'm going to build me my house—my real home. Think you'd like it?"

"This spot was made for a home," said Sally Dawn. "It's been waiting for it thousands and thousands of years. Poor little lonely hilltop!"

"I can pump water up out of the creek," said Torrance. "I can pipe it here easy as downing a mug of cider. That was the best cider ever, Sally Dawn."

"Funny we met here; I was sort of restless tonight. Know what I was going to do? You've never asked me to call on you, but I was doing it anyhow."

"That's great. Come ahead."

"Well—no. As long as I've had my visit with you, as long as you've made your duty call—I love to ride at night."

"I was coming over to thank you for the cider.—Ever see a nice deep pool, all shady in summertime, on top of a hill like this?"

"They don't grow that way, do they?"

"Big enough and deep enough for a swim. And ducks always waddling into it or out of it—"

"I know. White ducks with nice curly tails. And yellow bills and feet—they keep them so nice and clean, don't they?"

"Look here," said Torrance, "I don't like your riding off alone like this after dark."

"Mercy!" cried Sally Dawn. "Sounds like you'd lock me

up in a dark closet and make me go to bed without any supper if I didn't mind you!"

"It's Steve Bordereau," said Torrance in dead earnest. "He hasn't finished down here. He's got the toughest crowd with him that you could think of. They're headed this way before long, and I know it. I wouldn't want you running into them."

It was too dark for them to see each other's faces at all clearly, to capture any play of expression, but he did see the liquid flash of her eyes in the starlight as she turned slightly and lifted them to his.

"I don't believe it," she said presently. "He has gone for good. You have just thought about him so much and for so many years—"

"No. It isn't that. He is coming back. I don't know that he will come near you; but I don't want to think of your running into that crowd alone. Not at night, off in the woods like this. Remember what you did to him once. Think he's the sort to forget?"

They rode for an hour, well up to the benchland of the Harper place, and they stopped many times and looked off across the wide acreage, and he sketched for her his budding plans against the time when this was all his, when his ranch and hers had a common boundary line.

. . . And somehow, though nothing quite direct was said about it, both thought:

"Maybe someday the fence along that line will come down."

By this time Jim Torrance had his bunk house fixed up so that his men, three of them now, ate and slept there. He himself, though no one knew, slept in the barn. He'd go to his house first, then after a while put out his light, lock up and betake himself to a loft over the stalls where his favorite horses were kept at night. It was his thought that Steve Bordereau, did his path ever lead him anywhere near the ranch in passing, might take off time to shoot a few finely bred horses, if he didn't find it handy to drive them off.

Lights in the bunk house were out by nine or ten o'clock. Torrance had got into the habit of taking a nap in his own house; about two or three in the morning he saddled and went for a ride; when he got back he went to the barn for any more sleep he might have coming.

There were nights when a couple of hours of sleep were all that he got, all that he wanted. With every passing hour he felt surer and surer that not much longer did he have to wait; he thought the thing over from every possible angle, dead set against letting himself trick himself into the old pit of simply believing what he wanted to believe; he thought of all that he knew of Steve Bordereau, one way and another, and could see only the one logical conclusion—Bordereau was coming back, and soon.

If Bordereau struck Sundown, thought Torrance, he'd strike where most loot was to be had, and that was the Stag Horn where games ran high and where the house made money hand over fist. Wouldn't Bordereau know all about that? And just where the money would be kept? And at just what hour to strike?

One day Sam Pepper came nosing in, and had hardly had a drink—Sam always favored a free drink—when he gave speech with the newest of Sundown news.

"I just seen a feller," said Sam, "that I ain't clapped my peepers on since Steve Bordereau played dead and buried pore old Doc Taylor. A feller named LeSarge, Jake Le-Sarge."

"Jake LeSarge? Who's he? Tell me about him."

"I can tell you plenty!" said Sam, and did.

LeSarge, if you'd take his word for it, was tougher than the plank steaks they sold over to Joe's Lunch Counter. Still a young feller, maybe twenty-three-four, he had hung around Sundown off and on for ten years. Always in trouble, always hell-raising. Quarrelsome. A cheap skate, a tin-horn, as crooked as a dog's hind leg—and a sort of pet of Steve Bordereau's. Two years ago he killed Larry Mc-Kibben, and Larry was an up-and-up boy, well liked. Le-Sarge had skipped out, stayed away six months or so, and had crept back under Bordereau's wing. And a good many things were said of him that nobody could prove—not nice things.

"And he's back," said Sam. "Me, I was wondering, if

Steve has a gang like you say, why Jake LeSarge ain't one of 'em.

Jim Torrance was more interested than Sam had hoped to find him.

"What's this LeSarge doing in town now?" he asked. "Where's he hanging out?"

"He's hanging around the Stag Horn. He's buying drinks, free with his money, which he ain't always. I seen him making a play at the Señorita—Florinda, you know. Looked like he was stuck on her, trying to corner her, like maybe he'd like to go out and buy a dog collar that would fit that white neck of hers. Outside all that, he wasn't doing much of anything I could see."

Torrance tilted his chair back, his lean brown hands behind his head, his eyes, with a sort of vacant look in them, going up to the cross beams and smoky rafters above.

It was so long before he moved or spoke that Sam began to fidget. At last, however, he kicked his chair back and stood up.

"All right, Sam," he said. "Thanks for the tip-off. And now— Well, good night."

"Hey!" cried Sam Pepper. But Jim Torrance was gone, off to the barn to saddle and ride. And Sam Pepper couldn't even be sure what direction his ride was taking him, since Torrance cut straight across the road into the pines and might have gone anywhere.

So he had to yell after the departing figure: "Hey, Jim! Where are you going?"

And it just happened that this time Torrance answered him.

"Over to the King Cannon Ranch," he said.

Only half a dozen words, not an outstanding word among them, but as things were to happen those six words were fateful.

CHAPTER XX

TORRANCE hit the high spots streaking over to the King Cannon Ranch. But he got only about halfway, to the top of that pine-and-oak studded knoll where some day the home was to be, when he rode into a sudden, unpresaged rain. It was a rain of bullets, and the streaks of light were orange-red flames from a rifle, and, like a man shot through the head, he spilled out of the saddle. As he went down, untouched by any of those flying leaden pellets, he snatched out a gun with one hand while with the other he gave his horse a resounding slap to send the animal racing straight on. And Torrance, striking earth and rolling adroitly, brought up standing behind a thick-boled oak.

He had hardly come up erect on his toes when he glimpsed the man shooting at him. His assailant was scarcely twenty steps away, sitting a black horse in the shadows and all but invisible, and yet the wonder remained that Torrance wasn't killed and that he didn't shoot the man dead at the first shot. It was just one of those odd happenings which so thickly besprinkle life wherever life is running strong and swift.

The heavy slug from Torrance's forty-four, winged on its way by the several chances of haste, uncertain light and moving figures, slammed into the narrow margin of the other man's rifle barrel, striking it so near the trigger guard that the flying wrath of the bullet came next door to raising a blister on the hardened trigger finger. It was like slugging the gun with a sledge hammer; anyhow the rifle flew out of the would-be killer's hands and the man who thus relinquished his gun gave voice to an involuntary howl of rage, pain and fright commingled. For the fragment of a second he thought he had been shot—he didn't quite know where. And he wasn't granted much time to think about things.

Torrance saw, because of the star glint on steel, the flash of the weapon flying out of his attacker's hands, and then asked no better than to get the man in his two hands. He had fired the one shot only; he had his gun up for the second; he was nicely balanced on his toes. Obeying impulse, a thing he did far more often than most men realized, he hurled himself forward across the few steps intervening between himself and the man who just tried to kill him. And in some few seconds the two were gripped together like two wildcats.

There in the dark, shot through with starlight, with their horses snorting and stamping and watching and wanting to run away, yet not moving out of their tracks, the two men fought as two men will when there is only one thought in mind and heart and sinew, to win anyhow. To win with a blow of a clubbed fist, with a strangle grip, with a sudden knee or a brutal boot—to save your own life by beating the other fellow into insensibility or by the directer method of killing him. Yet, like a small bell beating in his brain, there was in Jim Torrance the urge: "Get him, but get him alive so he can talk!"

It was Jake LeSarge whom Jim Torrance jerked down off his horse, though at the time Torrance had not the least inkling of the man's identity; and Jake LeSarge, half Cherokee and sinewy and slippery, was as hard to deal with as a young panther. He was like a snake for quick-darting elusiveness, like a driving rod on the new western locomotives for the blows he struck. Jim Torrance came to know all this within some ten seconds, during which the two gave and took some measure of each other.

It just happened that Jim Torrance had what no other man that Sundown ever knew had in the superlative degree, the something which made him what he was, the one Town Marshal of Sundown whose memory will linger a long, long time after so many other things mundane are forgotten. He had the indestructible spirit. He took a smashing blow on the jaw and reeled backward and tottered on his heels and took another blow under his heart and felt the living breath jolted out of him, and all he did was set his teeth and bore back into the tornado that had struck him. Head down, chin protected, arms flailing and driving hard fists like knobby clubs, he paid back in full for all he got.

He landed by chance, or luck, on LeSarge's Adam's apple, corded and tight and hard, and the blow was like that of a sledge beating on an anvil. Almost it broke young Jake LeSarge's neck. It did knock him flat at the same time that it choked him up so that he thought he was dying for lack of breath. Before he could master his muscles and command them to jerk his lean, battling body upright, Jim Torrance was on top of him, battering him with merciless fists. Then Torrance's hands, the fingers like steel hooks, shut down on his throat until LeSarge's tongue lolled like a thirsty dog's, and his eyes bulged. A tremor, which the other man could feel, ran through his body from head to foot.

"Got you, damn you!" panted Jim Torrance.

Then his own head cleared. He kept a strangle-hold on the other man's throat, yet he no longer squeezed so hard; he remembered that he did not want to kill but to ask his questions and get them answered.

"Who the hell are you?" he demanded. "Quick, or I'll put a bullet square between your eyes!"

The other man, in sudden fear of death, answered:

"Me, I'm LeSarge, Jake LeSarge. I made a mistake—got the wrong man—"

"Sure!" said Torrance. "Sure! Now, where've you been? Down at the King Cannon Ranch, huh? Lie to me, and I'll know it! I'll batter your brains out!"

"Yes," said LeSarge. "Yes. At the Cannon ranch. I just come from there!"

"Bordereau sent you?"

"No! I swear—"

"I tell you I'll batter your brains out!"

"Leave up on my throat, will you? Yes, then. Bordereau sent me. He told me—"

He stopped there. Torrance eased up on him a bit, came into a squatting position over his captive and said:

"He sent you to get me didn't he? He told you to snoop around the King Cannon place, to ride over and meet up with me, or to get me over at my place or wherever you could find me. Am I right?"

"I don't even know who you are! I tell you I made a mistake; I was looking for another man. Can't you understand, pardner? I don't even know who the hell you are right now!"

"That's funny," said Torrance. He withdrew his hands then entirely from the other man; balanced on his heels he was grinning the way a wolf grins at the kill. He said, "It's mighty funny." He had jammed his gun back into its leather; now he jerked it out and set its cylinder spinning with its small-voiced metallic clicks. He said, "Tell me what my name is and tell it fast, or so help me I'm going to kill you!"

Then, in all haste LeSarge, knowing the voice of fate when he heard it beating on his ear drums, gasped out:

"You—you're Torrance, Jim Torrance!"

"Sure." Torrance shoved his gun back into its holster. He stood up.

"You're coming along with me, LeSarge," he said "Sabe? You're coming sweet and soft and willing, wherever I say. Sabe?"

"Yes," said LeSarge. "Yes. I'll come. You got me, Torrance."

"You're damn well right, I got you," said Torrance. "Now watch your step."

"All right," said Jake LeSarge. "All right. I know when I'm licked. I'm playing good dog. Where do we go?"

"I don't know!" said Torrance. "I don't know. You see, I do know who you are now; I know you for a crook and a yellow dog. But I don't know about you and Steve Bordereau. I don't know how much he is paying you. I don't know how easy it would be to buy you, to get you to double cross him. You ought to be cheap. Let me get you somewhere in the light where I can look at you."

"I'm on the square, Torrance. I've always been on the level—"

"Shut your trap, you dirty liar! Climb on your horse. Let's ride. Never mind about your rifle; I'll take it for you."

"Where're we going?"

"It isn't far to the King Cannon ranch house. We might as well look in there."

There was a light in the bunk house and as they rode nearer the hushed and sentimental strains of a guitar floated out to them. Then a voice was raised in song, a doleful rendition, and thereafter something was thrown, no doubt at the musician; it sounded like a heavy piece of crockery crashing against the wall.

"Dry up, can't you?" said the voice of the man who had been goaded into throwing things. "I've stood all I can."

Torrance and his captive dismounted and went to the door.

"Here's company, boys," said Torrance.

Curly and Drennen and young Pardee—it had been Pardee strumming and vocalizing—looked at them curiously.

"Hello," said Drennen. "This is LeSarge you've got with you, Torrance. What do you want him for?"

"I'm not sure. Is he any good for anything?"

"Absolutely not. Unless maybe we could chop him up and use him to poison coyotes with."

LeSarge, sullen and vicious looking, strove also to look bold and defiant but remained furtive and couldn't keep the apprehension out of his restless eyes.

"I wanted a look at him by lamp light," said Torrance. "So I'd be sure and know him if I ever saw him again. Just now he tried to shoot me. He's been snooping around the ranch here tonight, I don't know what for. You boys wouldn't know?"

No, they couldn't figure it out. And they agreed there was no use asking him; he couldn't tell the truth even if he tried, even if you played Indian with him and cut his hide into strips.

"What are you going to do with him?" asked Curly.

"I ought to have shot him while I had the chance," said Torrance, and sounded regretful. "At the time, though, I was sort of curious and— Oh, we'll let him go. You can go now, LeSarge. And you're to keep on going, sabe? And you're never to come back this way. We're asking men like you to keep out of Sundown for good. I'm town marshal now; it would be just a matter of duty to kill you on sight. Now, scat!"

LeSarge ducked out through the door, got onto his horse and was off like a streak. From some little distance he screamed something back, his voice high and breaking with rage.

"I don't like his poking around here," said Torrance. "He's one of Bordereau's men." He looked at Curly and Drennen and Pardee. "Sally Dawn oughtn't to be out after dark," he said. "And whenever she is, can't one of you boys always be on hand?"

The three young fellows glanced at one another and seemed anxious.

"She's already gone somewhere tonight," said Dick Pardee. But none of them knew where. "About half an hour ago." They were of the opinion that she had ridden into Sundown for something.

"I'm going into Sundown now," said Torrance. He set down LeSarge's rifle and went to the door. "I'll look for her. And it's just as well to follow LeSarge a ways; he's headed back toward town."

"It might be an idea if we rode along?" suggested Dave Drennen.

"It might. I won't wait, though, for you boys to saddle. You'll most likely meet up with me."

CHAPTER XXI

FLORINDA, though as nervous as a cat and all hot impatience, awaited her chance to slip out of the Stag Horn gambling room without drawing any curious attention to herself. She found the hallway empty and darted across it like a vivid flash; she caught up her skirts and ran down the back stairs.

At the rear of the Stag Horn was a long low shed where riders left their horses; between the shed and the main building was a dark, narrow alley. She sped along this, turned the corner of the house and came around to the front of the saloon where the continuation of the alley, making a right angle, gave upon Sundown's main street. There, lurking in the shadows, glancing eagerly up and down, she forced herself to wait another impatient moment.

She was looking for someone, anyone whom she knew well and could depend on, someone to carry a message in all haste. She saw a man coming along the plank sidewalk, a young fellow on high heels with their spurs still on them and jangling like small iron bells at every stride. She started to speak to him; she hesitated, frowning; she even put her hand out as though to stop him and draw him into the shadows with her.

But she drew back and let him pass on without seeing her. That was because of a sudden she had heard the measured clop of a horse's hoof beats and made out who, of all people, was riding this way. When the rider was just opposite and but a few feet away, she darted out, catching the bridle rein.

"Oh, Señorita!" she gasped. "For the love of God!"

A startled Sally Dawn stiffened in the saddle, and said coldly:

"You? What do you want with me?" She stiffened still further, saying, "Will you please take your hand—"

"But, Señorita! Quick! I must hide, but you must talk to me for one minute. Quick! Ride here where it is dark."

"Are you crazy! Or do you think I am?"

"It is maybe life and death! I swear it!"

"Whose?" said a suspicious, utterly incredulous Sally Dawn. "Yours or mine?"

"But neither! Of Señor Jim Torrance. I have to send word to him. I can't go because they would miss me and pretty soon they would guess where I am. So it must be you!"

Sally Dawn was still inclined to be stand-offish and suspicious. She didn't like the Mexican girl; she didn't trust her—and somehow or other she didn't enthuse at the thought of messages passing between her and Jim Torrance.

"Quick, I tell you!" she exclaimed, and began to sound angry. "Ride your horse here where it's dark; let me tell you what it is all about."

"Tell me now. Where you are!"

Then Florinda flamed out: "Don't you care if they kill him? Don't you love him?"

Sally Dawn pretended to scoff with soft cool laughter at loving any man, but suddenly shot back, "Maybe it's you who love him!"

"I do! Yes, with all my heart. I always have since the time I saw him first. But that is nothing; he does not love me. It is you he loves! He loved you that first night, when he ran away with you. And now you do not want to help him? Well then, little crazy fool, go away! I will find some man—"

Sally Dawn at last rode into the dark mouth of the alley. "Tell me! What is it all about?"

"It's about Steve Bordereau. He's in town! It's about Clark Murdo; he's here, too, with Steve. They've got a gang with them— Oh, I don't know how many men; maybe ten, maybe twenty. They're out for trouble; then they're off on the run for the other side of the Mexico border. But what Steve wants most of all, and what I guess Murdo wants just the same, is to kill Jim Torrance."

"But—but," stammered Sally Dawn, beginning to believe, yet not sure, and finding it hard to understand, "how do you know all these things?"

Florinda lifted her clenched hands above her head, her rings glowing in what faint light there was, and shook them and came near screaming. But she contained herself and said in a hushed voice:

"I can't talk all night. Well, then, a man told me some of this; he is one of Steve's men, he is young and a little bit drunk and he loves me and wants me to go with them, back to the border. And I have told you all I know. And if you will ride out to Jim's ranch—if you'll ride like the devil—before they finish up here and then go out to get him—"

"I'm going!" said Sally Dawn breathlessly. "And I'll tell him you sent me."

She whirled her horse and raced away. And Florinda, catching up her skirts again, ran back down the alley and to the rear of the house—and then crept softly up the back stairs.

While the two girls were talking, while Sally Dawn thereafter was racing on her errand, Jim Torrance was riding toward Sundown from the King Cannon ranch; and some minutes before he came within sight of the few lights of the little town, Sally Dawn had struck off into the north road which led to his place.

He had quitted the Cannon bunk house so sharply on the heels of LeSarge's precipitate departure that when he came out into the county road and rose to the crest of the first low-lying hill he not only heard the beat of flying hoofs somewhere ahead but, a moment later, caught a glimpse of the dark, hurrying silhouette of horse and rider. There went LeSarge straight back toward Sundown as fast as he could go. Torrance dipped his spurs as he shot down the hill; from the next rise he again saw and heard the horse and rider ahead of him, hammering straight along the road.

Torrance didn't try to overtake the other; he merely meant to keep him in sight for a while. LeSarge might turn to look back; not likely, though, since he'd ridden off in such rage, in such haste and without having any inkling that he might be followed.

Torrance saw him come to the crossroads and pass on, then swing into the main street, clattering straight on into town. He saw him with the dim street lights making him a more distinct figure, lights above and below the swing doors of saloons, when at last he made a swerve. LeSarge had come to the alley flanking the Stag Horn and had swung into it. He had had his warning to keep away from Sundown and was ignoring it.

It might be that he had some important business here tonight—

After that for a few minutes Torrance proceeded leisurely, jogging slowly along the street, watching for some sign of Sally Dawn or of her horse. She might have dropped in at the general store, at the post office, at the drug store. He saw nothing of her anywhere, for the good and sufficient reason that she was already out on the north road, hurrying to his place.

He thought, not exactly anxious yet: "Where in thunder did she go? Just out for a ride maybe? Maybe over to drop in on the Sam Peppers? Well, as long as she keeps to the county road I guess she's all right." So he dismounted in front of the Stag Horn, tied his horse, hitched up his guns and stepped around the corner into the darkness of the alley which had swallowed up Jake LeSarge.

At the rear of the building he saw that in the long shed there were several horses, a dozen or so. They were fidgety and kept stamping and blowing. He put his hand on three of them and discovered they were still hot and wet. That made his brows cock up. Something like a dozen men just arrived—and all together! And Jake LeSarge, though warned, had come hurrying, and LeSarge was a Bordereau man—

Torrance returned to the front entrance. He went into the downstairs bar, pausing just within the door, looking things over. The place was quiet; there were only eight or ten men there, all peacefully minding their business, which had to do with putting raw, red liquor down where it would do the most good—not a man in the place whom he had anything against. He went upstairs.

He came into the gambling room just on time.

It was a Saturday night and the place was jammed, and games were running high even for the Stag Horn. And every man there who had been playing or drinking stood with both arms stretched straight up in the air. Six or eight other men, all wearing bandanas for masks over their faces, were busy cleaning till and pockets down to the last dime.

The instant Jim Torrance came to the threshold a voice shouted, "Stick 'em up!" It was a voice Torrance didn't recognize. But before the three crisp words were finished, another voice boomed out, and Torrance did know whose it was; and this voice yelled joyously, "You! Take this, you—!"

That was Steve Bordereau. His shout and his act precipitated turmoil. His bullet cut through Torrance's coat. Torrance, not being sure which of the masked men was Bordereau, yet making his guess without worrying, had both guns in his hands and blazing before they came up waist high. With this diversion created, men who had been taken by surprise by the raid and who had paid to the high card in jerking their hands up, now went for their guns, and the room was filled with the thunder of shots and the acrid bite of powder smoke.

Then some one of the raiders yelled, "Let's go! We've finished here," and he or someone else started shooting the lights out. There were six coal oil lamps in the room; as fast as six bullets could go streaking out of the barrel of a quick six gun, the six lights were out, with glass tinkling and the smell of oil mingling with burnt powder. Then there was a concerted rush for the rear door.

That way, Torrance knew, Bordereau and his men were departing. He whipped about and ran back to the front stairs. He hadn't seen Florinda until then; even now he didn't see her immediately, but heard her voice. From the top of the stairs when he was halfway down she was calling him, and in her words, and most of all in the tone of her voice, there was something that checked him almost in mid-air.

"Jim! Señor Jim! For the love of God!— Oh, one little minute, Jim!"

"Quick! What?" he called back.

She started down the stairs; he could see her dimly because of the light in the room below, flowing out into the lower hall. She balanced strangely, then plunged down toward him headlong, falling like a dead weight. She struck against him; he gathered her up in his arms, at first impatient and angry, thinking, "The fool girl has fainted." But his hand, touching her breast, was wet; wet and hot with Florinda's blood. A convulsive shudder shook her; she tried to speak coherently and gasped out:

"He shot me. I saw. It was Steve. I don't care. I want to

be dead. I love you, Jim Torrance." Only she said it all in Spanish, and it was "Jeem," and the "Tor-r-r-ance" still was softly running water, very faint yet softly musical. "And, Señor Jim—"

"Listen, Florinda." He stood there on the stairs holding her in his arms; her own arms, with a spasmodic effort, their last, went up about his neck. "Listen," he told her. "You're not going to die; you're too young and beautiful and gay. I'll have a doctor—"

"I am not gay any more, Señor Jim. And in a few minutes I am not going to be young and beautiful any longer. So now I can tell you without shame what you know already in your heart. *Yo te amo con toda mi corazon.*—But there are other things; they won't matter to me, but to you who will go on living. Steve is here to kill you. He sent some of his men to rob the bank while he and the others robbed the place here. Next, they were going to ride to your ranch, to kill you—"

"But I'm here, Florinda. And now I am going to carry you—"

"So I saw your Sally Dawn. And she rode to your ranch to warn you. Oh, only a few minutes ago. And if Steve and Murdo and all the rest go there they will find her—or meet her coming back—and Steve hates her like he hates you. And then they are riding to Mexico.—And—Jim— Oh, Jim, kiss me just the one time! And hold me tight—tighter —very much tighter, Jim—and say, '*Hasta la vista, Florinda mia!*'—That would be funny, no?"

Then she tried to laugh, but when her head dropped down against his chest he knew that Florinda was dead.

He carried her the few steps down to the room below; the best he could do for her was to lay her slim, still body on the bar. Men, already excited from the shots they had heard upstairs, looked at him and his burden with bulging eyes. He spoke briefly to the bartender.

"She is dead," he said. "Steve Bordereau shot her. Get some women to take care of her—women who will treat her tenderly—or I'll come back and kill you, so help me God."

Then he ran out of the room.

CHAPTER XXII

JIM TORRANCE dabbed at his eyes as he ran, and cursed under his breath and longed with all his heart for just one thing then—to come up with Steve Bordereau. Perhaps because his sight was at the moment blurred, he crashed full tilt into three men advancing across the sidewalk in front of the Stag Horn like the three Musketeers. They were Dave Drennen, Dick Pardee and Curly Redmond, just arrived from the King Cannon ranch.

He told them in a few words, low-toned but as emphatic as the crack of a whip, what had happened; how Bordereau and his men had got away with their fresh loot; how Sally Dawn had ridden only a few minutes ago out to his place; how the Bordereau crowd were on their way at last to the border.

"They killed Florinda. She told me that they were headed out to my place to get me. Now they know I'm in town, they may not ride that way. But maybe their plans, already made, call for that direction. They may run into Sally Dawn. Unless you boys, riding in just now, met them on the county road?"

They hadn't seen any riders, hadn't heard anything.

"I'm on my way back to my place," said Torrance, and went up into his saddle.

"We're with you," said one of them and the three hurried to their horses. As they did so several men came out of the Stag Horn; one of them was Bill Yarbo. He shouted:

"What's up, Jim? Where you headed for? After them fellers?"

"To my ranch," Torrance called back as his horse jumped under him. "All you boys that are not friends of Steve Bordereau come along."

He rode first, taking chances of an ambush, into the

alley and to the shed where he had found the sweat-wet saddle horses; there was not a horse there now, not a man. He spurred on and into the back road and out of town to the north road, and still had no sight and caught no sound of the raiding party. Already they must be well on their way. And he began to feel pretty sure that they were headed back toward the hills, toward his ranch—in the direction Sally Dawn had taken. So he took that same road, shook out his bridle reins and touched his horse with the spurs.

He reloaded before he was out of town; both guns were empty. How many men had been burned down there in the gambling room before the lights went out—and even after—he did not know. But already Bordereau knew that he had left three of his band behind him. And that did not trouble Steve Bordereau, so long as he sped on his way with a whole skin and his job up here done. There'd be fewer men to pay off, more money for him from the loot already taken and slung to his saddle strings.

Torrance had not ridden far before he heard the hammering of hoofs; at first he thought they were ahead of him but presently realized they were at some considerable distance behind; they told him that Curly and Pardee and Drennen, perhaps Bill Yarbo and others were following him; their horses' hoofs rang out on a bit of hard road where they swung off from the main street.

He kept storming along, anger in his heart, and sorrow, too, for he could not forget bright Florinda dying in his arms—and fear, too, for Sally Dawn. He would put nothing beyond Steve Bordereau tonight, and he knew Bordereau must hate the girl if only for all the wrongs he had done her.

Ten minutes later he again heard, faint and far, the hammering of rushing hoofs, and this time he thought at first that he was hearing again the men behind him, though he had thought to have outdistanced them. But listening intently, hearing the faint flutter of sound above the pounding of his own horse's hoofbeats, he made out that it was ahead of him. This time it was Bordereau and his men that he heard, and they were speeding on northward, still on the road toward his ranch, and he was slowly coming up with them.

But before he had covered another mile he was delayed by Sam Pepper, riding in furious haste toward a meeting with him. Torrance would have pressed on but for Sam's insistence; Sam had a lot to say and said it.

"I was on my way when I heard them hellions come swooping along," said Sam. "Me, I pulled aside the road and let 'em have it. But I was close enough and there was light enough for me to make 'em out; there was one man leading the way and if he wasn't Steve Bordereau I'll swallow your spurs."

"Sally Dawn—"

"I know about her, too. She rode over to your place just a little while ago; I was still there; had went out to the bunk house and was gabbing with your men. She was looking for you; said Florinda sent her and she was to tell you Bordereau was high-tailing out this way to get your scalp. I told her you'd cut across the hills to her place; so she done the same. Then I told your hired hands that they'd better look out for Bordereau and his killers, and I did some high-tailing on my own."

Torrance breathed easier.

"So Sally Dawn's left and gone home? That's good news, Sam. Now in a couple of minutes you will meet up with some of the boys following me; tell them what you've told me. I'm on my way."

"Hey, there!" yipped Sam. "There must be ten or a dozen of them boys with Steve. You better—"

But Torrance was already off, his horse at a run. Sam sat undecided a moment; then he heard a drumming of hoofs coming along from Sundown-way, knew that here must come the boys who Torrance had said were following him, and waited out in the middle of the road for their arrival. As they slowed down he made out who several of them were, friends all, and called to them all he knew of the night's happenings.

"Jim's overtaking them hellers," he said, "and he'll do it, and it's just him against the crowd. His men, this being no fight of their'n, skipped out of the bunk house as soon's they heard what Sally Dawn had to say. And—"

"Come ahead!" sang out Dave Drennen. "We'll be with Torrance before they can burn him down."

"Listen to me—" began excited Sam.

They listened no longer. Bill Yarbo, riding by him, almost riding him down, drenched him with big, booming, mocking laughter.

"You hang back here, Sam," he said. "Safer. Or run get Mrs. Sam to hide you under her apron!"

Whatever Sam screamed after him was drowned out by the thunder of hoofs. Sam whirled his own horse about, dug his heels in and followed them. But long before any of them got to Jim Torrance's ranch, before even Jim himself had reached there, they knew that Bordereau had already arrived, had tarried briefly and had gone on his way.

That was because they saw the red flare in the night sky. Jim's house, his bunk house, his barn, all were in flames.

So it was as bright as day out in the road when they pulled in at Torrance's gate and came up with him. He was on foot, and waved them to a stop; he was stooping low, looking for tracks in the road.

When he straightened up, "They've cut across the road here," he said. "They're headed across the hills, over the old Parker place. They're headed toward the King Cannon ranch. And they're riding hell-for-leather!"

Again he led the way, this time with the others keeping as close to him as they could; very close at first, but within ten minutes he was far out ahead of them.

So he came alone through the trees dotting the hills of the old Parker ranch to an open spot from which he could look down into the valley that was the heart of the King Cannon ranch, and he saw first of all a flush against the sky, like a hot summer dawn. But it wasn't dawn and it wasn't summer, and he knew that he was right in judging that Bordereau had come this way. That rosy, softly fluttering light was the light of a fire down where the ranch buildings were.

It struck Torrance that Bordereau must be mighty sure of himself! Already the bunk house was blazing; the first spears of flame began to stab through the barn's walls. Torrance came rushing on. He saw men—just dark, running figures—and he thought: "The house isn't burning. Why?" And then he was so close that he slid down from his saddle and ran forward on foot.

A woman—the light was so flickering and false and filled with trickery that at first he thought it was Sally Dawn—came running out of the ranch house back door. She was screaming as she darted out into the yard, trying frantically to gain the grove just back of the house. It was the Indian woman who worked for Sally Dawn; Torrance made that out just as he saw a running figure pounce upon her. Torrance, still running, shot the man and saw him fall and saw the woman scramble to her feet and vanish among the trees. He himself kept straight on to the house, not stopping even while he fired and glanced aside. He thought: "She's running out of the house, so the house is being attacked. Maybe Sally Dawn is in there now. Then Bordereau will be there."

The first door he came to, at the side of the house, was locked. He ran around to the rear and up the three steps to the kitchen porch. The door there, too, was locked. He threw his weight against it.

Just then several men, he never knew how many, whether four or five or six, came running from the direction of the barn shouting, "That you, Steve?"

"You rats!" shouted Torrance. "Get to hell out of here if you can travel any faster than a bullet!"

They opened fire on him, all of them together, and he, with his back against the wall and a gun in each hand, his body partly in shadow, gave them as good as they sent. How many of them he hit, how many he missed, he was never to know. But he did see three men drop before, simultaneously, two things happened. One was that the boys from Sundown came swooping down the slope of the timbered hill, yelling like Comanches and already beginning to shoot at what running targets they saw. The other was that Jim Torrance's two guns, both with cylinders emptied, brought their hammers down with a click.

That was two things. A third came so swiftly that Torrance had not even reloaded when he got its import. From within the house came the sounds of an angry voice, shouting, and of the explosion of a shotgun. The voice was Steve Bordereau's! Who but Sally Dawn had fired the shotgun?

Torrance struck the door again with his shoulder, and this time its ancient bolt dragged old screws out of the woodwork, and the door flew open and Torrance burst in.

There was a coal oil lamp burning in the dining room, and the door was open, so he had light enough to guide him. He hurried on through the dining room. Just then all within the ranch house was perfectly still. Outside, however, there was the Fourth of July. Out there hell was riding on bullets.

Then, above the lively young inferno outside, he again heard sounds within the house. They came from upstairs; it sounded like a man battering a door down. He ran to the staircase and when his foot was at the bottom step he heard quite clearly Steve Bordereau saying stormily:

"Out you come and quick, and I won't hurt you. Stay in there and I'll burn the house down, you in it. I've already set fire to your other buildings. And when you open the door, shove that shotgun through, butt-end first, or—"

No, Jim Torrance hadn't heard all this from the bottom of the stairs. By the time Bordereau had got that far he was nearly at the top, making his rush in a sort of twilight, for all the light that came into the upper hall was from the burning buildings, flickering through the muslin curtains. Bordereau heard him and broke off and was still a minute, then called out:

"Who's there? That you, Clark? I told you—"

As Torrance's eyes reached the level of the second story floor they discovered Bordereau, who had quitted the locked door behind which Sally Dawn was, and had turned to make out who came.

And when no one answered and he knew it wasn't Clark Murdo his gun was in his hand.

Torrance knew the shot was coming and lurched sideways before it came, and completed his upward rush. Bordereau fired again and at the instant Torrance hurled a heavy forty-four, useless now save as missile or club, and heard the thud of it as it struck the other man somewhere in the body.

"Torrance!" yelled Bordereau, and there was a world of gloating in his voice, and triumph. "I've been waiting for now!"

He waited a split second too long, for while he was speaking, realizing that he had his enemy unarmed and so sure of shooting him dead, Torrance hurled his forty-four straight into Bordereau's face, and followed it up by catapulting his own body on Bordereau's as the man reeled back. Bordereau came up with his shoulders against the wall; he fired a third time.

But now Torrance was on him and had locked one hand about Bordereau's gun wrist, and with the other was battering into an already bleeding face. An instant later the two crashed to the floor, and a door was whipped open and Sally Dawn came running to stand over them, a shotgun in her hands.

"Jim! Jim!" she cried wildly. "Let him go—get away from him—give me a chance—I'm going to shoot him—"

Torrance snapped at her:

"Stand back! He's got a gun in his hand! You run!"

"I won't run! I'm not going to let him kill you! I tell you I am going to kill him this time!"

She would have asked nothing better just then, knowing that it was going to be Jim Torrance's life or Steve Bordereau's. But in the faint light, with the two men now battling like a grim pair of wolves, never still for an instant, rolling and twisting and flailing about, she couldn't even make out which one of them was Jim, which Bordereau.

Those moments were to her like a nightmare. She could hear the shouts outside and the gunfire; a man screamed terribly and an even more terrible sound in her ears was another man's laugh cutting across the tragic outcry. And she could see on the wall down the staircase the flicker of a light that grew rosier and brighter as buildings burned with higher leaping flames. And worst of all was it to stand there, her weapon gripped so determinedly in her hands, and not be able to shove its muzzle down against Steve Bordereau's body and so end the thing. At that second she would have pulled the trigger with no more compunction than she would have slapped at a mosquito.

The two men in that fierce death-grip of theirs rolled to the top of the staircase. Somehow Bordereau wrenched free and stood up. Sally Dawn saw him clearly enough to make out who he was, and jerked up her shotgun. At that same instant two other things happened. Bordereau still had his gun in his hand and crooked his finger to the trigger, sure this time he had Jim Torrance where he had long wanted him. But Torrance wasn't out of the fight yet; he rose as Bordereau rose, and hurled himself forward. Bordereau's gun exploded; a terrified Sally Dawn didn't know whether it had found its mark or not; all she knew was what she saw, and that was the two bodies hurtling down the stairs, all the way to the floor below.

Down there men were running into the house through the kitchen. She couldn't tell who they were but supposed and feared they were Bordereau's men. She was at the head of the stairs; she was on the verge of emptying a shotgun among them when a roaring voice which she knew, the voice of Lying Bill Yarbo, shouted:

"Jim! Where are you? We got 'em on the run."

Sally Dawn screamed down to him:

"He and Steve Bordereau—they're fighting. Bordereau has a gun—"

She ran down then, only to encounter the same condition which had already made impossible her taking any hand. Torrance and Bordereau were again struggling hand to hand, body to body. Then she heard Jim Torrance laugh. Never in her life had she heard a man laugh like that; never would she forget it.

"Bordereau!" he shouted. "You've dropped your gun—and now I'm going to kill you! For what you've done to Florinda tonight, for what you've done to Sally Dawn, and to me, and to a lot of others—I'm going to kill you—now—with my hands!"

"Jim! You damn fool!" roared Lying Bill Yarbo. "Stand out of my way. Let me shoot the —— —— ———!"

But Jim Torrance didn't have it in him to stand aside for any man. His lean hard fist was already on its way, and caught Bordereau under the chin and sent him staggering back so that he came close to falling and only gained his uncertain balance when he brought up against the hall door which happened to be closed. He saw other men come running in from the kitchen until the hall was filled with them, and in desperation he tried to get the door open behind him and make his escape.

Then Jim Torrance laughed again, and again bore down on him. For as long as it takes two infuriated men to exchange a dozen blows, they stood there, hammering at each other. Again Torrance's fist beat Bordereau back as a club beats a man, and again Bordereau tottered—and this time, before he could get control of himself, Torrance was again on him, battering him. Once more the two men went down. They lay on the floor rather more quietly this time. Their hands were at each other's throats.

Now and then a convulsive shudder shook them. Men crowded close; one of them brought the lamp from the kitchen. Bordereau lay on his back; Jim Torrance was on top of him; Torrance's hands were at his throat, the fingers almost sunk out of sight. Bordereau's glaring eyes, horrible to look at, seemed about to spring from his head—

It took four men to pull Torrance off, and when he was on his feet and stood and looked down at the man he had beaten so close to death, Sally Dawn saw his eyes and was afraid of him.

She threw the shotgun down and came running to him and caught his arm in both her hands.

"Jim! Jim! Oh, Jim, please—for God's sake, don't! Just let them take him away."

At first he just tried to shake her off; he didn't hear what she was saying; he didn't even know who she was.

"Let him get up," he said to the men standing over the fallen man. "Let him up. I'm going to beat hell out of him. Then I'm going to kill him just as sure as he killed Florinda —just as sure as he killed my pardner six years ago."

Sally Dawn kept clinging to him, shaking his arm, pleading. He couldn't seem to brush her aside. Angrily he looked down at her and saw that it was Sally Dawn.

"Jim!" she pleaded. And then, there before them all, she said huskily, "Jim—if you love me—"

He put a hand up to his face; it was battered and torn and bloody. He shook his head as though to get his thoughts clear, the way a horse shakes its head when summer flies are at its eyes. Then he put his hand down on her two and patted them gently.

"I won't kill him, boys," he said. "Maybe it'll be a good thing if we let this country know that the law is nosing in here and is coming to stay. The law will hang him. Take him away."

They took him away swiftly, men thick about him. And under a big oak, from which Bordereau could take full advantage of the spectacular view of buildings burning, they hanged him and let him kick his life out. By this time there were thirty Sundown men on hand to officiate; not a single dissenting voice was lifted when someone called for a rope.

CHAPTER XXIII

MEN stood around and watched the outbuildings burn to the ground. There was nothing they could do beyond making sure that the fires did not spread, an unlikely thing at this time of year after the first rains and snow flurries. Jim Torrance, staring frowningly at the devastating flames, suddenly awoke to the fact that he was standing slightly apart from the rest of the men but that he was not alone. At his side was Sally Dawn Cannon, and for a little while she didn't seem to realize any more than he did that they were holding hands.

But this inactivity was of the shortest duration. Men scouted around to check up on the results of the battle in loss of lives and injuries to combatants on both sides. Dave Drennen, clutching a bleeding shoulder on his way to the house and first aid, said in passing Torrance,

"They say Bordereau's gang was thirteen strong tonight in Sundown. Three of them got shot down at the Stag Horn. The boys have picked up five more out here, dead or as good as dead. That's not counting Bordereau. Murdo was along; he's dead out by the barn, shot through the head."

"Better go get that shoulder fixed up, Dave," said Torrance. And to young Pardee, passing close, he called: "Will you streak for a doctor? Or be sure someone else goes?"

Just then a newcomer rode up, swung a pair of saddle-bags down into Pardee's hands and dismounted.

"I thought there'd be a job for me," he said. "So I followed on just as soon as I heard there was apt to be a scrimmage tonight." It was Dr. Frank, the new man who had settled in Sundown recently, after the taking off of Doc Taylor.

"There's something else that's got to be done right away," said Torrance to the several men who began to gather where he was. "Catch up all the Bordereau horses; see how many are missing. Remember, he was on his way out of here; there's every chance he was carrying a lot of money with him down to the border. And there happens to be a sizable amount of gold that belongs to Sally Dawn Cannon. If the stuff is missing, if some of the men got away on horseback, we've got to run 'em down while the trail's hot."

They scattered on the run, and the round-up began.

Curly Redmond was carried into the house with three bullet holes in him; Dr. Frank immediately set to work, and Sally Dawn, though pale and shaken, aided him so ably that he grinned at her and patted her on the curly head and said, "Good kid."

One of Bordereau's men, badly wounded, was brought to where Torrance was. It was Joe Tortillas. Questioned, he was sullenly stubborn until a rope was mentioned; then, in exchange for a promise not to hang him, he answered. Yes, Steve had all the moneys with him; they were always on his saddle. He rode the same horse he nearly always rode, a big bay with white forefeet and a white nose. The horse had been left with the other horses, two men guarding them; Joe didn't know what had happened to any of them, but thought they had stampeded when the shooting began.

Bill Yarbo came swaggering up. He had a lot to tell. You would have thought—if you didn't know him!—that he had just about cleaned up on the whole gang single-handed. He himself had killed Clark Murdo; he had shot Joe Tortillas; he had clubbed a couple of other jaspers over the heads with his gun, saving ammunition—

"Here's Bordereau's horse!" someone sang out.

And here indeed came Bordereau's horse from some-where in the semi-dark on the side of the house farthest from the fires. A man was riding it, a little man looking all the littler from being established so high upon such a big animal.

"Here she is, Jim," the little man called down, and only then they recognized Sam Pepper. "I grabbed Bordereau's cayuse soon's I seen it, thinking most likely Steve would have Sally Dawn's gold with him. Got it, too."

A man laughed and said: "Why, old Sam's got more sense than all the rest of us put together! He kept his mind on what counted."

"Hell," snorted Lying Bill Yarbo. "What Sam did was see a chance to grab a horse and run for it! And it just hap-pened to be Bordereau's horse!"

"The way I found the horse," said Sam Pepper wasp-ishly, "was that I made out Clark Murdo running to grab it and skip out. I reckoned it would be like him to grab all the loot, give him a chance." He looked down on Lying Bill, took a long, deep breath and rapped out, "So, me, I shot Clark Murdo down, shot him through the head and—"

"You damn little liar!" roared Bill Yarbo. "You must of been eavesdropping just now and heard me—"

A shout of laughter went up, drowning his voice.

"Seems to me," said Jim Torrance, formerly marshal of Sundown, now just an enthusiastic young rancher to whom the country looked for big things, "that we've got a bully good chance—Steve Bordereau gave it to us!—to save our-selves a lot of money right at the jump."

Maybe Sally Dawn guessed what was coming, for she smiled at him and made a brave endeavor to stifle her smile, and her cheeks grew a bit pinker. It was a glorious winter morning. There had been rain and hail and a light snowfall during the night, but now the skies were blue and the sun was bright, and there was just enough snappy cold in the air to make breathing a delight and to send one's blood along dancingly.

"So we're going to save some money," she said, "when I feel so rich so all of a sudden, and so unexpectedly?"

They rode on through the pines. She said, "Where do you think we are going?" quite as though she didn't know perfectly well.

On top of the gentle oak-and-pine-studded knoll where once he had said something about one day building a home —not just a house, but a home—they stopped. He said:

"I got a letter yesterday from three old friends of yours up in Canyon City, sheriff, banker and medico. The banker suggested that someday I might be able to use some additional funds, developing here; he said, 'Come and get it; the bank's yours.' And the two other old boys wrote together, 'Let us know, so we can dance at the wedding, for we're the two damn best dancers either side of the Rockies.'"

"Wedding?" said Sally Dawn. "What wedding?"

Jim Torrance eased himself sideways in the saddle and started rolling a cigarette that never got rolled to completion.

"I was thinking," he said. "My place is pretty well burned down, thanks to Bordereau. So's yours. Now, if we tore all the fences down between us, and if we made us a place right here—"

"Duck pond, and everything?" said Sally Dawn.

It was then that he threw his cigarette away.